NEW YORK TIMES BE

LORI HAN

HEAT OF THE
MOMENT

*Love is like
magic. It can
change everything
you believe in . . .
and leave you
breathless.*

SISTERS OF
THE CRAFT

**ST. MARTIN'S
PAPERBACKS**

U.S. $7.99
CAN. $9.99

Don't miss these thrilling novels from
New York Times bestselling author

LORI HANDELAND

Sisters of the Craft
IN THE AIR TONIGHT

SMOKE ON THE WATER
(Available August 2015
and turn to the back of this book
for a sneak preview!)

The Phoenix Chronicles
ANY GIVEN DOOMSDAY
DOOMSDAY CAN WAIT
APOCALYPSE HAPPENS
CHAOS BITES

The Nightcreature Novels
BLUE MOON
HUNTER'S MOON
DARK MOON
CRESCENT MOON
MIDNIGHT MOON
RISING MOON

ISBN 978-1-250-02013-0

5 0 7 9 9

Availd

He

Praise for the Phoenix Chronicles by
LORI HANDELAND

DOOMSDAY CAN WAIT

"A striking series . . . with a decidedly sexy edge. Readers again view the world through the eyes of ex-cop-turned-humanity's-savior Liz Phoenix [in] this complex mythology." *—RT Book Reviews* (4 stars)

"We really enjoyed it . . . and are looking forward to [more] in this series." *—Robots & Vamps*

"Cool . . . exciting." *—Lurva à la Mode*

"Fascinating, vivid, and gritty."
—Fallen Angel Reviews

"Handeland does an amazing job of packing so much punch into the pages of this story without ever leaving the reader behind. *Doomsday Can Wait* ups the paranormal and emotional content of the series, adding strength to the heroine and a more human touch to one of her closest allies. This is an action-packed series that urban fantasy readers should thoroughly enjoy, and I'm looking forward to seeing where the author takes us next." *—Darque Reviews*

"Handeland pens another tale that captured my heart . . . with captivating characters [and] an absorbing plot that will keep readers on the edge of their seats."
—Romance Junkies

ANY GIVEN DOOMSDAY

Heat of the Moment

Lori Handeland

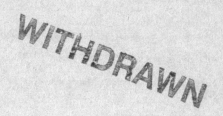

St. Martin's Paperbacks

This is a work of fiction. All of the characters, organizations, and events portrayed in this novel are either products of the author's imagination or are used fictitiously.

HEAT OF THE MOMENT

Copyright © 2015 by Lori Handeland.
Excerpt from *Smoke on the Water* copyright © 2015 by Lori Handeland.

All rights reserved.

For information address St. Martin's Press, 175 Fifth Avenue, New York, NY 10010.

ISBN: 978-1-250-02013-0

Printed in the United States of America

St. Martin's Paperbacks edition / July 2015

St. Martin's Paperbacks are published by St. Martin's Press, 175 Fifth Avenue, New York, NY 10010.

10 9 8 7 6 5 4 3 2 1

For our Reggie.
Best. Dog. Ever.

Chapter 1

I glanced up from my examination of a basset hound named Horace to discover the Three Harbors police chief in the doorway. My assistant hovered in the hall behind her.

"Can you take Horace?" I asked, but Joaquin was already scooping the dog off the exam table and releasing him onto the floor. Before I could warn him to leash the beast—my next scheduled patient was Tigger, the cat—Horace had trotted into the waiting area and found out for himself.

Indoor squirrel!

Since childhood, I'd heard the thoughts of animals. Call it an overactive imagination. My parents had. That I was right a good portion of the time, I'd learned to keep to myself. Crazy is as crazy does, and a veterinarian who thinks she can talk to animals would not last long in a small northern Wisconsin tourist town. I doubted she'd last long in *any* town. But Three Harbors was my home.

Woof!

Hiss.

Crash!

"Horace!"

Tigger's owner emitted a stream of curses. Joaquin fled toward the ruckus.

"Kid gonna be okay out there?" Chief Deb jerked a thumb over her shoulder then shut the door.

"If he wants to keep working here, he'd better be." The waiting room was a battleground, when it wasn't a three-ring circus.

I sprayed the table with disinfectant and set to wiping it off. "What can I do for you, Chief?"

"I've got a missing black cat."

My hand paused mid-circle. "I didn't know you had a cat."

She'd never brought the animal to me, and as I was the only vet within thirty miles, this was at the least worrisome, at the most insulting.

"Just because you picked up a stray," I continued, "doesn't mean the animal doesn't need care." Ear mites, fleas, ticks, old injuries that had festered—and don't get me started on the necessity for being spayed or neutered. "A stray probably needs more."

"Chill, Becca, the missing cat doesn't belong to me. Neither do the two other black cats, one black dog, and, oddly, a black rabbit that seem to be in the wind."

I opened my mouth, shut it again, swiped an already clean table, then shrugged. "I don't have them."

"If you did, you'd be my newest candidate for serial killer of the week."

"I . . . what?"

"After the first two cats went poof, I suspected Angela Cordero."

"She's eight years old."

"Exactly," Deb agreed. "But when the dog disappeared, I started to think maybe it was Wendell Griggs."

"Thirteen," I murmured.

"Missing small animals are one of the first hints of pathological behavior."

Apparently Chief Deb liked to read that healthy and growing genre, serial killer fiction.

"Missing small animals are usually an indication of a larger predator," I said. "Especially this close to the forest."

Three Harbors might be bordered on one side by Lake Superior, but it was backed by a lot of trees, and in those trees all sorts of creatures lived. Perhaps even a few serial killers.

My imagination tingled. If I weren't careful I'd be writing one of those novels. Maybe I should. Writing might be good therapy for my overactive imagination. Ignoring it certainly wasn't helping.

"I know." She sounded disappointed. Apparently the chief would prefer a serial killer to a large animal predator. Worse, she was kind of hoping that the serial killer was someone we knew, who'd yet to hit puberty.

This surprised and disturbed me, though I didn't know her well. We'd gone to school together, but Deb had occupied the top of the pyramid in high school—literally. Someone of her tiny stature and blond-a-tude had been a given for cheerleader of the year.

She'd worried me when she'd danced on top of those ten-people-high pyramids. Now I was worried that she'd fallen off, once or twice, and hit her head.

"Have you had any animals in here that have been bitten, scratched, mauled, or chewed on?" she asked.

"Not lately."

"Any farmers complain that they've seen coyotes or wolves closer to town than they should be?"

"Wouldn't they report that to you, not me?"

She tilted her head. "Good point."

Deb had cut her blond ponytail years ago and now wore her hair in a short cap that, when combined with her tree-bark-brown police uniform, Batman-esque utility belt, and Frankenstein-like black shit-locker boots, only made her appear like a child playing dress up.

Dress up.

I tapped the calendar. "Less than two weeks until Halloween."

"I *hate* Halloween." Deb kicked the door, which rattled and caused Horace to yip in the waiting room. Wasn't he gone yet? "Second only to New Year's Eve for the greatest number of morons on parade."

"You said all the missing animals were black."

"So?"

"A wolf or a coyote wouldn't know black from polka dot."

While dogs and cats, and by extension wolves and coyotes, weren't truly color-blind, they didn't see colors the way we did. Most things were variations of black and gray and muted blue and yellow. Or so I'd heard.

"Might be kids playing around," I continued.

"Sacrificing black animals to Satan?"

"You think we have a devil-worshipping cult or maybe a witches' coven? In Three Harbors?"

She drew herself up, which wasn't very far, but she did try. "There *are* witches."

"From what I understand, they're peaceful. Harm none. Which would include black animals."

"*Something* weird is going on."

"Kids messing around," I repeated. "Though I doubt

they're stealing black animals and keeping them safe in a cage somewhere just for the hell of it."

Which brought us right back to budding serial killer. Or two.

"Would you be able to give me a list of all the animals you treat that are black?" she asked.

"If the owners agree."

Wisconsin statues allowed the release of veterinary records with permission from the owner.

"Why would anyone care about the release of the color of their pet's fur to the police?"

"Never can tell," I answered.

If there was one thing I'd learned in this job it was that people were a lot stranger than animals.

At five-thirty, Joaquin flicked the lock on the front door and turned off the waiting room lights, then followed me through the exam room to the rear exit.

Trees ringed the parking lot that backed my clinic. Only my Bronco and a waste receptacle occupied the space. However, I'd had a night-light installed, and it blazed bright as the noonday sun.

"Sorry to leave you with the Horace and Tigger problem," I said.

"It was my fault for letting Horace run free."

It had been, and I'd bet he'd never do it again. Between patients I'd seen him sweeping up dirt from an overturned potted plant and wiping the floor beneath one of the chairs. It was anyone's guess if Horace had peed and Tigger had knocked over the plant or vice versa.

I'd never had a better assistant than Joaquin. His long-fingered, gentle hands calmed the wildest pet. He also had the best manners of any adolescent in town, not that there'd been much of a contest. From what I'd seen of the Three Harbors youth, being a smart-mouthed überdelinquent was the current fashion.

"You going home or did your mom work today?"

Joaquin lived in a trailer park outside of town. Not a long trip, but one that involved a sketchy stretch of two-lane highway, with only a bit of gravel on the side. I didn't want him walking it after dark, and at this time of year, dark had come a while ago.

"She's working."

"You're going straight to the café?"

His lips curved at my concern. "If you saw where we lived before we came here . . . This place is safe as houses, my mom says. Although I don't really know what that means beyond really safe."

Three Harbors *was* safe, at least for people, which reminded me. "Have any of the kids been talking about . . ." I wasn't sure what word to use. Did they call Satanism something else these days? And if so, what? "Cults?" At his blank expression, I kept trying. "Sects? Devil worship?"

"That's why the chief wanted the list of black animals?" His voice was horrified. "Someone's killing them?"

"We don't know that."

"What do we know?"

I hesitated, but now that I'd opened the door, I couldn't close it without freaking out Joaquin worse than he already was.

"There are several cats, a dog, and a rabbit missing.

They're all black, which almost surely rules out a feral dog, coyote, or wolf."

He nodded. The kid knew nearly as much about animals as I did.

"I was thinking that since it's so close to Halloween, maybe some kids were messing around. Hear anything?"

"No one talks to me at school." He twitched one shoulder in an awkward, uncomfortable half shrug. "I'm Mexican."

Three Harbors didn't have a lot of Mexican-Americans. In fact, now that Joaquin and his mom were here, we had two.

"I don't fit in," he continued. "I'm dark and foreign and new."

Joaquin was a beautiful boy—ebony hair, ebony eyes, ridiculous lashes—also ebony—smooth cinnamon skin.

"Doesn't that make you exotic and exciting?"

"Not," he muttered.

"No one's talked to you?"

"Teachers. I heard one of the kids saying that I didn't speak English."

"And what did you say to that?"

"Hablo Inglés mejor que usted habla Español, estúpido."

"You didn't."

"You understood me?"

"I'd have to be *estúpido* not to understand *estúpido.* Once I got that much, the rest wouldn't really matter. Have you been participating in class?"

"Have to."

"In English?"

He cast me a disgusted glance. "Have to."

"Then why would anyone think you couldn't speak the language?"

He rolled his eyes the same as every kid I'd ever met. "Hence my use of *estúpido*."

I pursed my lips so I wouldn't laugh. I liked this kid so much. Why didn't everyone?

Because kids were mean. I knew that firsthand.

But were they mean enough to sacrifice helpless, harmless animals?

I hoped not.

I lived in an efficiency apartment above my clinic. When I'd taken over Ephraim Brady's practice after college, it was part of the deal.

My mother hadn't wanted me to move to town, but it wasn't practical to live on the farm when over half of my business was done in the office. Not to mention the small kennel where we housed post- and pre-op patients, boarders, and strays. In the winter, I might be prevented from making it into the office for a day or two, and then what? If I was already there . . . half the battle was won.

I exchanged my khaki trousers—which repelled animal hair better than most—for track pants, my white blouse—out of which anything could be bleached—for an old T-shirt. I covered that with an equally old sweatshirt, switched my comfy shoes for the expensive running variety, then grabbed a hat and gloves, put my cell phone in one pocket, my keys in the other, and trotted down the stairs and out the door. Time for my nightly wog—my twin brothers' word for the walk-jog I did to stay in shape.

Instead of wogging down Carstairs Avenue—the main street of town was named after my family. The Carstairses had lived in Three Harbors from the beginning, which, according to the welcome sign, had been in 1855—I took the path into the forest.

Three Harbors was a small town, but it was also a tourist town, and these days that meant bike paths and hiking trails. They were well lit and meticulously maintained. I still kept Mace on my key ring. I couldn't very well jog with a nine-millimeter. Even if I owned one.

The forest settled around me, cool and deep blue-green. The trail had lights every few feet, some at ground level, others high above. Still, I rarely ran into anyone after dark, and I loved it.

My feet beat a steady *wump-wump*. That combined with the familiar crunch of the stones beneath my shoes at first drowned out the other sound. But eventually, I heard the thud of more feet than two.

At the edge of twilight, loped a huge black wolf.

Chapter 2

I'd been seeing this wolf since I was a child, which would make her one old wolf. Wolves lived eight to ten years in the wild. At that rate, I should be on wolf number three. One of the many reasons I'd never told anyone about her.

Considering the nature of today's visit, I should have mentioned the wolf to Chief Deb. Except I still wasn't quite certain the wolf was real.

I'd never gotten close enough to touch her. No one had ever seen her but me. While I heard the thoughts of every other animal I came near, not a whisper from this one. Add to that her seemingly eternal—or at least freakishly long—life span, and her oddly human, bright green eyes, and she seemed even less likely to be fact than fiction.

I continued to wog, soothed by both the forest and her presence. These runs had come to be as much a part of my life as breakfast.

For the past several days, my wolf had been oddly absent; I'd even wondered if she were gone for good. The last time I'd seen her, she'd been nervous and twitchy, then she'd howled for no reason at all, and run off. Hadn't caught a glimpse of her since. I was so glad she was back.

I reached the end of the trail, paused, stretched,

straightened, and a light flickered in the distance. I stepped off the path, and the wolf growled.

The hairs on my arms lifted. She'd never growled at me before. One look in her direction, and I realized she wasn't growling at me now. She was growling at that light. Which was exactly where no light should be—the McAllister place.

In every small community there was often a woman who skated the edge of sanity—a recluse, a druggie, in this case all three—who from time immemorial was branded the local witch.

Mary McAllister heard voices, even when she was on her meds. Sometimes she self-medicated. Then she heard them more.

I started toward the light. I should have pulled out my cell phone and called Chief Deb. Hindsight always has the best damn ideas.

The wolf bounded in front of me. At first I thought she would crowd me back, growl again, maybe even bare her teeth. Instead, she led the way along a well-traveled and narrow deer trail.

About a hundred yards in, the dark closed around us and I was glad for her superior eyesight. Every once in a while we reached an area where the trees weren't so thick and the moon shone down, but I still would have been lost without her.

Tiny animals skittered away from us. A doe started up, and danced off, white tail shimmering beneath the silver night-light.

The wolf glanced at them, but she didn't follow. Another oddity. Predators didn't ignore prey. I hadn't thought they could.

The distant light became less distant, less a flicker, more a window. Then the house loomed up from a small clearing sooner than I'd thought it would. Traveling as the crows fly, rather than the roads do, cuts off a lot of time.

The witch's house stood not far from my parents' place. Long ago it had been a farmhouse too. But in the intervening years, government programs which gave tax breaks to farmers who planted trees instead of crops had led to the previously cleared fields becoming forest again.

The windows were broken; the front porch listed north. Local kids liked to dare one another to sneak inside and stay overnight—especially at this time of year—so close to All Hallows' Eve.

The light, this place—and the missing animals—converged to give me a nasty, bone-deep chill. I pulled out my cell phone and discovered I had no signal. Too many trees.

If there were just a bunch of kids inside, I could probably disperse them with the threat of telling their parents. However, if Chief Deb's idea of a budding serial killer were true, I didn't really want to volunteer as his, or her, first human victim. I had no choice but to head back toward town, at least as far as I needed to go to get a cell signal.

A door opened; the figure of a man appeared in the halo of light. He held a shovel.

The door closed; the silhouette disappeared. But the porch creaked as he walked across it, then the steps groaned. A minute later, the distinct sound of digging filled the night. What could possibly be urgent enough to bury in the dark?

Something he wanted no one to see, which meant I could not let him see me.

My heart pounded; my palms had gone damp. I took one step backward.

Snap.

I swear the entire forest froze. Not a single bug buzzed. Not an owl hooted. Not a dog barked anywhere. More importantly . . .

The digging stopped.

I remained still as an opossum confronted with anything. Sooner or later he'd think a deer had tromped past and go back to digging.

Wouldn't he?

Slowly, quietly I let out my breath, equally slowly and quietly I drew in another and waited.

There. Had he slammed the shovel into the earth again? It had sounded . . . not quite right.

Because it had been a huff from the wolf and not the shovel. She followed that warning with a low, vicious snarl as the man materialized from the darkness.

I stumbled back, arm up to deflect the downward slash of the shovel. I closed my eyes, braced for the impact.

"Becca?"

I opened one eye, closed it again.

Of all the people in the world to find me cowering in the bushes, sweaty, tired, and wearing workout clothes, why did it have to be him?

Owen McAllister's fingers loosened on the shovel that he'd brought along for protection. Against what, he wasn't quite sure. But considering what he'd found in his house, he was understandably on edge.

At the first crack of a branch in the darkness, his hand had gone to his hip and found only hip, no gun. He'd had to check his weapon in his luggage when he'd flown home, and he hadn't yet taken it out. He hadn't thought he'd need it.

Becca lowered her arm, straightened, then glanced longingly toward Three Harbors. The movement caused her riotous red hair to slide over one much-missed breast before she glanced back. "What are you doing here, Owen?"

"I'm the one who should be asking that." It was, after all, his house. Just because he hadn't been in it for ten years, didn't make it any less so.

"I saw the light."

Her parents' place lay in the opposite direction from where she stood. Even if she'd seen the light from there, which she couldn't because of the ridge in between, she would have had to circle around to arrive where she stood, and why would she? He had no more explanation for that than he had for her being here in the first place.

"You saw the light from where?" he asked.

"Town."

"Did not." There was no way his single battery-operated lantern had shone that far through the forest.

"Not town exactly. I was at the end of the hiking trail."

"What hiking trail?"

"I'm not going to explain all the changes to Three Harbors since you left. If I hadn't seen a light do you think I'd be out here?"

"Why are you? It certainly wasn't to make sure the house hasn't been vandalized. From the looks of the place that ship sailed nine and a half years ago."

She lowered her gaze. Guilt? Why? It wasn't her house. Maybe she'd been the first one to throw a stone through the window. Considering what had happened between them, or hadn't, he could hardly blame her.

He shouldn't blame anyone. Why he'd thought he could leave the place untended for ten years and everything would be right where he'd left it, he had no idea. In truth, he hadn't cared. He hadn't ever planned to return. Now he had, and it was worse than he could have imagined.

Of all the people to turn up on his first night back in town he never would have expected Becca Carstairs.

"You're right," she said, gaze once again returning to the distant glow of Three Harbors. "I shouldn't be out here." She contemplated the shovel he leaned upon. "What are you burying?"

"Bodies."

She blinked and took a step back, landing on another stick. The resulting crack made her flinch, and he felt bad for scaring her. But didn't she know him better than that?

Owen rubbed a hand over the back of his neck. He might have been gone from this town for ten years, but he would always be "that McAllister boy." When there was trouble, everyone pointed his way. To be honest, a lot of the time they'd been right.

Even after he'd found football and discovered he was pretty good at it—knocking heads on the field kept him from knocking heads anywhere else—folks still saw him as Mary McAllister's son. And Mary had never met a pharmaceutical she didn't love.

As she'd gone about obtaining them in both creative

and illegal ways . . . Well, in a town like this that was hard to live down. Certainly it wasn't fair to visit the sins of the mother on the son, but when had life, or small towns, ever been fair?

Still, Becca had always believed the best of him. She'd befriended him, stood up for him, protected him. She'd loved him.

Which was why he'd had to leave.

"Animals," he blurted. "I found dead animals in the house. I'm burying the bodies."

"Are they black?"

"Well . . . blackened." The moon cast just enough light over her face to reveal her confusion. "They were burned."

The scent of charred flesh and fur still lingered—in the house, the yard, his nose. For an instant when he'd walked into the place, he'd thought he was having a flash-back—wasn't the first one, probably wouldn't be the last.

"Show me."

"I don't think so."

"Why not?"

A lot of reasons, the most obvious one—

"It's not pretty."

"I'm a vet. You wouldn't believe what I've seen."

"You don't want to see this." He wished he could unsee it. But he'd wished that about a lot of things, and that never, ever happened. Which was how most wishes went.

"I'm sure I don't want to see it." She made a "move along" gesture with both hands. "But I have to."

Owen shook his head, refused to move, and she stomped her foot. More twigs died.

"There are missing pets."

"You think these are them?"

"Only one way to find out." She tilted an eyebrow. He stayed where he was.

"Maybe we should call the police."

"We will. But if the bodies are burned like you say, they'll call me to identify what they are. Better if I take a peek first. Besides, my phone doesn't work. Does yours?"

He hadn't checked, and his phone was in the house anyway. "After you," he said.

The ground was uneven; Owen leaned on the shovel a bit. He still had a slight hitch in his giddyup he didn't want anyone to see.

Ten years and Becca didn't seem to have aged at all. The light wasn't good but what there'd been had seemed to shine right on her, like a beacon from above.

Not a wrinkle around her hazel eyes. Her skin was still redhead pale and smooth. Her only freckles dotted places no one could see. He remembered tasting them, tasting her.

Owen took a deep breath, but that only served to reveal another thing that hadn't changed. She still smelled like lemons and sunshine. He hadn't drunk a glass of lemonade since he'd left.

Lemonade had always tasted like her.

He stumbled, badly. Lost his grip on the shovel, which fell into her, and she stumbled too. He reached out and snatched her arm—just because he was lame didn't mean

he was . . . lame. His hands were still quick, even if the
rest of him wasn't.

The snarl that rumbled from the darkness had his skin
prickling. His free hand went to his empty hip again as
a huge, black wolf loomed from the night.

Becca stepped in front of Owen. He still had a grip
on her arm and pulled her back, which only made the
wolf snap, jaws clicking shut centimeters away from
Owen's free hand. Again, quickness was everything.
He'd learned that the hard way in Afghanistan.

"He isn't hurting me," Becca said.

The wolf crouched, still grumbling but no longer
snarling and snapping, its freakishly light green gaze
fixed on Owen.

"You have a pet wolf?"

She stared at the beast as if it were the first time she'd
seen it, and considering the animal's behavior that
couldn't be the case. "Wolves aren't pets."

"Got that right."

The beast showed Owen her teeth. If he'd been confused before, he wasn't now. Definitely not a pet.

Frantic barking commenced. A bolt of brown fur
vaulted through one of the now glassless windows of the
house and hit the ground running.

Owen had time to shout, "Reggie, *nein*!" an instant
before the two animals slammed into each other and
rolled. Snarls filled the air. Spittle flew; teeth snapped.

"Call her off," he ordered.

"She isn't a pet. Call him off."

Reggie wasn't a pet either, but he had been trained
by the best.

"Nein!" Owen ordered. *"Aus!"*

Reggie released the wolf's leg, as ordered. The black beast circled the brown one.

"Hier!"

The dog hesitated, his eyes flicking to Owen, then back to the wolf. Owen couldn't blame him, but he also couldn't let Reggie disobey.

"Lass das sein! Hier!"

This time Reggie followed the commands of "don't do that" and "come." Though his neck craned so that he could keep the wolf in his sight, he trotted to Owen's side and sat without being told to *sitz!*

"What was that?" Becca asked.

"German."

She cast him an exasperated glance. "I got that much, but why?"

"Reggie's a military working dog. *Er gehorcht auf Kommando.* He obeys German commands."

Most K-9 working dogs were purchased from Germany. There they not only nurtured the bloodlines necessary for K-9 work, but they had the best training programs for the same. Even dogs purchased young and trained in the States still learned commands in German to match their initial training—sit, come, stay—as well as to align them with all the other dogs.

"That's a Belgian Malinois."

Most people thought Reggie was an oddly unmarked and slightly small German shepherd. Not Becca. She knew her dog breeds. Always had.

"He is," Owen agreed. "A lot of Belgians are bred in Germany."

Becca offered her hand to Reggie, palm down, non-threatening. He glanced at Owen. Military working dogs—MWDs for short—were not pets. They accepted admiration as their due, but only if it was allowed by their handler. Anyone who knew anything about MWDs would never touch one without asking first. That was a good way to lose a finger.

Reggie was better than most, he didn't need a muzzle in crowds, but he still wasn't cuddly and probably never would be.

"In ordnung," Owen said. *Okay.*

The dog sniffed her fingers. The wolf growled, and Reggie pulled back, with a low *woof*.

"Hush," Becca murmured, to one or both of them, Owen wasn't sure, but they both hushed. The wolf paced back and forth a dozen yards away. There was something odd about the animal that went beyond its far too human eyes.

"What kind of military work does he do?"

Owen didn't want to say, but from Becca's expression she already knew or at least suspected. It wasn't rocket science to figure it out, and for a veterinarian even less so.

"Explosive detection," he answered.

"Then why is he here?"

The world shimmied, as if something had exploded nearby, though Owen knew nothing had. He was still hoping that remnant would fade along with the constant urge to hit the dirt after any loud, sudden noise. It was embarrassing. Though much better now than it had been when he'd first woken up. Back then, a door closing could make him shake like a tree in a strong breeze.

"There was an accident."

"An accident with a bomb-sniffing dog would involve a bomb."

"Can't put anything past you."

"Must you be sarcastic?"

"Apparently."

She looked like she wanted to smack him, except that would involve contact, and from the way she hovered just outside his reach, that wasn't going to happen. Was she keeping her distance to avoid setting off the wolf, or to avoid setting off Owen?

Owen wasn't sure what he'd do if she touched him. That single second of touching her—before the wolf took offense—had been bad. Or maybe it had been good. He couldn't decide.

"You're in one piece," Becca said, "and so is he."

Only because they'd been put together again better than Humpty Dumpty, but he wasn't going to tell her that. He also wasn't going to walk where she could observe him long enough to register that he still couldn't walk quite right. While the coldness in those eyes that had once gazed at him so warmly was hard to stomach, the pity would be even harder.

"We're fine," he lied. "Home on leave. I plan to get this place ready to sell, then we'll be out of here."

"You're staying in the house?"

"Where else?"

She eyed it as if it might collapse in a heap any second. He wouldn't be surprised.

"I've slept worse places," he said.

Her hazel eyes flicked to his. "Where?"

He wasn't going to talk about that. Not now. Not with her.

Actually, not ever and with no one.

"I'll only be here until I sell the place."

"Sell?" she echoed, as if hearing the word for the first time. "But your mother—"

"Isn't ever going to be well enough to come back."

It had taken him a long time to accept that, even longer for his mother to, but now that they had, the house was an unnecessary burden.

"You don't want to live here when you—"

"No," he interrupted. Here was the last place he wanted to live. Here was too close to her.

"Shouldn't your enlistment be up by now?"

"I re-upped." Several times. "I'm due to re-up again." And he would if he could. "Men die if I don't do my job."

Her gaze narrowed on Reggie. "If he's a bomb-sniffing dog that makes you his handler."

"Becca, you had to have known all this—"

"How would I?" she interrupted. "You never wrote, Owen, except to tell me you wouldn't be writing."

He'd had his reasons. They still applied.

"I'm sure there was plenty of scuttlebutt on the Three Harbors grapevine."

And as the local veterinarian, Becca had to have heard all of it.

"If it concerned you," she said. "I didn't listen."

That shouldn't hurt, but it did.

Chapter 3

I was being a bitch.

Heard it. Knew it. Couldn't help it. He made me so damn mad.

Ten years since Owen had left Three Harbors, left me, and he hadn't come back. You'd think I would have gotten over it, over him.

Guess not.

"I . . . uh . . ." Why was I here? What was I doing? "I should check those animals."

"No one's stopping you."

Now he was being a bitch too. Great. I headed for the house.

Owen was different. Why wouldn't he be? He'd been gone a long time.

He'd always been handsome, with a grin that could charm the socks off just about anyone. He'd charmed more than the socks off me.

Back then his dark brown hair had been long, curling over his nape, sloping across his equally dark eyes. I'd loved how those eyes could go from icy—when he was glaring at someone who'd dissed him—to smoldering whenever they stared at me.

His hair was now brutally short, and his eyes seemed darker, sadder—though there'd never been anything light

about Owen McAllister. He'd always been a big kid—
taller than everyone else, muscular long before the
other boys. That hadn't changed. He was taller by over
an inch, shoulders wider by more than that. His biceps
bulged; his thighs seemed too large for his jeans.

We'd been friends first. Good friends. Best friends. I
missed that. You could always find another lover—
theoretically; I certainly hadn't—but a friend like Owen
didn't come around every day. Or any day apparently.

Then again with a friend like him, who needed ene-
mies? He'd broken my heart, and I hadn't yet figured out
a way to mend it.

I reached the listing porch, glanced back. Owen and
his dog hovered, unmoving, at the edge of the yard.

"Go ahead." He bent and pulled something from Reggie's coat. "He's got some burrs that I don't want in the
house."

From the appearance of the house, a few burrs
wouldn't hurt it. Perhaps Owen had seen enough of what
was inside. I didn't blame him. I didn't want to look
either. But I had to, so I climbed the steps and went in.

I stopped just past the threshold—not only because
of the smell—charred flesh and fur—but the sight. The
place was ruined. Not that it had been in that great a
shape to begin with, though Owen had done the best he
could. He'd been a kid with very little money—all he'd
had was time and hope.

The years had taken a toll. Damage had been done
not only by the elements but by the teenagers that had
come here to drink, dope, and screw. I saw evidence of
all three—bottles and cans, the stubs of cigs and joints,
several used condoms—scattered everywhere.

What I found in the living room was worse. The other had been kids being kids. Asshole kids, but still kids. This . . .

I stared at the charred remains.

This was evil.

Owen waited for Becca to disappear into the house.

Though she'd probably seen worse, or at least seen similar, he didn't want to let her go inside and face that alone. But more than that, he didn't want her to see him walk.

Childish. Foolish. Selfish. He silently berated himself with every *ish* he could think of as he gimped in her wake. He could have added *gimpish*, but he didn't think it was a word.

Should be.

Shrapnel had made a mess of his leg. Tendons were damaged, nerves too. The break in his femur had been ugly. The doctors had said he wouldn't be able to walk again. He'd refused to believe them, and he'd been right.

They'd also said he wouldn't be able to return to active duty. He refused to believe that either. Owen had nothing else. He was good at nothing but the job he'd learned in the Marines. If he wasn't Sergeant McAllister, who was he?

Reggie yipped. Owen had stopped walking to rub his thigh. The dog, which had healed much faster than Owen had, stood at the bottom of the listing porch steps.

"I'm okay," he said, as if Reggie could understand. Sometimes he swore the dog could.

He'd certainly understood when Owen had shouted, "Run," that day Reggie had found the turned-up earth at the same time Owen had seen the boy with the cell phone.

Which was why Reggie was in better shape than he was.

The kid had activated the IED a bit too soon, which meant that Owen and Reggie were alive and not dead after the big—

"Kaboom," Owen said.

The dog climbed the steps. Now he was gimping too. Owen sat on the top step, patted the area next to him. *"Sitz."*

Owen ran his palm over the animal's injuries, masked now by fur, but still there. When he reached the worst one, Reggie flinched.

Owen moved the hair away from the scar. No blood at least. This far out, there shouldn't be.

"Looks like you've bought yourself an aspirin in your kibble, pal. Shouldn't have been rolling in the dirt with a wolf today. Probably not any day with a wolf."

Speaking of . . . The wolf had disappeared as quickly as it had appeared. Where had it gone? Why had it gone? Why had it come in the first place? Becca seemed to know the animal, which wasn't surprising. She'd always had a strange affinity for them.

When they were children, she would entertain Owen with tales of "what the bunny said," and "what the fox thought." Forest creatures would walk up and eat out of her hand. The first time his mom had seen them surrounded by raccoons and opossums and squirrels, she'd flipped out. Started screaming about rabies, scared all the little beasties away.

He'd been six years old and already adept at knowing when he could calm her down and when he needed to call the EMTs. He avoided the latter as much as possible. Because if his mom went to the mental health facility, Owen went to foster care—at least until they'd moved here. Once he and Becca became friends, the Carstairs allowed him to stay with them while his mom "rested."

He owed that family more than he could ever repay. Another reason he had left when he had.

Reggie's tongue lolled. He appeared to be smiling. Owen rubbed behind the dog's ears. "You liked tussling with that wolf, didn't you?"

Reggie barked.

Owen had heard the Belgian Malinois described as the "sugar-hyped kid" of the dog world, and that could be true when they weren't handled correctly. A Belgian did not make a good pet, unless you had a huge amount of land and all day to spend throwing sticks. Without constant activity, they got into trouble. Left alone and bored they would destroy anything, everything, just for something to do.

But that drive to go, go, and keep going was what made them excellent bomb-sniffing dogs. Belgians didn't stop until they found something; they weren't afraid of much, and most didn't get twitchy when bullets blazed all around them. Owen thought Reggie kind of liked it.

"Steh." Reggie stood, but he didn't move until Owen showed him the red rubber ball that was his reward, then gave the forward command, *"Voran."*

Reggie nosed open the door, which Becca had left ajar. Owen followed at a slower pace, using the railing, the wall, the door for balance. He should probably use a cane. He had one, but he hadn't been able to make himself hold on to it for more than a minute, let alone walk with it.

He'd been on a plane since yesterday. Exhaustion, combined with more walking and more sitting than usual, then driving from Minneapolis, as well as the digging, had made Owen shakier than he liked.

What he should do was take a pain pill, then sink into a warm bath and fall into a fluffy bed. However, thanks to his mother's drug issues, he didn't take pain pills. He doubted the water heater worked any better now than it had when he lived here. Considering the electricity was off, along with the water, it wouldn't matter if it did. The mattresses were as trashed as the rest of the furniture, and even when they hadn't been they weren't fluffy.

He'd grit his teeth and get along. One of the first things he'd learned upon joining the Marines.

Inside there was no sign of Reggie. As Owen had mentioned kibble, he'd thought the dog would be waiting outside the still-closed kitchen door to the right. When he'd gone out to dig the grave, he'd put Reggie behind it, not wanting him to mess with the disgusting scene in the living room.

Reggie was a well-trained dog, but he was a dog, and sometimes he grabbed things he wasn't supposed to—like a terrorist—and dragged them around. While Owen often enjoyed that little mistake, having Reggie ingest charcoal pet remains wouldn't be at all amusing. So he'd confined him in the kitchen. That the windows were broken wide open had escaped him until the dog vaulted through one.

Becca spoke in the living room. Was she talking to

Reggie or herself? Owen had told the dog to *voran,* which was a command to go forward, in working-dog-speak to do what he was supposed to do. While Reggie was usually searching for explosives, he might also find and detain insurgents if he came across one. Though Becca was neither, she was standing in front of a scene that had to smell pretty nifty to a dog.

Owen swallowed. But not to him.

"I know," she murmured, and Owen frowned. Had he said that out loud?

He entered the living room as she smoothed her palm over Reggie's head. The dog's tail thumped once. She'd been talking to him. Nothing new. When they were kids she'd believed that dogs talked back.

Becca eyed the display atop the old table that some-one had dragged in from the kitchen, which gave Owen a chance to move closer unobserved and take a seat on the arm of the water-stained couch. Reggie hurried over and sat, waiting for his beloved red ball.

Owen handed it over, and, enthralled, Reggie dropped it, chased it, chewed it. The dog would do anything for the red ball, which meant Owen kept the thing in his pocket 24/7—and carried a spare in his duffel.

"The chief had reports of three missing cats, a dog, and a rabbit," she said. "There's more than that here."

"Some people must have figured their pets ran off or got plucked by a wolf." Becca cast him a narrow glance, and Owen held up his hands in surrender. "I didn't say it was your wolf."

"Not mine."

"A wolf, coyote, fox, bear." He paused. "Do bears eat meat?"

"Yes. Though they don't digest it well. Which is why most of their diet is plants and berries."

"They still might snatch a Pekinese that's wandered into the woods."

"No 'might' about it," she agreed.

"But if an owner lives close to the forest and Fluffy disappears, most of them wouldn't report it to the police. The cops aren't going to arrest Yogi."

"As Yogi is smarter than the average bear, he'd probably be above stealing then eating Fluffy, but I take your meaning."

Owen smiled. Even before he'd fallen in love with her, he'd liked her so damn much. He still did.

Be honest, dumbass.

He still loved her. He always would.

Becca pulled out her cell phone, looked at the display, cursed, and put it back in the pocket of her track pants. "I need to call Chief Deb."

"Chiefdub?"

"Deb. Debbie Waldentrout is the police chief now."

"Debbie Waldentrout is three feet tall." The idea of her in a police chief's uniform was somewhat cartoonish.

"Is not." Becca headed for the door.

As she went past, Owen took her elbow and she stilled. He should have let her go, especially when she shivered. Instead he rubbed his thumb over her ulna, and she shivered some more. Because he was sitting on the edge of the couch and she was standing, his gaze was level with her chest, which rose and fell so quickly he was captivated.

That scent of lemons overshadowed the scent of death, and Owen breathed in, out, and in again. From the moment he'd met her, she'd cleansed him, healed him, elevated him. He'd become so much more while he'd been with her. He'd become so much more *because* of her. She had loved him. She had saved him. He'd always wanted to tell her that, but he'd never been quite sure how.

What he saw in her gaze made Owen tighten his fingers—to push her away, or pull her closer. He never knew, because she leaned over—so quick he had time to do nothing but say her name. A whisper. A plea. A prayer. And then she was kissing him; he was kissing her.

The years fell away. It was their first kiss. Their last.

That first one had been tentative—soft, a little afraid, yet so full of hope. The last had been shocked, a little tearful, and full of despair. This one tasted of both. How strange. What did she hope for? What did she fear? Why did she despair?

Questions for another time, right now he delved, taking her mouth, tasting her teeth, wishing, hoping, praying for more, even though he knew it could never be. For so many reasons . . .

Suddenly she was gone. His mouth followed hers in retreat, seeking those lips he still dreamed of. His arms reached; his empty fingers closed on nothing. He started to stand. The pain sent him right back.

His breath hissed in. Reggie yipped and rushed over, shoving his precious ball into Owen's hand, sharing what always made him feel better. Owen put the toy into his pocket, then pushed his fingers into Reggie's fur to keep them from doing what they shouldn't.

Rubbing his leg. Yanking her back. Making a fist and punching a wall.

"I don't know why I did that," she said. "It's just—"
She waved a hand toward the table, and he suddenly remembered what he had completely forgotten.

The travesty in his living room.

How could he have kissed her and dreamed of doing so much more, with that only a few feet away? Because, for him, a room that contained Becca Carstairs was devoid of anything else worth noticing.

"You always made everything better," she blurted to the wall and not to him. "At least until—" Her breath rushed out.

"Until I made everything worse."

After a few seconds of silence, during which Reggie glanced back and forth between the two of them, brow wrinkled, mouth open, she straightened. "I'm going up on the ridge to see if I can get a signal."

The ridge lay between this house and her parents' farm and was the highest point for miles around.

"Try the porch first." Owen jabbed his thumb toward the stairs that led to the bedrooms on the second level. The largest, his mother's, had a flat, porchlike area that extended over the garage. The trees had been shorn away from the utility poles more than once in the past ten years and created a tiny avenue to the sky. "Higher might help."

She started for the stairs. "If I can't get through I'll have to head to my folks' and use their landline."

He wanted to say he'd go with her, but the idea of climbing up one side of the ridge and down the other made his leg pulse.

"If you go, take Reggie."

She paused. "Why?"

"That wolf is still out there."

Becca glanced at the front door. "In the yard?"

"I didn't see her, but—"

"Yeah, no," she said.

"What do you mean, no?"

"Did I stutter? The last time your dog saw a wolf, he attacked her."

"Exactly."

"She wasn't doing anything but protecting me."

"And why was that?" he asked.

"Because you had a shovel and you appeared ready to use it. On my head."

"I didn't mean why did she protect *you*, but why did she protect anyone? She's a wild animal. They don't protect humans."

"Wolves are different."

A long, low, mournful howl rose toward the moon.

"That one sure is," he muttered.

I escaped upstairs while Owen was distracted by the wolf howl.

He hadn't looked so good. I suppose finding a pile of charred fur in your living room wasn't the best welcome home, but it hadn't been aimed at him. Had it?

No. No one could have known he'd be coming home. Could they?

I hadn't lied when I said I hadn't listened to scuttlebutt about him. I couldn't bear it. I'd loved him so damn much. His leaving had been difficult, but I'd tried to understand.

I have nothing, Becca.

You have me.

I wasn't enough. I'd tried not to let him know how

much that hurt. I got up every morning hoping for his letter. When it came at last it was agony.

So why had I kissed him tonight like the foolish girl I'd once been—crazy in love with a boy who would only hurt me?

My father's words. He couldn't help it. He loved me.

He'd loved Owen too. But us together . . . Not so much.

In the end he'd been right. Owen had left me. I'd been so devastated my first year of college was still a blur. I'd managed not to flunk out, and at the University of Wisconsin that wasn't easy. The school was hard and my major, zoology, not for sissies.

Considering our history and my heartbreak, why had I kissed him? Because he'd been sitting on the couch where we'd first touched? Because when he came near me all I could do was remember every single other time that he had?

Or had it been because the sight on that table had scared the shit out of me, and I'd needed to forget for an instant in the arms of the only man who'd ever made me feel strong, capable, and adult?

Hell, be honest, Owen was the only man who'd ever made me feel anything. The first brush of his mouth and I'd been lost.

I was twelve, and he was taking my hand, holding it tight during *The Blair Witch Project*. The movie had struck a little close to home. I had no idea why we'd watched it.

I was thirteen, and he was kissing me in that very room, tasting my tongue, his palm hot at my waist, his thumb almost brushing my breast.

We were fifteen, and they'd just taken away his mother for what would be the last time. Those damn voices had told her to kill him. Was it any wonder I'd never mentioned hearing voices of my own?

The expression on his face—confused, crushed, helpless. I'd held him in my arms; we'd both fallen asleep on the couch. My parents had found us. I'd begged them to give him a home, and they had. Soon after, I'd tried to give him me. To his credit, he'd refused.

For a few years more.

Memories tumbled through my mind as I ran up the steps, down the hall, through a room as trashed as those below. At least the windows weren't busted, but the door leading onto the porch was warped, and I had to put my shoulder into it to get the thing open enough to slip outside. I was just glad I didn't have to ask Owen for help. I needed some distance, and I needed it now. Damn him for bringing everything back. I hadn't thought of Owen McAllister in . . .

Days.

I moved to the edge of the porch. There wasn't even a railing to keep stupid people from tumbling off. Obviously not up to code—if Owen tried to sell the place, there was going to be a lot he'd have to add, subtract, and update first.

I stood there breathing for a minute—lovely fresh air that didn't smell of blood and fire, flesh and mold. But mostly it didn't smell of sun and grass, hay and midnight.

Of him.

The wolf called to the moon that swelled heavy and ripe and cool straight above, but she was so far off maybe it wasn't even the same wolf. And about that wolf . . .

Owen had seen her. His dog had rolled around with her. Which made the animal a lot less imaginary. I had to wonder why she'd shown herself to someone after all these years and why that someone had been Owen.

I glanced at my phone; I had a signal. Yay! I didn't want to go to my parents'. I didn't want to explain why I was here, what I had seen.

And who I had seen it with.

I located the police station's direct number in my contact list. Less than a minute later, the dispatcher put me through to Chief Deb.

"You know those animals you were looking for?" I asked. "I found them."

Chapter 4

The living room window gave Owen a perfect view of the ridge. If Becca couldn't get a signal upstairs, she'd appear on top of it very soon. She'd no doubt shimmy down the drainpipe before she'd come back through here.

While Owen didn't like the idea of her being alone out there, she wouldn't be for long. The bright moon would catch the reflective stripe on her track pants. He'd be able to follow her progress up, up, up through the breaks in the trees until she popped out on top like a piece of toast.

Then Owen would give Reggie the command, *voraus,* or *run out*. He'd be hard-pressed not to tell him to *bringen,* or *fetch*. But Reggie didn't *bringen* nice people back any less chewed on than he brought back the not-so-nice.

"If necessary I expect you to vault through that window." Owen pointed; Reggie followed the line of his finger. "And kick the ass of whatever is anywhere near her."

Reggie gave a low *woof*. Owen took that to mean "Happy to."

Ass kicking was Reggie's specialty. Once, it had been Owen's. He very much feared it might never be again, and he wasn't certain what else he could do.

In the Marines he had excelled.

Running fast? Check.

Hitting hard? Check.

No home, no family, no life? Check and double-check.

He'd been a shoo-in for K-9 Corps. Add to that his love of animals, which he'd had even before he'd met Becca, and he had been accepted into the canine program without a hitch.

There was something about dogs that healed or at least helped. Your mother was a druggie, a nut, often a thief? You were an average student on a good day? No place to go? No future to dream of? A dog didn't care. They didn't even know.

Becca had known, and she hadn't cared either. Owen had loved her so much he couldn't think straight. Luckily her father had loved her enough to think straight for both of them.

What would the man say if he knew Owen was back? Did it matter? He wasn't going to stay.

Owen rubbed his hand over his mouth, which still tingled from hers. Would he be able to look Dale Carstairs in the face any more now than he'd been able to look at him then? Certainly this time he'd only kissed her, then he'd—

Owen stood and paced, ignoring the pain. He was no longer a kid with nothing; he was a man with . . .

"Not much more."

He threw a glance toward the ridge. No sign of Becca. He whirled, planning to pace some more, and nearly tripped over Reggie. He'd decided to pace too. Owen gave the dog a pat. "I have you, don't I, buddy?"

Reggie panted and drooled.

However, if Reggie went back to active duty and Owen did not, he wouldn't have the dog either. The idea of turning the animal over to another handler after all they'd been through together made Owen sick.

The more he thought about things, the worse things got, and that was without even considering . . .

He lifted his gaze to the table full of *ick*. There was something about it from this angle that made him get the lantern and move closer, lifting the light, then setting it on the mantel and stepping back where he'd been.

"Damn," he muttered, just as Becca pounded down the hall and out the front door.

I wanted to meet Chief Deb in the yard, give her a heads-up before taking her inside, and from the volume of the siren and the peek-a-boo flash of headlights through the trees, she was breaking land speed records to get here.

The click of toenails on wood announced Reggie an instant before he descended the porch steps and stood at my side. He shook like he'd just jumped into a very cold lake, tilted his head, whined a little.

Hate that noise.

A lot of dogs howled along with a siren, protest rather than performance. However, Reggie did nothing but take a seat and stare in the direction of the sound. I suspected the places where he'd sniffed bombs had a lot of sirens blaring.

I rubbed his ears. "Sorry, buddy. It'll stop soon."

"What did he say?"

Owen leaned against the porch railing. I hadn't heard him come out. Nothing new. For such a big guy, he'd always moved very quietly.

"Dogs can't say anything." Didn't stop me from hearing them.

At first my parents had thought my recitations of "what the doggy said" adorable. As time went on and those recitations had expanded to include every animal I met, with a bizarre measure of accuracy, they got a little spooked.

As it wouldn't do for the local GP to know their little girl was a fruitcake, they took me to a pediatrician in Minneapolis. The fancy city doctor told them to ignore my stories. Without attention for the behavior the behavior would eventually go away.

It hadn't, but I had stopped sharing. Even at the age of six, no one wants to be weird.

Chief Deb's cruiser shot out of the trees like the DeLorean in *Back to the Future* shot out of . . . the future. Considering what I'd found here, I couldn't blame Deb's need for speed.

She threw the car into park when it was still moving, the gears grinding so loudly that Reggie growled.

Owen jumped; I thought he might fall off the porch, then he had to steady himself with a hand on the broken railing, which shimmied, and then so did he. Something tickled my brain, and I stared at him so long he noticed.

Instead of making a sarcastic comment, or even sticking out his tongue like he would have when we were kids, he glanced away, and that just made the tickle tickle even more.

Chief Deb vaulted from the car, nearly catching her hip as she slammed the door. "Where are they?"

Reggie scrambled in front of her. The *back off* in his head came out of his mouth as *grrr*.

Deb frowned at the dog as if she hadn't noticed him until that moment. Though he wasn't that large a dog, Reggie was still kind of hard to miss.

She tried to move around him; he sidestepped; another warning rumbled free. Deb's eyes narrowed. "Am I gonna have to shoot you?"

His lip lifted, and the rumble became a snarl.

"Becca, call off your dog."

I'd always picked up strays. Folks didn't know from one day to the next how many animals and of what variety might belong to me—until I managed to foist them off on someone else. Right now, though, I didn't have any. I was sure it wouldn't last.

I pointed at Owen. Deb's eyes widened. She hadn't noticed him either. In her defense, he was hovering at the edge of the porch, just out of the moonlight's reach, and she'd no doubt been distracted by the oddest case to land in Three Harbors since the glacier came through.

"Owen?" She looked him up and down.

He *was* a whole lot bigger. It was no wonder I hadn't recognized him earlier when he'd been fooling around in the dark with a shovel.

"What are you doing here?" Deb continued.

"My house."

"And the dead animals?"

He leaned against the wall, crossed his arms, and his biceps expanded more. I thought Deb was going to drool.

"Not mine."

Deb stared for so long, I finally poked her in the back.

She jumped. The movement made Reggie growl again. "Get him outta my way."

"Reggie, *hier.*"

After another glance at the chief, the dog took the steps with a hitch in his stride I hadn't noticed before and didn't much like.

"Is he named after Reggie White?" Deb's voice lifted on the sainted name.

Like every other person in town, she counted the days between Sundays. I wouldn't be surprised if she wore a green and gold T-shirt under her uniform. She wouldn't be the only one. In Wisconsin, especially in small towns like these, the Packers were more of a religion than a football team.

"I didn't name him," Owen said. "But he does have a helluva pass rush."

Reggie snorted. Had he understood that? Doubtful. Though most dogs knew a lot more words than anyone gave them credit for, *pass rush* probably weren't two of them.

"Shall we?" The chief indicated the house.

I wanted to ask about Reggie's limp, but Owen waved us on. "You two go ahead. I'll make sure he stays here."

I thought Reggie would stay anywhere Owen put him for as long as he put him there, but I didn't comment. As Deb was shifting back and forth so fast she was either beyond impatient or really needed the bathroom, I made a mental note to discuss the dog's health, or lack of it, later.

I did wonder for an instant why Owen didn't want to join us. Perhaps he'd been in too many caves to stomach being inside anywhere for very long. Or maybe the smell of death didn't agree with him. Did it agree with anyone?

Chief Deb gagged as soon as she went in. Considering most of the windows in the place were broken, you'd think the smoky-meat smell would be gone. You'd be wrong.

Deb paused in the entryway of the living room. "You didn't tell me about that."

"I said I'd found the animals." I'd been hovering in the hall, not wild about going back in there either. Now I joined her, and I saw what she meant.

The lantern, which had previously resided just inside the room and thrown a muted glow over the table—the less light on *that* the better—now sat on the mantel, perfectly illuminating a five-pointed star etched on the wall.

Owen waited until the two women disappeared into the living room. Their attention captured there, he ordered Reggie to stay with the German command, *"Bly'b,"* then followed.

He reached the others just as Deb whirled. "Owen!"

If she'd been a normal-sized woman, she'd have yelled right in his face. Instead she yelled right in his solar plexus. He didn't step back, but she did, emitting a little "Eep!" before she shoved him.

"Don't do that!"

"You screamed. It's not my fault I was already here."

Deb pointed to the chalk outline of a star on the wall above the table. "Is that yours?"

The place might not be an interior decorator's wet dream, but it also hadn't been like this when he left. "No."

"Where'd it come from?"

"No idea. I didn't draw it."

"Did your mother?"

"What? No. Why?"

"This *is* the witch's house."

He contemplated the drawing. It did appear kind of witchy.

"My mother isn't actually a witch."

"You sure?"

"Yeah."

Reggie barked once from outside. Owen must have said that too loud and too angrily. Big shock.

"Becca?" Chief Deb asked.

"His mother isn't a witch," she agreed. "And this . . ."—she waved her hand at the graffiti and the table—"is all new. Wasn't here the last time I was."

The annoyance that had already sparked over Deb's words, flared at her needing someone else's confirmation of his own.

"Could your mom's friends have come here?" Deb continued. "What are they called? A coven?"

"She didn't have friends." She'd had dealers. And if it weren't for that damn star on the wall, the dead animals on the table, and the lack of a meth lab in the kitchen he would have figured those dealers had gone *Breaking Bad* on the place. It made more sense than a coven.

"She isn't a witch," he repeated. Did the woman listen?

"Maybe a coven met here because they knew the place was abandoned."

"It wasn't abandoned."

Sure, he should have come back before now, but—

His gaze went to Becca, who continued to study the

table, probably because she didn't want to look at him. And that meant she *really* didn't want to look at him because who would choose to look at that?

"Couldn't tell it by the appearance of the place," Chief Deb muttered.

"And whose fault is that?" he snapped. "If the Carstairs' farm was left empty you can bet someone from your office would have driven by often enough."

"The Carstairs' farm would never be left empty." Deb's voice was so reasonable, and her words so true, Owen was at first furious, and then so empty he felt drained.

He'd been foolish to think the house would be in decent shape, that he could come here and, with a few minor tweaks, have the place ready to sell in a few weeks. But he'd been foolish about a lot of things.

Believing his mother would get better. That his life was finally on track. That he'd ever get over Becca Carstairs.

"I need to call Otto," Deb said.

Otto Dubberpuhl, the GP in Three Harbors, was the only doctor they had and had been for as long as Owen could recall. Owen had figured the guy would be in his grave by now. Doctor D had been old when they were kids, or maybe he'd just seemed so. Back then, forty was old, so Doctor D might be all of fifty now, but Owen doubted it.

Because the town was so small, Doctor D performed any autopsies. But those consisted of an explanation for a thirty-five-year-old farmer dying on his tractor and the occasional crib death. Once in a while, a domestic disaster. Still, Owen doubted he was the one to call for this.

"Maybe you should find someone with more experience in . . ." Owen waved at the mess. He wasn't sure what to call that.

"Doctor D took a course on forensics," Deb protested.

"I think it was called 'Accurately Portraying Forensic Science in Your Novel,'" Becca said.

Owen took a deep breath in an attempt not to laugh, choke, or cough. As the air was still heavy with the scent of *ick,* the gulp took care of any urge to laugh, though the choking and the coughing were touch and go for a while.

"This isn't a murder," Owen pointed out.

Becca cast him a disgusted glance. "Is too."

"Would forensic techniques work in a case involving animals?"

"Probably not," Becca said. "But there was a class in veterinary forensics in college."

"Great!" Deb bounced on her toes as if she might actually start to cheer like the good old days. G-R-E-A-T! GRRREAT! "Go nuts, Becca."

"I didn't say I took it."

"You didn't?" Deb's face became crestfallen.

Becca shook her head so hard her hair flew around her like a fiery dervish. "Too ghoulish for me."

"Ghoulish?" the chief repeated. "I love all that CSI stuff."

"CSI on people is one thing, animals another."

She had a point. How many books, movies, and television shows portrayed the graphic deaths of animals? Few to none. While a lot of people seemed to be overly okay with human mutilation, torture, and bloody death, they were equally squeamish about the same in regard to animals.

Owen cast a glance at the table, swallowed, and turned away. He could see why.

"Veterinary forensics involves cases of abuse, mutilation, fighting rings—dogs, roosters." Becca jabbed a finger at the spectacle that had ruined Owen's living room. Probably forever. "And that. Whatever it is."

"What are we going to do?" Chief Deb asked.

"We?" Owen repeated. He had no clue about forensics—human, animal, or otherwise.

"I can call the professor," Becca said. "See if he has a recommendation."

Deb hesitated. She probably didn't want to admit the inadequacy of her force—who would?—but in the end what choice did she have?

"That would be good. Thanks."

Becca took her phone out of her pocket, touched the screen. "I've got his number."

If she hadn't taken the class, then why did she have the professor in her contacts list?

She lifted the phone to indicate upstairs, where the cell signal lived. "I'll give Jeremy a call and be right back."

If she hadn't taken the class, why was he *Jeremy*? If she *had* taken the class why would he be *Jeremy*? Wouldn't he be Professor Whatever?

Owen stood in the hall stewing while Chief Deb poked around the crime scene. He didn't think that was a good idea. Wouldn't it be better to leave it alone until an expert showed up? But she was the cop, not him.

At the sound of footsteps on the staircase, Owen moved into the living room so Becca wouldn't see him hovering in the hall trying to eavesdrop on a conversation he had no prayer of hearing over that distance. He didn't have ears like Reggie.

"He's coming himself," Becca said.

"Swell," Owen muttered.

"He's the best forensic veterinarian in the Midwest."

"How many are there?"

"Don't know, don't care. Jeremy will be here in the morning."

"Doesn't he have a class to teach?"

A coed to boink?

"He'll cancel." She waved a hand toward the five-pointed star on the wall. "The pentagram intrigued him."

"That's a pentagram?" Deb asked, tilting her head right, then left, then right again as she studied it.

"Isn't it?" Becca glanced at Owen.

"My geometry grades were shit." Along with the rest of them.

"Mine were more like crap, but I think that's what they call those. If not, Jeremy should know." Becca bit her lip, sighed.

Owen knew that look, that sigh. "What else?"

"Jeremy said that a pentagram is a Wiccan symbol."

"He thinks witches did this?"

"No."

"You just said—"

"A pentagram *is* a Wiccan symbol, but those who practice Wicca believe that they should harm none." She pointed at the table. "That's pretty harmful."

"I never thought I'd see anything like this in Three Harbors," Owen said.

"None of us did."

Silence settled over them.

"Well, let's move along." Chief Deb made a shooing gesture.

Becca moved; Owen did not.

"Good night," Owen said.

The chief blinked. "You can't stay here."

"It's my damn house."

"It's a crime scene."

"Not really."

"Yes, really," Becca interjected. "Jeremy said we should leave it as undisturbed as possible."

Owen had to force himself to unclench his teeth, which had automatically ground together the instant she said *Jeremy* again. He indicated his trashed house. "I think that ship sailed a long time ago."

"Nevertheless . . ." Chief Deb shooed him again.

Though he didn't want to stay here, not with that there, Owen refused to be shooed. He'd taken great pains not to be seen walking today; he wasn't going to ruin that now.

"You'll have to stay somewhere else, Owen," Deb said.

"I don't have anywhere else."

The silence that followed that statement made him wish it back even before Becca spoke.

"You can—"

"No."

"You don't even know what I was going to say."

"I'm not staying at your place."

"I didn't ask you to."

"She can barely fit in her place." Deb eyed Owen. "You never would."

"Where do you live?" he asked.

"Above the clinic."

"In Doc Brady's room?"

Owen had been there once with Becca when they'd brought him a bird with a broken leg. Oddly, by the time they got there, the creature was hopping around on it pretty well, and it had flown off as soon as Doc Brady held it out the upstairs window of his teeny-tiny abode.

There wouldn't be room for him and Reggie in Doc Brady's—make that Doc Becca's—place, even if he were willing to go there.

"I can stay at a bed-and-breakfast. There must be a hundred of them."

More like a dozen, and at this time of year, just after prime leaf viewing, they should be pretty empty.

"Unfortunately none of them accept pets," Becca said.

"Reggie's better behaved than most of their clientele."

"No doubt," she agreed. "But their clientele doesn't drool and shed."

"I bet some of them do."

"What about Stone Lake?" At Owen's confused expression Chief Deb continued. "Big-city lawyer got sick of lawyering and bought Stone Lake Tavern. Built some cottages on the water."

"He lets dogs stay in them?" Owen asked.

"Only when they bring along their duck-hunting owners to pay the bill."

Stone Lake was more of a pond than a lake but ducks still floated on it.

"Sounds perfect. I'll just pack up and be on my way. Don't feel you have to wait for me. I promise not to touch—" He waved at the altar.

"Not so fast." Chief Deb held up her hand like a crossing guard stopping traffic. "I have questions for you that I want answered before you go anywhere."

Her shoulder mike squawked static. "Say again," she ordered, moving into the kitchen, nearer to both an open window and town.

Chapter 5

Owen was acting strangely. Not that finding dead things in your house wouldn't make anyone kind of off, but—

"Why is it your house?" I blurted. "I thought it was your mother's."

"She signed everything over." Owen's gaze went to the mess and stuck there. "Lucky me."

"I'm sorry."

"You didn't trash the place." His eyes came back to mine. "Did you?"

"Once upon a time, I might have." I'd been hurt, angry, young, but I also hadn't been here. By the time I'd returned to Three Harbors for good I was Dr. Carstairs, and I had better things to do.

"Doubtful," he said. "You were always a Goody Two-shoes."

He was right. The one rebellion I'd ever made was him. That had worked out so well, I hadn't bothered with rebellion, or men, since. Animals were more my speed. They were honest about their feelings. If a dog loved you, you knew it. If it hated you, you knew that too. Pretty damn fast.

Chief Deb reappeared and beckoned me. I followed her into the kitchen. She tapped her shoulder mike. "Emerson's asking for you. Duchess has been in labor for hours."

As the only Emerson in Three Harbors was Emerson Watley, we were talking Duchess the cow, rather than Duchess the dog, or Duchess the duck. I did count all of them as patients.

"That's not unusual. But . . . how did he know where I was?"

"Office is closed. Your cell isn't getting a signal."

So he'd called the cops. I wasn't really surprised. It had happened before with other clients. Usually people called my parents first. Emerson might have, but they wouldn't have been any help.

Often, if I knew I was going to an area where my phone would be useless I left word with dispatch. Three Harbors was a small town. Eventually, everyone called dispatch. Though this time I hadn't left word because I hadn't planned on a side trip. Thanks to the nightmare in the living room, the cops still knew where I was.

Deb's mike hissed with static loud enough to crack a window if there'd been any left to crack. She leaned out the gaping hole in the wall in an attempt to get a better signal.

I joined her, standing as close as I could to hear the dispatcher—sounded like Candy Tarley, whose hair color fluctuated between cherry Gummy Bear and lemon Life Saver, depending on the month and her mood.

"He says—" Snap, crackle. ". . . doesn't like—" Pop! ". . . looks of her."

Emerson Watley had been a dairy farmer for over forty years, like his father before him, and his father before him, and knew what a calving cow should look like.

"Tell him I'll be right there."

"Okay, Becca." Deb turned her head toward the mike, obviously waiting for the atrocious static to clear before she did so.

No one had called me Dr. Carstairs since I'd graduated. A few went with Doc Becca. Didn't matter. As long as the checks they sent to Three Harbors Animal Care didn't bounce—I had *huge* school loans—they could call me anything they wanted. I just needed them to call.

I had my hand on the front doorknob before I remembered I had no car. But Owen did.

The hall was empty. I walked back to the living room.

"Huh."

The living room was empty too.

The instant Becca moved into the kitchen with the chief, Owen gimped as fast as he could to the front door. Thankfully Deb and Becca faced away from the hall, the chief leaning half out the window as she tried to hear what the person on the other side of the fizzy radio was saying.

Owen quietly opened the door. Reggie sat on the porch, right where he'd left him. Together they headed for the rental truck.

After his injury Owen had been airlifted out of the field and taken to Bagram Air Base. Once he was stabilized he'd been flown to Ramstein Air Force Base in Germany, then transported to Landstuhl Regional Medical Center for surgery. Within a few days he'd been on another plane across the Atlantic to Walter Reed in D.C. Reggie had followed the same general trajectory— Bagram to Germany, though he'd been taken to Dog Center Europe, about fifteen minutes from LRMC.

It was unusual for a working dog to return to the U.S., which on the one hand had made Owen nervous about the extent of Reggie's injuries. On the other hand, Owen was glad he wasn't alone. He was used to being with Reggie twenty-four/seven. Without him, he'd be more lost than he already was.

Once Owen had been released from Walter Reed, he'd met Reggie's plane in New York. They'd flown from there to Minneapolis. They could have taken another hop to the small airport in Ashland, but the cost was astronomical.

Instead, Owen had rented a pickup truck, released Reggie from crate bondage, and driven several hours to Three Harbors. He couldn't remember the last time he'd slept, eaten, or showered, and the desire for all three suddenly overwhelmed him.

Reggie climbed into the cab more slowly than he'd gotten out of it. He was favoring his injury more than Owen had ever seen. When he sat, he did so with his haunches against Owen's. Reggie only did that when he was overtired, stressed, or ill.

The tap on his window made Owen jump so high he banged his bad leg on the steering wheel. Becca stood on the other side of the glass.

"I need a ride."

He was so tempted to put the truck in gear he actually reached for the shift.

"Don't you dare." Becca yanked open the door.

Damn. If he'd put the vehicle in gear the door would have locked automatically.

"Always go with your instinct," he murmured. One of the very first rules in bomb detection.

"I'm not letting go until you agree to give me a ride." She glanced toward the house. "And if you don't want to be stuck here answering questions you don't know the answers to, we'd better move before Deb gets done talking to the station."

"Then move." He indicated the passenger side.

She ran around the front, shooed Reggie, who'd come over to greet her, back to the middle, and hopped in. Owen put the truck into gear, and they lurched toward the trees. Just in time too. In the rearview mirror, Chief Deb emerged from the house. At the sight of his taillights, she kicked the porch railing and it fell into the overgrown flower bed.

"Thanks," Becca said. "I figured you'd drive off the instant I let go of your door and leave me behind."

He would have if he'd thought of it. But he wasn't thinking very clearly or very fast on so little sleep.

"How'd you get out here?" he asked.

"Wogged."

Owen blinked.

"That's what my brothers call my pathetic attempts at jogging. Faster than a walk, slower than a jog makes—"

"Wog," he finished. He'd always liked her brothers, though not half as much as he'd liked her.

Owen cast a sideways glance in Becca's direction, then had to lean forward to actually see her since Reggie's big fat head was in the way. The dog stared at Becca too, mouth open, tongue lolling. Couldn't blame him. She was stunning.

Her hair was long, thick, and fire red. She'd braided it; she always did. Otherwise the heavy mass got into everything—her eyes, her face, her food, his mouth.

Owen swallowed and dragged his eyes back to the road. He should never have kissed her. Though, to be fair, *she* had kissed *him*. It didn't make the taste of her that still lingered on his tongue, nor the memory of how different things were—how different *he* was—any easier to bear.

"You—" he began, and his voice broke. He cleared his throat, tried again. "You always jog in the forest in the dark?"

"No. I wog."

The dirt path had some deep ruts, the result of years of snow and ice and mud with no grading to even it out. The trees and bushes had encroached from the sides, narrowing the trail until branches scraped the truck. He was going to wind up paying for a new paint job by the time he returned it.

"Isn't that a little dangerous?"

"In Three Harbors?"

"If you were jogging—"

She lifted her eyebrows.

"Excuse me, wogging, in Three Harbors I wouldn't be worried."

"You're worried?"

He glanced at her; Reggie tried to lick him in the nose. "You saw my house. There's something weird going on here."

"I didn't know that when I left, and I doubt it has anything to do with me." She held up a hand. "Or you either. It's one of those things. Sick, weird, freaky, horrible, all of the above. But in the end, probably stupid kids behaving badly."

"You believe that?"

"Nope," she said.

If what they'd been talking about hadn't been sick, weird, freaky, horrible, and all of the above, her response might have made him laugh. As it was, he muttered, "Shit."

"Yeah," she agreed. "Good times. I need you to drop me at Emerson's place."

The only Emerson Owen knew was Emerson Watley, a dairy farmer older than God, with plenty of hair in his nose and his ears but none at all on his head.

"Hot date?"

Why had he asked that?

"Date?" she repeated as if the word were a new one. "With Emerson? He's ancient."

"He could have a grandson, named after him and everything. Or maybe you just like ancient."

Owen really needed to shut up now.

"I have no idea what you're talking about. There's a cow having trouble calving, so drive this truck like you own it and get me there yesterday."

"I don't own it."

"Pretend."

For a few seconds the only sounds were the tires on the road and Reggie's staccato breaths. He could feel the heat coming off her skin. If he touched her hair, would sparks ignite? Maybe she'd just punch him. Wouldn't be the first time.

"It's none of your business," she blurted.

"The cow?"

"Me." She sat stiff and straight, chin lifted, gaze forward. "Even if I had a date with Emerson, or any other man in this town or the next, you gave up the right to care about it a long time ago."

"No," he said.

"No?" Her shrill voice made Reggie inch so close to Owen he was practically driving.

"I might have given up the right to date you, but I never gave up the right to care."

Watley's driveway appeared, and Owen took the turn so fast, Reggie was thrown into her side. He yelped.

"Hey." She set her hand on the dog's shoulder at the moment Owen did the same.

Their fingers met. They both jerked back; the dog snorted.

"What were his injuries?" Becca asked.

As if he understood, Reggie offered the paw on his injured leg. She smiled and ran her fingers down the appendage. Owen couldn't believe the dog allowed it. Most MWDs had to be sedated for veterinary care. They weren't the kind of animals who submitted to anyone other than their handler. But Becca was different.

"Just here?" she asked, palm directly over the inflamed area. Reggie started to pant.

"He's fine." Owen negotiated the long, gravel lane then parked next to the brilliantly lit cow barn.

She lifted her hand from Reggie and opened her door,

then hesitated, clearly wanting to argue, to examine the dog further, but duty called. "Bring him by the clinic."

"I'll do that."

Her eyes narrowed. Had she heard the lie? She should be getting better at it by now—thanks to him.

"Becca?" Emerson stood in the circle of light just outside the open barn door. The man looked exactly the same as he had the day he'd chased Owen off his land with a rifle.

Was this place caught in a time warp? Owen had yet to run into anyone who had changed as much as he had.

Then again, he was the one who'd left. Which only made the time-warp theory more plausible.

"Thanks for the ride." She got out of the truck.

"Don't you need your doctor bag or something?" Owen asked.

"I'm hoping all I have to do is turn the calf, and it'll come out easy-peasy."

Owen had been around enough cows to know that if the delivery was going to be easy-peasy, it would have happened already with no need for veterinary assistance. "You're gonna be up all night, aren't you?"

"Probably." Becca rubbed Reggie's head one last time then slammed the door and went into the barn. The old guy cast a dubious glance in Owen's direction before following.

Owen rested his hand on the gearshift, but he didn't throw the truck into reverse. Reggie nudged his arm.

"Gotta go?" Owen opened the door and got out. After a curious glance in his direction, Reggie jumped out too. The dog had just been outside for hours, if he'd had to go, he would have. But Owen wanted to watch Becca work—or maybe just watch Becca. Either way, Reggie was a good excuse.

"*Voraus.*" Owen pointed to the tall grass at the side of the barn and the dog trotted off, nose to the ground. He'd probably already caught the scent of a field mouse and would be occupied tracking it for the foreseeable future.

Owen crossed the short distance from his truck to the barn. He'd been on his feet so much in the past few hours, his leg both ached from overuse and moved with less of a hitch for the same reason. Nevertheless he was glad the darkness shrouded him. Once he reached the barn door, it was an easy matter to steady himself with a hand on a stall, a stanchion, a pitchfork, a wheelbarrow.

The only people in the barn were Emerson, Becca, and Owen. One cow stood in a well-lit stall, her head confined in a portable gate. The rest lowed from the corral. At this time of year they should be walking free in the pasture, but for some reason they crowded around. Several hung their heads over the half back door. The way they chewed their cud and mooed every so often, dark, limpid gazes on the mother, they seemed to be giving advice.

Owen must have made a sound or a movement because Emerson glanced in his direction. "Whaddya want?"

Becca, elbow deep in the cow, glanced Owen's way. "I thought you left."

"I wanted to watch."

"It's not a reality show." She turned her arm so her shoulder spun forward. The cow stomped, narrowly missing her toes.

"Watch it," Owen said.

Becca gifted him with an evil glare. "I know what I'm doing."

The cow mooed—long, low, and mournful. He couldn't blame her.

"Do you need help?" Owen asked.

Obviously Becca had delivered calves before, though he wasn't sure how she'd managed to yank a hundred-pound animal out of a thousand-pound animal when she didn't weigh much more than a hundred pounds herself. She'd need to use the calf chains at her feet, once she grabbed hold of something to wrap them around.

"I can help," Emerson muttered.

Owen cast him a dubious glance. Once upon a time the old man had possessed Popeye forearms. Most dairy farmers did, especially the ones who'd grown up hauling buckets of milk from the cow to the holding tank. When dairy farming went high tech—i.e., the lines ran from cow to holding tank, no more hauling—it got easier. However, there was plenty of work to keep a farming man fit. Pitching hay, shoveling manure, driving a tractor, lifting . . . everything.

Emerson still had some impressive forearms, but the rest of him appeared more Olive Oil than Popeye. He was skinny as an exclamation point, and his back had started to hook like a question mark.

"I don't mind," Owen said.

"The last time you were here you didn't mind helping yourself to my beer."

"About that—" Owen began.

"Betcha didn't expect to get shot."

"Does anyone?" Owen murmured.

"You shot him?" Becca straightened, though she still had her hand in the cow. She seemed to be mining for gold in there and not finding any.

The cow mooed, stamped, and shifted her huge rump. "You probably don't wanna do that, Duchess." Becca patted her butt. "Lord knows what I'll pull out if you don't stand still."

Duchess blew air through her nose like a bull.

Owen didn't much care for that sound. Duchess might not have horns, or a ring through her nose, but she was as big as any bull and she could do some damage, even with her head in that gate, if she wanted to. In his present condition Owen wouldn't be able to reach Becca in time to help. In his present condition he probably wouldn't be any help even if he got there in time.

"She seems upset," he said.

"How'd you like to squeeze a watermelon out your back end?"

"No, thank you?" Owen ventured.

"Damn right," Emerson agreed.

Becca narrowed her eyes on the old man. "While I'm fishing around in here for the hoof I just lost because Duchess couldn't be still, why don't you tell me why you shot someone over a few beers."

"Stealing is stealing."

"And shooting might be killing."

"It was a pellet gun. Just stung a bit. Right?"

Owen rubbed his rear. "Right."

"You ever gonna pay me for that six-pack?"

"Sure." Owen took out his wallet, removed a ten, and held it out.

Emerson lifted a furry eyebrow, waiting for Owen to

bring it closer. When Owen didn't, the old man, who still got along fairly well for his age, though his legs were as bowed as any lifetime cowboy's, crossed the short distance and plucked the ten from Owen's hand, tucked it into his overhauls, then peered up, up, up Owen's length. "Heard you got some fancy medal."

"Nothing fancy, sir." He'd gotten a Purple Heart. The medal they gave you for not running fast enough or ducking quick enough. He'd prefer to be back on the front line, sans medal.

"Don't be modest." Emerson slapped Owen on the shoulder so hard his teeth rattled. "I always thought there wasn't anything the matter with you that a kick in the butt, or some basic training, couldn't cure." He held out his hand.

Owen was so surprised he stared at the large, thick, scarred appendage until Becca cleared her throat, then Owen's hand shot out to take the other man's.

"Guess I was right." Emerson shook, released.

Owen wasn't sure what to say to that, so he went with what he'd learned in the Marines was the best answer to everything. "Good to go, sir."

The old man shuffled his dirty boots, glanced at his watch, then peered longingly toward the house. Morning milking loomed only a few hours away. At his age he could use some sleep before that. At any age, dairy farming wasn't easy. Owen preferred the Marines.

"You don't have to stay," Becca said. "If I need a hand, I can always call you."

"You sure?" Emerson asked, but he'd already taken a step toward the door.

"I have my cell." Becca pointed to the phone, which

lay atop an overturned bucket out of harm's way. Lord only knew what kind of damage it could sustain during a calving.

Emerson ran a hand through hair that wasn't. "I'll take you up on that. It's been a long day's night, y' know?"

"I know," Owen agreed. He should be dizzy with exhaustion; he had been only about fifteen minutes ago.

But the proximity of Becca had revived him.

Chapter 6

The calf did not come out easy-peasy. I hadn't expected it to. I'd just wanted to get rid of Owen.

That had gone well.

While I'd been fishing around inside Duchess, he'd snuck closer and now leaned over the open stall door.

"Where's Reggie?"

I didn't need a strange dog trotting in here and scaring my expectant mother. She was twitchy enough already.

"He's chasing field mice."

" 'And bopping them on the head, ' " I sang under my breath.

"What?"

"The song?" He continued to stare at me blankly. " 'Little Bunny Foo-Foo.' " My mother had sung it to me so often I'd named my first bunny Foo-Foo.

"The white rabbit with the black nose," Owen said.

He remembered the pet but not the song. I shouldn't be surprised. Owen hadn't had a mother like mine. I didn't even want to think of what his might have sung to him while drunk or high or both.

"Just make sure Reggie doesn't race in here and spook this cow. She's got enough on her mind."

"I'll close the door."

"Will he bark if he's out there and you're in here?"

Owen cast me a disgusted glance. "He's a military working dog. He'd sit out there waiting for me until the cows come home."

"Ha," I deadpanned.

He grinned, and for a minute I was dazzled by that smile the same way I always had been. Then Duchess bore down and squeezed my arm hard enough to make my eyes water. Something that felt like a hoof brushed the tip of my fingers, and I lunged.

Duchess grunted. *Bitch!*

"Sorry."

"You talking to the cow?"

"That a problem?" I asked.

"Only if they answer."

I wasn't even going to go there.

"The door," I reminded him.

Duchess lifted her nose and let out a very loud *moooo.*

You'd think she was the first cow to calf.

Just because it's her first doesn't mean it's the first.

If you'd relax, sugar, this would all end sooner.

Duchess swung her head right, then left. But because of the head gate, she couldn't see the others. Didn't stop her from "talking" to them.

If you don't shut up I'm going to end you.

The cows shifted, huffed. I swear one even rolled her eyes. They were all named for the nobility—Duchess, Lady, Countess, Marchioness, Majesty, Queenie, Princess, Victoria, Bess, Kate, and so on. Despite those names, they reminded me of a gaggle of housewives in a fifties hair salon.

I stifled a giggle at the idea of that image immortalized on velvet, then leaned my head against the warm rump of Her Grace for an instant.

"While you're at it, could you shut the door to the corral too?"

"Sure." The door creaked. "Good night, ladies."

Well, I never!

We were just trying to help.

The nerve!

You'll be so—

The door closed. The comments ended.

I knew their dialogue was all in my head, as were the pithy retorts of Duchess. That the laboring cow huffed and glared in perfect syncopation with the remarks was most likely her response to my heightened tension.

I wished my mind would stop its running commentary in animal voices. But I'd been wishing that all my life, and my wish was never granted.

"Could you bring some warm water?" I called. "There are buckets next to the sink in the milking parlor. Should be some soap up there too, if you'd squirt some in."

"Got it." A few seconds later the sound of water hitting the bottom of said bucket commenced.

I should have insisted that Owen get lost, but Emerson hadn't looked good. He was getting too old for this job, though I'd never tell him. Comments like those would only insure that he'd work even harder to prove me wrong and wind up with a hernia. Farmers were as stubborn as bulls. I swear the term *bullheaded* was coined just for them.

Unfortunately for Emerson, he and his wife had four daughters—all grown, married, and gone. Not one of their husbands was interested in taking over the farm, which meant Emerson would hold on to the place as long as he could, then sell it. Or he'd keel over trying to prove to me, or some other moron who'd said he should slow down, that he shouldn't, and his wife would unload the place so she could live in a condo on the lake. The farm that had been in the Watley family for so long that the road to the east had been dubbed Watley Road would be no more.

It was a common enough occurrence. Very few people of my age group wanted to be dairy farmers. Very few people in my age group had the stones for it.

In my family, my brothers—the twins Jamie and Joe—certainly didn't. At seventeen, they were strong and able and they did what they were told, but they also counted the days until they didn't have to any more.

My sister, Melanie, was the best bet for the next generation at Carstairs farm. She attended the University of Wisconsin–River Falls where she was studying dairy science.

I think my dad developed a permanent twitch in his right cheek after she told him that. He preferred hands-on learning to books, but Mellie had her own ideas. And as our mother said, "At least one of them's interested."

Duchess gave a low, annoyed moo—couldn't blame her, my mind had been wandering—and swung her head in my direction.

Get it out.

"Arm or calf?"

Get them both out of my ass before I kick yours.

Funny how she sounded an awful lot like me. They all did. Because they *were* me.

"You okay?" Owen set a steaming bucket of water at my side.

Had I been talking to her out loud? God, I hoped not.

I glanced up. He only appeared mildly curious about the process and not concerned over my sanity.

"I'm peachy," I said as Duchess bore down again.

I'm sure I had unmentionable gunk everywhere. Wasn't the first time, wouldn't be the last. If I had a problem with gunk, I wouldn't be a vet.

I fished around a bit more for a hoof, a nose, something, found nothing, and withdrew my arm.

"It's going to be a while," I said.

Duchess stomped—once, twice, again.

"You'd almost think she understood you."

"Almost." I made use of the water.

Owen seemed as tired as I felt. It was after three A.M. Who knew how long he'd been awake. At this point I couldn't remember how long I had.

He sat on a hay bale just inside the stall door, leaned his head against the wall, and closed his eyes. "Do you ever get called to a calving in the bright light of day?"

"Not yet."

When a minute or more passed and Owen didn't respond, I turned my head. His eyes were still closed, his breathing had evened out. I waited a while longer to make sure he was truly asleep before I crossed the distance and gently touched his too short hair. Spiky now, sharp where it had once been soft, the ends made my fingers tingle.

I drew back, then found my own hay bale and just watched him breathe.

* * *

Owen came awake, and he didn't know where he was.

What else was new? Lately, if he knew where he was that was cause for celebration.

He hadn't been dreaming. Hadn't heard loud noises and woken on the floor, or worse, in a corner or under the bed. He was in a barn, but not one he knew. The cow didn't look familiar either, but most of them looked alike to him.

"Reggie," he said, but the dog didn't appear, and unease trickled over him. There was something about the dog he should remember.

Owen stood with a lurch, then nearly fell when his leg shouted with pain and gave out. He caught himself on the stall and sat again with a muted thud, as everything came back.

The dirt. The kid. The cell phone.

Click. Boom. Then screams.

It wasn't until he'd woken in the hospital in Germany, and asked who else had been hurt, that he'd understood those screams had been his. He rubbed his leg where it throbbed.

"You're awake." Becca set a fresh bucket of warm, soapy water on the floor.

Had she seen him try to stand and nearly fall? As she didn't stare at him with pity, disgust, or even curiosity, he thought not.

"How long was I out?"

"An hour?" She shrugged. "Little less? Maybe more? Time drags in the dead of night."

She should try it walking around Afghanistan without a flashlight.

He needed more sleep. But these days, he had a hard

time falling asleep and an even harder time waking up and remembering where he was.

Except tonight. Tonight he'd dropped off, slept without dreams, and while he had woken confused, he'd been less so than usual. He even remembered what they'd been talking about when he'd gone lights out.

"Why are all calves in Three Harbors born in the dark?"

She had her hands on her hips as she contemplated the back end of her patient. "Is this a riddle?"

"You're the one who told me that before I fell asleep. Did you answer and I missed it?"

"I didn't say they're all born in the dark. Just that they never seem to need me to help unless it's three A.M. We've got another hour, maybe two, before we're done."

"How do you know that? Something you learned in school? Something you've figured out since delivering a dozen or two?"

He leaned forward. He was fascinated with her.

He leaned back. Fascinated with what she *did,* he corrected himself. *How* she did it. Who wouldn't be?

In the field he was responsible for Reggie, had taken a few courses so that he could detect if the dog was overheated, overstressed. He'd also had to learn what to do for both—lots of water, ice, keeping the footpads and the belly cool, there was a reason a hot dog would flop into a mud puddle—as well as minor cuts, abrasions, stomach issues, and the like.

"I've yet to attend a calving that didn't take place in the dead of night. I've yet to deliver a calf at any of them before dawn." She spread her hands. "Which at this time of the year is . . . six-thirty?"

"I'll take your word on that."

"That the calf won't be born until dawn, or that dawn is around six-thirty?"

"Yes," he said, and she laughed.

"I should probably . . ." She flexed her fingers.

Duchess snorted, stomped, and swung her butt in the other direction so fast she nearly knocked Becca over.

Becca shoved her back where she'd been with a shoulder to her rump. "Stop that, or you'll never have it out."

The cow grumbled, but she quit moving.

"You have a way with animals. You always did."

"Hence the DVM after my name."

Becca inserted her hand where it had been earlier, closed her eyes, appeared to listen. Her forehead crinkled. "I can just get my fingers around a hoof, but when I pull—" She gritted her teeth, braced her legs and—"Dammit."

She stepped back and stuck her hand in the bucket of water, washing with more enthusiasm than was probably necessary. Though maybe not considering where that hand had been. She paced over to Owen, head down, muttering, then to the bucket, then over to Owen again.

"If I don't get that calf out soon, I could lose it and the mother."

"Why are you whispering?"

She glanced at the cow, which was staring at them both. "No reason."

She laid a palm on the animal's side. "Relax." She stroked the heaving rump. "I haven't been in labor. I don't know. I'm sure it isn't easy."

Why did it seem as if she were answering the cow's

questions? Probably because Owen was so tired he could almost hear them.

"What?" she asked.

"I didn't say anything."

"Shh!" She set her cheek against the animal's side, spread her fingers along the rib cage, closed her eyes again, breathed in, out, in. Then she straightened as if she'd been goosed. "They're stuck."

She returned to the rear end. "*They're* stuck." Joy sparked in her eyes. "Not one in there but two."

As dawn tinted the sky, twin calves teetered on spindly legs while Duchess licked them all over.

"They're beautiful," Owen said.

You're beautiful, he thought.

This was why he'd left. So she could become Dr. Rebecca Carstairs, DVM. It was what she'd wanted. What she'd dreamed of. What she was meant to be.

And if he'd stayed, she never would have been anything but his.

Chapter 7

By the time Emerson arrived to do the milking, the twins were having breakfast.

"Two," he said as proudly as if they were his doing. "Both heifers. Thanks."

I nodded. Too tired and hungry and happy to say anything.

I'd been at a loss as to what was wrong, panicked that I was going to lose my first cow and calf. It happened, but it hadn't yet happened to me, and I wanted to keep it that way.

Was that why I'd "heard" the little voice say: *We're stuck!*

When I reached back in, I'd found the same hoof I'd been tugging, but this time I ran my fingers up the leg until I found the chest, a head, and then another head. I'd disentangled them like a reverse jigsaw puzzle and guided them both into the dawn. I hadn't needed any help from Owen or the calf chains after that. Duchess did most of the work.

Quite obviously the hint had been my subconscious adding all the things my hands and eyes and ears and brain had gathered into a solution and projecting that solution into the "voice" of one of the twins. Did it really matter how I'd figured out the problem so long as I had?

My gaze went to Duchess and her girls. They wouldn't think so.

Owen was nowhere to be seen. Emerson opened the back door and allowed the housewives into the barn for morning milking. I lifted my hand in good-bye and hurried out the other door before I "heard" any more from them.

I was half afraid Owen had left me to find my own ride. That would be rude; then again, I hadn't expected him to stay all night. But he sat behind the wheel, engine idling. As I emerged, he whistled.

Reggie bounded out of the tall grass and onto the seat. He was moving a lot easier than he'd been last night. Animals were like that. Around me, they were like that a lot.

I climbed in too, and we were off. We weren't even to the top of the long driveway when my phone vibrated. I groaned. All I wanted was food, a shower, and a few hours of sleep, in that order. However, if duty called I had no choice but to answer.

I glanced at the text message. "Hallelujah!"

"Win the lottery?"

"Better. My mom made waffles."

Owen reached the road but didn't pull out. I pointed in the direction of the farm. "That way."

"I know which way. Don't you want me to drop you at your apartment so you can get your car?"

"I want waffles ten minutes ago. If you have somewhere to be at . . ." I glanced at my phone again. "Seven A.M. one of the boys can take me home."

"I don't but I . . . uh . . ."

"You know my mom. She made enough to feed you too." And probably most of the French Foreign Legion, though once my brothers got done, the Foreign Legion would be eating scraps. "The least I can do after all your help is make sure you have breakfast."

"I didn't *do* anything."

Laughter spurted. "That's exactly how you always said it."

"Said what?"

"That you didn't *do* anything. Every time someone—" I broke off.

"Every time someone accused me of whatever criminal act had been committed in the city limits," Owen finished.

"Sorry." He still hadn't turned onto the road, and I waved to the right. "Whether you're leaving or staying for breakfast doesn't really affect your direction at this point. I'll expire if I have to wait for you to take me to town so I can get my car and drive back to the farm. We're over halfway there."

"You will not expire," he grumbled, but he turned right.

"Thanks. And thanks for staying with me at Emerson's. It was nice to have more company than the ton in the middle of the night."

"What's *the ton*?"

"Old-time British word for the aristocracy. It's what I call Emerson's herd since he named them after the peers of the realm."

Owen continued to look confused.

"Duchess, Lady, Countess."

"That's weird."

"Weird is what you make it." I was weird, but I'd done my best to make sure no one knew it but me. "You didn't have to stay."

"I had no place to be."

"You could have slept in a bed."

"Maybe," he said. "But probably not."

Before I could follow up on that statement he blurted, "People are treating me differently."

"Okay."

"Chief Deb didn't accuse me of animal mutilation."

"No, she accused your mother."

"Actually she accused my mother's imaginary friends."

"She accused your mother's coven."

"My mother isn't a witch, so she doesn't have a coven any more than she has friends."

Poor woman. She'd been a miserable mother but not on purpose. I'd always hoped that someone could help her, but apparently crazy like that was beyond help.

"Emerson shook my hand," Owen continued. "The last time I saw him he shot me."

"So?"

"So?" he echoed. "Once someone shoots at me, they don't come back later and shake my hand."

"What do they do?"

He didn't answer, and I didn't press. I probably didn't want to know. The very idea of someone shooting at Owen made me twitchy.

"I doubt it'll be the last time someone shakes your hand around here."

"Why?" He seemed horrified.

"Heroes get their hands shaken."

"Reggie's the hero, not me. I just hold his leash."

"I highly doubt that's all you do. But you can always have them shake Reggie's paw if you want to." Owen cast me an exasperated glance, which I ignored. "Why do you downplay what you've accomplished?"

"You have no idea what I've accomplished."

"You've been in the service for ten years, Owen. I doubt you had your thumb up your ass."

He choked.

"If it bothers you to have your hand shaken, get over it. It's going to happen a lot."

"Not if I hide."

"Good luck with that." Once people knew he was in town, and why, they were going to come searching for him. And a guy of his size, with a dog of Reggie's size, in a town of this size?

He wasn't going to be able to hide for long.

"I didn't join the corps to be a hero," Owen said.

"Why did you?"

He cast her a quick glance. "You know why."

"I know what you told me." Her mouth tightened. "You had to make something of yourself. But to me, Owen, you were everything."

She'd been everything to him too, which was why he'd had to go. This place had made him feel like nothing, like no one, and even her love couldn't change that. But how could he tell her that she wasn't enough?

"I didn't mean to lie." Which was a great, big lie. He hadn't *wanted* to lie, but he *had* meant to.

"You lied?"

"I said I'd write."

"You were going to leave and never write?" Her face crumpled, confused, in the soft, early morning light.

He'd also said he'd come back. But one lie at a time.

"I should have told you, but I . . ."

He had a sudden memory of her eyes—stricken. Her tears—salty. Her kiss—desperate. Her touch . . .

Everything.

How could he tell her it was over when all he'd wanted was for it not to be? Then he'd made love to her and . . .

He certainly couldn't tell her then.

"I didn't want to hurt you," he finished.

She laughed, one short, harsh burst of sound. "You think it hurt less to wait and wait for that letter, then open it and find out how stupid I was to believe in you, than it would have hurt to know you didn't love me in the first place?"

That wasn't true. He'd left *because* he loved her. He'd leave again for the same reason. But he couldn't tell her that any more now than he could then. Just because Emerson Watley had shaken his hand didn't mean anyone else would.

In Three Harbors, Owen would always be the delinquent son of a crazy drunk-druggie. Just as Becca would always be the daughter of one of the founding families. People used the word *doctor* before her name. Just because he carried the rank of sergeant before his wouldn't change anything. If he lost that rank, then what would he be?

No one all over again.

"It was a long time ago." Becca stared out the passenger window where the tip of one of the silos on the Carstairs farm had just become visible.

"Feels like yesterday." She looked the same, smelled the same; he wanted to kiss her . . . just the same.

"Sometimes it does," she agreed. "Then other times it all seems so long ago, so far away, so hazy, like it happened to someone other than me. As if you were a story I told myself."

He didn't care for that at all, but who was he to judge? He'd coped with the loss of her by throwing himself into his training. Becoming so exhausted he could do nothing but move forward with little energy left to look back. Because looking back hurt so badly he could hardly breathe.

Owen turned into the long, gravel lane that matched the one at Watley's and led to a similar farm at the end. House, barn, sheds, machinery, all pretty much the same, though in slightly different locations.

A big, floppy tan mutt came racing out of the barn, braying either a welcome or a warning. From Reggie's grumble, he thought it was the latter.

Owen set his hand on the dog's shoulder. "Easy, boy. His place."

"Moose is harmless," Becca said.

"Reggie isn't." He didn't play well with dogs not of the working variety. Probably because he'd never had much chance to. Or maybe because, to Reggie, work was play and vice versa. He had no time or patience for anything else. He lived to sniff out bombs and terrorists. But, hey, so did Owen. He rubbed his bad leg.

Becca rolled down the window a few inches. "Barn, Moose!"

The dog appeared crushed, but he went where he'd been told, leaving a looming, waiting silence behind.

Owen shifted the truck into park. "Becca, I'm sorry—"

"Me too," she interrupted, then took a deep breath. "I know I asked you to breakfast . . ."

His lips curved. "I wasn't going to come."

She nodded as if she'd known that. She probably had. She'd always known him better than anyone. And despite other people treating him as if he were a completely different person than the one who'd left, he wasn't. Deep down he would always be the same.

Just like his mother.

"It's probably best if we don't see each other any more than we have to while you're here."

Owen blinked. Hadn't seen that coming.

"Not at all would be my vote." She scrubbed her nails lightly between Reggie's eyes. The dog practically drooled. "However, with the problem at your house, that probably isn't going to happen."

"You kissed me," he said stupidly.

She gave Reggie one last pet and got out of the car.

"Won't happen again," she said, and slammed the door.

Kissing Owen had definitely been a mistake. Despite how good it had been, how right and familiar, I'd known that the instant I'd done it.

Because now all I could think of was doing it again. Which would only lead to a much, much bigger mistake. Sleeping with him. And *that* would be a lot harder to forget than a mere kiss.

"Mere." There'd been nothing "mere" about it. Not now. Not then. Not ever.

The thunderous swoosh of my shoes through the ankle-deep fallen leaves seemed to announce my presence even louder than Moose had.

The door wasn't locked. Never was. No one got past that dog.

A steaming cup of coffee sat on the table. At Moose's first bray Pam Carstairs would have glanced out the window and seen that someone was coming. She would have stayed at that window until she knew just who. I had seconds before the questions began.

Where had I been? What had I done? Whose truck had I arrived in?

I sat at the table and slurped from my cup as if I'd been lost in the desert and just found an oasis. Sometimes coming home felt like that. My mother's coffee definitely tasted as good as clear spring water after a long summer's drought. No matter how hard I tried to replicate it, I'd never been able to.

"What's new, baby girl?"

I hadn't been a baby for years, and I wasn't "the" baby, but Mom had always called me that, and I let her. I liked it. Mostly because it annoyed Mellie. Her nickname was "squirt." Drove her bonkers, which meant that the boys and I called her that as often as we could.

"Twin calves at Watley's," I said between slurps. "Heifers."

"Nice." She began to line her cast-iron skillet with thick strips of bacon. First came the sizzle, then came the scent, and I wanted to lick the air the way Moose did whenever he smelled it. Seriously, what *wasn't* better with bacon?

Chocolate? Yes. Lettuce? Hell, yes. Ice cream? Bizarrely, yes.

I refilled my cup. At this rate, I'd have to start another pot before Dad and the boys came in for breakfast. Wouldn't be the first time.

"Emerson called here."

Just as I'd thought.

"Did that woman get hold of you too?"

"What woman?"

"Didn't leave her name."

I lifted my eyebrows. That didn't usually stop my mother from knowing who any local caller was. And tourists didn't call my parents' house.

"Weird," I murmured.

"She was. Asked why you weren't at home or at work, demanded where she could find you."

"What'd you tell her?"

"That I had no idea. People that rude can take their business elsewhere."

Since I'd never heard from her, she no doubt had.

I leaned against the counter and watched my mother work. She'd done this dance every morning for the past thirty years. The particulars might vary. Sausage instead of bacon. Eggs instead of waffles. Some days brought pancakes, others toast. Ham or hash? Who knew? But that skillet was always sizzling, and the kitchen smelled like heaven.

Which meant it smelled like home.

"Was that Owen in the truck?"

She'd been able to see him in the cab of the truck from a hundred yards away? My mom had always had the eyes of a hawk. When combined with the ears of a bat and a nose that probably detected as good as Reggie's she'd been a terrific mother. Still was.

I took another sip of coffee, swallowed, then took another while I decided what to tell her. I would have preferred to skip how I'd run into Owen. She didn't need to hear about the animals and the altar.

Except this was Three Harbors. She probably already had. Which explained how she knew Owen had been in the truck.

Grapevine, not spidey sense.

She let out an impatient huff.

"Yes," I blurted. "Owen."

If she peered at me just right I'd spill everything in my head. I wanted to avoid that as much now as I had when I was a kid.

She continued turning the bacon slices one by one. "It's unfortunate that he's back in town at the same time something so awful appears in his house."

Just like I'd thought. She already knew.

I was both glad that I didn't have to tell her about the *awful* and annoyed at her use of *unfortunate*. "He didn't do it."

"Of course not."

"Then why is it unfortunate?"

"Because the poor kid had to walk into the place after so long and find that. Why else?" She shook her head. "You're as defensive as he is."

"He was always blamed for everything."

"Times change," she said. "So do people."

I wasn't sure if she meant Owen had changed, or everyone else had.

"You don't look like you got any sleep."

"I didn't. I met Chief Deb at Owen's, then got the call to Watley's, then came here."

"You don't have office hours today so you can sleep."

"Maybe." There was something I had to do today, but right now I hadn't had enough coffee to remember what it was.

My mother was suddenly standing before me removing the now empty cup from my hands. "You should lay off the coffee if you plan to go home to bed." She set the cup in the sink and handed me a plate. "Eat, then I'll have one of the boys take you home."

I was knuckle deep in waffles and bacon when the men tromped in, bringing the scent of an autumn morning and cattle. The latter was better with bacon too.

"Ginge!" Jamie stole a bite of waffle from my plate. I gave him an elbow in the gut—not hard, but he got his own rather than stealing more of mine. Unfortunately, I could elbow him all day and most of tomorrow and he'd never stop calling me "Ginger."

If he'd been an aficionado of *Gilligan's Island,* the nickname would have been more appealing. Ginger Grant was a very hot redhead. Except *Gilligan's Island* had been popular during our grandparents' day and I doubted that Jamie had ever bothered watching an episode.

Jamie called me "Ginger" because of *South Park,* which didn't make the comment half as nice. Little brothers, even when they were no longer little, were mostly annoying.

Joe, who always let Jamie do the talking, just winked and followed him to the food. At least he didn't touch any of mine.

Like all the Carstairs, except me, my brothers had light brown hair. When they were three, they'd been blond, just like Mellie. Mellie still was, thanks to a monthly appointment for highlights and root control. All of them also had pretty blue eyes, which made my mud-green shade even more noticeably different.

My flame-red hair was as much a mystery to my parents as to me. I'd asked every relative we had if any Carstairs in memory had ever possessed red hair. None had.

Kids noticed how different I was from every other Carstairs on the planet, which led to a lifetime of comments about the "stork getting it wrong," and other oh-so-amusing jibes.

I loved my parents, my siblings, loved this town, or I wouldn't have come back after college, but there was always a part of me that felt as if I'd been plunked into Three Harbors by strange forces and not born here like everyone else.

"Sweetheart." My dad kissed the top of my head, paused, sniffed. "You've been playing with cows again."

You'd think he wouldn't be able to smell cows on me since he had enough cow smell on himself. You'd think wrong.

"Watley's." My mom brought my dad both his coffee and his plate. "Twin heifers."

I used to find it beyond frustrating that she waited on him like that. Then she caught the flu once—and only once, which is another subject entirely. She'd had four kids. Four! And we'd brought home all sorts of things—germs, foster sons, hedgehogs.

While Mom had been down with the flu, Dad had trashed the kitchen just trying to make cereal, and all became clear to me. She didn't wait on him because she was the woman and he was the man; she waited on him because he was a slob and she didn't want him anywhere near her kitchen.

"Trouble?" My dad stirred cream and sugar into his coffee.

"I wouldn't have been there if there weren't trouble."

Most of the time cows had calves all by themselves, sometimes the farmer didn't even know about it until the cow walked back in with an extra.

"Good point." He toasted me with his cup, drank.

My father's face was well lived in—weather crinkles around the eyes, smile lines framed his mouth. His hair had highlights without help from anything but the sun, though his roots were gray. As he said when Mom teased him, at least he still *had* hair. A lot of his pals didn't.

"Where's your car?"

"Owen brought her."

Silence fell. Everyone but my mother, who was pouring bacon grease into a tin can, stared at me.

"Owen's back?" Jamie asked.

"It would be a little hard for him to give me a ride if he wasn't."

"Ha-ha." Jamie took the chair across from mine. His plate was so full he really should have used two. "Why's he here? Where'd you see him? Is it true he's in explosives detection? What—"

I held up my hand. "I'll tell you all I know if you just zip it."

Jamie didn't have to be told twice. If his mouth was asking questions he couldn't eat. Not at my mom's table. So he zipped it, then tucked into the plate as I recited all I knew. Almost.

I wasn't going to discuss the new breadth to Owen's shoulders, the fresh calluses on his hands. I especially didn't plan to relate the same, great taste of his mouth.

My father began to make a waffle sandwich, something he did only when he had someplace else to be.

"Where are you going?"

He glanced up in the middle of squirting syrup on top of the butter he'd spread on two waffles like bread. "I need to check the fence on the north side."

Joe started to rise, and Dad shook his head, then proceeded to snap bacon in half and position it on a waffle. "One of you take Becca to her apartment. The other can do inventory on the feed. We'll need to place an order this week." He slapped the second waffle on top of the first, picked up his sandwich, and left.

I was still frowning at that abrupt departure when Jamie said, "Call it."

A quarter flipped end over end over end through the air.

"Tails." Joe shoveled the remains of his breakfast into his mouth.

Jamie slapped the coin onto the back of his hand, peeked and tucked it into his pocket. "You take Becca; I take inventory."

I kissed my mom then followed my brothers out the door.

My dad's truck was gone, which was odd. To check a fence he usually took a tractor or an ATV.

"Who won the toss?" I asked.

Jamie winked. "Wouldn't you like to know?"

Chapter 8

Joe was his usual silent self as we headed toward Three Harbors. I didn't mind. I half dozed with my forehead against the window.

The flash of brilliant blue from Stone Lake brought me out of my stupor in time to witness Owen's white rent-a-truck parked in front of a cabin. He'd taken Chief Deb's advice. He hadn't had much choice. With Reggie in tow it was Stone Lake or . . . my parents' house. I could understand his reluctance to return there. Too many people, too much action.

Too many memories.

I closed my eyes. Seeing Owen again had brought back just how hard it had been to get over him. I'd been right to say we should avoid each other as much as possible. Spending any more time with him might erase all the progress I'd made. Not that there'd been all that much. I dreamed of him weekly, thought of him daily, missed him hourly.

Yeah, I was over him all right.

"Lot of sighs coming from over there," Joe observed.

I made a snoring sound and kept my eyes closed. Because he was Joe, he let me.

A blip in the road tapped my head against the glass.

I opened my eyes. We were trolling down Carstairs Avenue.

Ahead of us, the newspaper delivery van rolled from business to business distributing a daily dose of information. While many small towns had lost their newspaper completely, or had at least had their daily subscription scaled back to biweekly, Three Harbors maintained a healthy circulation.

Perhaps part of the reason was that the owner of the *Three Harbors Herald* also owned the Lakeside Hotel, a thriving business that could fund the dying one. Perched on the shores of Lake Superior, the place had recently been filled to capacity with tourists in town for the annual Falling Leaves Festival.

Three Harbors had prospered on tourism. Summer vacations, autumn leaf viewing, winter snowmobiling and cross-country skiing, as well as various hunting seasons ensured that the town didn't struggle often. Even when the economy tanked, we remained busy. Folks that would have gone to Europe, or the Caymans, or some other expensive place, would instead remain closer to home.

Spring was our only down season, and in northern Wisconsin spring was mostly a myth. If it did make an appearance, people often blinked and missed it completely. I could probably make a bundle on T-shirts that read: *SPRING IN WISCONSIN? JUST LIKE WINTER EVERYWHERE ELSE.*

"Will you be able to catch some sleep this morning?" Joe asked.

"I think I can." No messages on my voice mail yet.

Almost a miracle. Still . . . there was something I was supposed to do today. What was it?

"Jeremy," I muttered.

"I'm Joe," my brother said, enunciating his name, drawing out the "oooo."

"Very funny. A professor from the university is supposed to come in today and take a peek at the crime scene."

"Why is that bad?"

"You didn't see the crime scene."

"Can I?"

"No!" I glanced at him, and he stuck out his tongue. "Why would you want to?"

Joe slid the truck to a stop at the curb in front of my building. "I'm a seventeen-year-old boy," he said, as if that answered the question. And it kind of did, along with raising another one.

"You know anyone who's got an unhealthy interest in Satan?"

"Is there a way to have a *healthy* interest in Satan?"

He made a good point. "I meant are there any kids at school that seem overly weird?"

"Define *overly*."

I rubbed my forehead. I was too damn tired for this. "What do they call kids who look very Ozzy these days?"

"I don't know what that means."

The only reason I did was because my college roommate had been obsessed with the reality show *The Osbornes*.

"Dyed black hair, black eye makeup, piercings, black clothes."

"Emo," he said. "They call it 'emo' now, and that's half the kids in school in some way or another."

"Really?" Sheesh, I was old.

Joe shrugged. I wasn't sure if that meant he was telling the truth or pulling my leg. Did it matter?

"If you hear anything about Satan, witches, covens, black magic, sacrificial whatever, you'll let me know, right?"

"Really?" he echoed. "Sheesh. People are sick."

"You have no idea." I got out of the car. I started to slam the door and had another thought. "You know Joaquin?"

Joe blinked.

"Joaquin Ramos?"

"You think there's more than one Joaquin in school? Of course I know him. Why?"

"Could you . . . I don't know . . . Ask him over or something?"

"You want me to plan a playdate with the new guy?"

"That a problem?"

"He's a sophomore."

"Meaning?"

"I'm a senior."

I lifted my eyebrows and waited.

"It's kind of strange for me to do that. Borderline creepy. He's a kid."

"You're not?"

"Not the same way he is."

"He doesn't have any friends," I said.

"He can't have mine," my brother muttered, but at my narrowed glare, he continued. "Tell him to join a club, try out for a sport, something. That's how you meet people and make friends. Not by sitting alone or working for you."

"People might be picking on him."

Joe frowned. *That* he didn't like. "I'll keep an eye on him."

Which meant Jamie would too. I shut the door. Joe did a U-turn and headed back the way we'd come.

Thank goodness no one stood outside the clinic with a pet in his or her arms. I might not hold office hours today, but that didn't mean people listened. Emergencies happened. However, a client's idea of what constituted an emergency—a cough—and mine—copious blood flow—were very different.

Another thing I'd learned—if I opened the front door in plain view of town, word got around I was open for business, so I snuck around to the rear.

I smelled like a duchess, and not the *Downton Abbey* kind, so I scrubbed up in the sink, I was too tired to do more, donned my idea of pajamas—pale green scrubs dotted with dancing dogs—then crawled into my bed, a daybed that served as both couch and sleeping area. The red numbers on the digital alarm atop the end table read 8:14. If I was lucky I'd be able to catch a few hours' siesta before Jeremy arrived.

I'd trained myself in college to fall asleep quickly and pretty much anywhere—night or day, dark or light. A talent perfected by med students, mothers, and soldiers everywhere. When the only sleep you got was sleep you took, you adjusted or you lost your marbles.

My ability to sleep quickly and deeply was augmented

by my ability to wake up and function within seconds
as well. Lucky for me.

The long, low wail of a wolf, closer than a wolf should
be, woke me, confused me. Wolves didn't often howl at
the sun.

I opened my eyes an instant before the pillow smashed
down on my face.

Owen was lucky that a duck hunter from Waunakee had
rented one of the cottages at Stone Lake, then slipped
on freakishly early ice and broken his wrist. Which
equaled no hunting for him and an empty cottage for
Owen. He even received a discount since said Waunakee hunter had canceled too late to get his deposit back.
Sucked for that guy.

"I'm not sure how long I'll be staying," he told the
fellow behind the bar, which, from the papers and the
laptop spread all over it, doubled as the front desk.
Since a sign announcing *OFFICE* had been hung directly
beneath the one that read *STONE LAKE TAVERN* that made
sense.

"This is the last week of duck hunting," said the man,
whom Owen decided was the owner since the pocket of
his bowling shirt read *KRAZY KYLE*, and the business
registration certificate on the wall read *KYLE KRASINSKY*.
"Next week I'm empty." He lowered his voice to a whisper. "Except for that guy."

Owen followed the wobble of the man's two chins
toward a table in the rear. As it was daytime, none of
the lights were on in the tavern except for those above the
bar, and the area was wreathed in shadows.

There was someone there, but Owen couldn't see whom. Then a door-shaped swath of daylight highlighted a tall, cadaver-thin, impossibly old man wearing a bandolier of bullets and more guns than Owen had ever seen draped over a single person, even in Afghanistan.

The door closed, eliminating the sunshine and the man. Krazy let out a relieved breath. "I'm glad he left. He makes me nervous."

"Can't imagine why. What's up with him?"

"He said he's hunting wolves."

Owen doubted the fellow had been hunting them with the pistols at his hips, but he'd also carried a rifle and a shotgun. "That legal?"

"Gotta have a permit, and they ain't easy to get, but yeah."

"It's wolf-hunting season?" Seemed early but what did Owen know? He'd never hunted anything but terrorists.

"Mid-October to February. Though if the quota's met, they end it early."

"You get a lot of wolf hunters in here?"

"He's the first." From the twist of his lips, Krazy hoped he was the last.

"You don't approve of wolf hunting?" Owen asked.

"I don't know. They say there are too many now. They've been protected so long. But around here I've only seen one. Black as the ace of spades."

Owen must have started because Krazy's gaze flicked from his perusal of the back door to Owen. "You've seen her too?" He didn't wait for a response. "She's beautiful, and she doesn't seem to be bothering anyone."

She'd bothered Owen, and Reggie too for that matter.

"They say wolves steal small dogs, cats, chickens, calves. Sometimes an old horse or cow. But I've never heard of any being lost around here."

Apparently the "lost" animals that had been found in Owen's house had not been widely reported. Which was odd considering every stray cat was usually cause for a bulletin. Three should have been front-page news.

"Wolves are hard to find," Owen said. "I've heard that wolf hunters have to bait them, like bears."

"True," Krazy agreed.

"You don't sound convinced."

"There's something about that guy . . ." He shook his head. "Weird smells coming from his cabin."

"Probably sauerkraut."

"I know what sauerkraut smells like."

"Kielbasa?"

"It was more metallic."

"He was cooking metal?"

"I don't know, dude."

"You didn't ask him?"

"He said he was making his own bullets."

"That would explain the metal."

"I've smelled melting lead. This wasn't it." Krazy shifted his shoulders, uneasy. "He creeps me out."

He'd creeped Owen out too, and he'd only caught a glimpse of the guy.

"Well, if creepy were against the law, half the world would be in jail."

"Preaching to the choir, brother."

Krazy was a lawyer. Guess he'd know.

"My place isn't next to his, is it?" Beggars couldn't be choosers but still . . .

"Nah. He wanted the cottage closest to the woods."

"I bet he did."

"Yours is up front. Closer to the bar, right?" He held up a hand, and Owen slapped a high five. "But after this week, it'll just be you and him, so you could move wherever you want. I'm not full again until the weekend before Thanksgiving."

"Gun deer hunting."

"Right." Krazy seemed like he wanted to high-five Owen again, but it was too soon. "You from around here?"

"I was," Owen said. He really didn't consider himself from here any more. He was a soldier. His home was the United States Marine Corps.

At least until it wasn't.

"Visiting family? I know how it is. Visiting's one thing. Sleeping in the same house's another." He tapped the keyboard of his laptop. "You're good for a month if you want. Though who wants to visit family for a month? Unless they're in Italy or something, right?"

"Right," Owen agreed.

He hadn't planned on being here more than a week when he'd arrived. Hence the sleeping bag and Coleman lantern in his truck. But more than a month?

No way in hell.

Owen took the proffered key and drove the white truck, which he was starting to think of as his, even though it wasn't, to cabin number 4. He could have walked there, but then he'd have had to leave the truck in front of the tavern, and at this time of day, that would cause talk. At the least someone might walk over to see who was drinking at eight A.M., and once they discovered his name—he hadn't told Krazy not to share it; maybe he should have—then they'd knock on his door and one thing would lead to another.

All of it annoying.

Owen parked at number 4, grabbed his backpack, and headed for the door, Reggie at his heels. In the distance, a gun boomed. For a minute he was afraid the wolf hunter had bagged one, even though it was broad daylight. But the guy stood on the porch of the cottage closest to the woods, staring into them.

A second shot sounded, and Reggie did a little spin in the grass, then glanced at Owen hopefully.

"Sorry, buddy. Not our fight." He opened the door and waited for the dog to go in.

With all those guns around, he didn't want Reggie loping off. No one in their right mind would confuse him with a duck. However, Owen knew better than most that the number of people in their right mind was fewer than anyone imagined. In certain light, with bad enough eyes, Reggie did look like a wolf.

Owen had enough problems without explaining to the military why their extremely expensive MWD—trained, Reggie was worth about fifty grand—had a bullet hole in him. Not to mention he'd have to take the dog to Becca for treatment, and he'd rather avoid seeing her. Especially since she'd said the same about him.

The cabin was small but new and very nice. According to the brochure, several of which lay on the barely nicked countertop, local craftsmen had fashioned all the faux rustic furniture and cabinets in both the kitchen and the bath. Local art hung on the walls. The quilt and the curtains had been purchased at the Three Harbors Arts and Crafts Fair.

"Now I just need to buy some local food and everything will match."

A creak, then a groan drew Owen's attention to the bed where Reggie already had his tail curled around his nose and his eyes closed. Owen could almost hear his thoughts.

If I can't chase and catch whatever they're shooting at, I might as well be asleep.

Owen had to agree. He unbuttoned his pants. Someone knocked on the door.

Reggie lifted his head; his ear twitched. While the majority of their time in the field required Reggie's go-go-go personality, there were other instances when they had to be silent and still and wait for something to develop. Reggie didn't like those times any more than Owen did. But he'd been trained, same as Owen, to respect them.

Owen closed all four fingers and his thumb into a fist—the hand signal for *quiet*—and the dog set his chin on his paws. Maybe if whoever was knocking heard nothing they would leave.

"Owen?"

Dammit. Owen knew that voice, and it wasn't going anywhere.

I flailed around, smacked someone's arms, grabbed onto them, and yanked. They didn't move, so I dug in with my nails and scratched. Instead of relief, the pressure on my face increased. My lungs labored for air. Behind my closed eyelids black spots danced across a bloodred landscape.

At first I thought the growling and snarling was in my head, lack of oxygen bringing about bizarre hearing issues. Then I considered it might be death coming for me. Like those creepy black crawly things that had skulked through the movie *Ghost* and taken away the nasty people.

But they'd taken those people to hell and . . . come on! I was one of the good guys.

Wasn't I?

Suddenly the pressure was gone, and I drew great gulps of lovely air into my screamingly tight lungs. The black spots cleared. I wasn't alone in my apartment. Obviously.

However, I didn't expect my wolf. She had a piece of brown cloth in her mouth that matched the shirt on the tall masked figure with the pillow still in one hand. Man? Woman? Couldn't tell. Not only had the person covered his or her face, neck, and head, but he or she wore oversized clothing too bulky to define. I got the impression of either a very tall woman or a slim man.

The wolf yanked the pillow from the intruder's gloved hand and tossed her head. The pillow thunked against the wall and hit the floor. The wolf's lip lifted in a silent snarl. She stood between the stranger and the door.

Where was my phone? Nine-one-one was in order.

Suddenly the masked attacker grabbed my end table, sending a lamp crashing to the floor, and threw it at the wolf. She sidestepped, but it caught her on the hip, sent her skidding into the coat rack. Both the wolf and the rack smacked against the wall pretty hard. Sweat-shirts, scarves, and coats rained down on the too still animal.

You'd think the guy/girl would have run. Instead, he/she picked up the pillow and headed in my direction once more. The eyes shining through the mask seemed crazed.

I couldn't get up. The harder I tried, the dizzier I became. The longer I waited, the closer my attacker got.

I lifted my hands toward the descending pillow. I doubted I'd be able to prevent its smashing into my face again, but I had to try. The cool, crisp cotton case brushed my fingernails, and I braced against the pressure.

It never came. He, or she, flew up and away, whapping against the far wall and hitting the ground just like the pillow had, but with a much louder *whap*. Something smaller and tinny bounced onto the floor as well. Perhaps a tooth. I wouldn't be surprised. Or sorry.

My attacker leaped up and ran out of the apartment, weaving a little, banging into the doorjamb, then stumbling down the stairs. The silence that followed rushed in my ears like a rolling river.

I was light-headed and dopey from lack of oxygen. I was having a hard enough time accepting that someone had tried to kill me. That the would-be murderer had flown through the air with the greatest of ease only proved I was still out of it.

The wolf remained unconscious, which left her off the hook for the tossing, even if she'd had the opposable thumbs to do it.

Tear the creep limb from limb. Yes. Pick up and throw? No. Pick up and throw without touching anything? I had no answer for that question at all.

I sat up, head spinning, got my feet on the ground and stood. I needed my phone but I couldn't think where I'd put it.

"I should call it," I muttered, then started laughing. How could I call my phone without my phone?

I put my hand over my mouth to stop the scary sound of my laughter. What was wrong with me?

My phone flew off the kitchen table then skidded a few inches in my direction. A shiver raced over me, raising goose bumps everywhere.

I dropped my hand. "That didn't happen either."

I sounded so certain, I nearly believed myself.

I brought up the keypad on my phone screen, then paused with my thumb poised over the 9. I really needed to get rid of the wolf before the cops came. But how? She still lay there, eyes closed, her ribs lifting and lowering steadily.

I moved closer, reaching out, pulling back. I was a veterinarian, for crying out loud. I knew better than to touch an unconscious animal of any kind. That was a great way to get bit. And a wild animal?

That was a great way to get rabies.

Which was the main reason I wanted her out of here. Not that she *had* rabies. But the authorities would think so. Wild animals—especially twitchy ones like wolves—did not venture into populated areas unless they were starving or rabid. As it wasn't the time of year for starving wolves, this one would find herself in a cage or worse while they waited to make sure she didn't foam at the mouth. She'd saved my life; I couldn't do that to her.

I whistled. One of the wolf's ears twitched. She had

a white circle of hair at her neck. Invisible if you weren't very close and her neck wasn't craned just right.

I clapped my hands. Her eyes opened.

Henry?

No one here but the wolf and me. Who was she talking—

Wait a second. I'd never heard anything from her before. Of course I never really heard anything from any animal. But why would I imagine she'd think—

Henry!

Exactly. I didn't know any Henry.

The wolf sat up. I stepped back and kept stepping back until my legs bumped into my daybed.

She flicked a glance at me, the eerie light green of her eyes even more so with the sunlight streaming through the window over the sink. But her gaze moved on, roaming the room as if searching for something. Or someone. Perhaps—

Henry.

She stared at the bathroom door, and that shiver I'd had before returned. Was there someone else in my apartment besides the insane masked man or woman?

"Who's Henry?"

The wolf's eyes returned to me.

"For that matter, who are you?"

Prudence.

My wolf was named Prudence. Hadn't seen that coming.

You can call me Pru if you like.

"Sure, why not? And Henry? Who's he? Where is he?"

Her gaze went to the bathroom again.

"In there?"

No. He is next to the bookcase.

"The only thing next to the bookcase is more books."
I needed a bigger bookcase, but who didn't?

You can't see him.

It didn't sound like a question, but I answered anyway. "No. Should I?"

Her blue-black fur rippled, a lupine shrug. *Probably not.*

"Why not?"

He's a ghost.

Chapter 9

"Sir." Owen moved back.

Becca's father stepped into the cabin.

"Bly'b," Owen said, and shut the door.

The man cast him a confused glance. "Excuse me?"

That *had* sounded like gibberish.

"The dog." Owen waved at the bed. "I told him to stay in German. It's how he was trained, the commands that he knows."

Dale Carstairs grunted. Owen hoped he had more to say than that. Then again, maybe he didn't. The last time they'd spoken this man had ordered Owen to leave his darling daughter alone.

"You need to leave Becca alone."

"Wow," Owen said. "Déjà vu."

"Don't be a smartass."

Owen moved into the kitchen to make coffee, more for something to do than for actual drinking. He was jittery enough just being in Three Harbors without adding caffeine. But Becca's dad had revived all the uncertainty he'd always felt in the man's presence.

Even before Owen had banged his daughter.

Owen tried to cover the flinch and his continued unease with a search for the coffee. There wasn't any. Why would there be? He hadn't been shopping.

"Listen, I . . ." Owen scrubbed his hands through his hair, turned.

Carstairs stared at Owen's leg. Hell. He'd gimped across the room without even trying to hide it. Not that he'd have been able to *keep* hiding it for much longer, but he'd rather not have revealed his weakness to this man first.

"What happened?" While Carstairs's gaze had been hostile when he'd walked in, along with his voice, both had softened. Pity did that.

"World went boom," Owen said shortly. "I was in the way."

"Sorry to hear it. I was also sorry to hear about the trouble at your place."

I bet you were, Owen thought. If it weren't for the trouble at his place Owen might already be on a plane.

"I should have kept an eye on the house."

"That wasn't your job."

"I'm the closest neighbor. I'd say it is."

"I doubt anything would have helped. You couldn't be there twenty-four/seven."

Owen had learned during his first week in Afghanistan that a determined kook was never deterred. Considering his mother, he'd probably learned that his first week on earth.

"Still, I'm sorry you came home to such a horrible sight."

"I've seen worse."

"I'm sorry about that too."

Carstairs was sorry about a lot. For an instant Owen wondered if he was sorry he'd done what he had all those years ago. Then Owen remembered the first words the guy had uttered today.

You need to leave Becca alone.

Which were nearly the same as the last words Owen had heard him say. Nevertheless . . .

"Wasn't your fault."

"Seems I was the one who encouraged you to join up."

"Encouraged? Is that what they're calling it now?"

The way Owen remembered it, he'd been "encouraged" to enlist or be charged with statutory rape. By the time he'd discovered that the statutory rape law in Wisconsin defined adult as eighteen and the age of consent as less than fifteen, and therefore did not apply to him and Becca, it was too late. He was in the Marines.

"What did you expect me to do?" Carstairs looked away. "I took you in; I gave you a home; I treated you like you were my own son. Then I caught you having sex with my seventeen-year-old daughter."

"I loved her."

"You would have ruined her."

According to this man, he *had* ruined her.

In the end, Owen hadn't enlisted because of the threat itself, but because the issuance of it had illustrated the truth. Owen would never be accepted in this town. He would always be seen as "less than."

Carstairs rubbed his palms along the hips of his stained overhauls. It didn't appear as if he'd changed after coming in from morning milking. He'd no doubt run right over here the instant he'd heard that Owen was back.

"You two were so intense, so young."

Owen had been intense, but he hadn't been young. Not

in the way everyone else had. Which meant he should have known better than to touch Becca. He *had* known better. But that hadn't meant he could stop himself. Then, once he'd started, once he'd known what love was . . . Nothing had mattered but her.

That was why he'd left. Owen had had nothing. If he'd stayed, Becca would have had nothing too.

"Young people make huge mistakes. They don't think. They only feel. And then it's too late. I wasn't going to let that happen to her. She was destined for great things, and she wouldn't have been able to achieve them if you . . ." His voice drifted off.

"If I'd have been hanging around her neck like a dead albatross."

Carstairs shrugged, which Owen took as a yes.

Owen felt again like that boy from the wrong side of the forest, with the crazy mom and no money who'd had the audacity to fall in love with the town princess. He'd been a fool to hope that Emerson Watley's change of opinion might translate to everyone.

Wasn't going to happen. Others might shake his hand and call him a hero, but this man never would. Owen had broken his trust, and he couldn't really blame Becca's father for still being angry about it.

"You aren't going to tell her, are you?" Carstairs asked.

"Tell her?" Owen echoed.

"What I said back then."

The man was afraid the truth would come out, and he'd become the villain instead of Owen. Owen wasn't certain that would happen even if he spilled everything to Becca. He'd still lied and left. Her dad had only lied.

"If I didn't tell her then, I sure wouldn't tell her now. I'm not staying."

"No?" Becca's dad glanced pointedly at his leg once more.

Owen ground his teeth. "I'm going back to my unit."

"And if you can't?"

Panic blazed. Reggie lifted his head, let out a huff, as if to clear his nose. His ruff lifted. Either Owen had given off the sudden scent of flop sweat or the dog had heard his breathing enter the freak-out zone. Maybe both.

Now that he thought about it, Reggie's behavior was similar to the behavior he exhibited to signal insurgent. Owen had always wondered how the dog knew the difference between bad guy and not a bad guy. The scent and the sound of nerves might do it.

"I'm okay," he said.

Carstairs snorted. Owen's fingers clenched. Reggie growled, gaze on Becca's dad.

"Bly'b," Owen repeated, then breathed in through the nose, out through the mouth several times the way he'd learned in rehab.

"How's your mom?"

"The same."

If she were any different—better or worse—someone from the Northern Wisconsin Mental Health Facility, where she'd been for a long, long time, should have called him.

"I'm selling the house," Owen continued. "Even if she ever gets well enough to leave the facility, she shouldn't live there."

The place was too isolated—creepy even before it had

become so broken down. Living there alone would make anyone crazy. If you were crazy to begin with . . . best to stay away.

"Don't you want to live there?" Carstairs asked.

"When I leave the service, I am not going to come back here."

"Why not?"

Owen cast the man an irritated glance. Even though Carstairs had done everything he could to make sure Owen left all those years ago, and seemed determined to ensure the same happened now, he seemed offended that Owen didn't want to stay.

"I can hope all I want that what I've accomplished might change people's view of me, but in a town like this that doesn't happen. I'll always be the son of the crazy lady."

"That's because you *will* always be the son of the crazy lady." Carstairs lifted his hand in a halting gesture. "You should be proud of yourself, Owen, but you can't change the truth. Crazy like your mom's doesn't go away and—" He let out a sharp sigh. "It's in the blood. Who knows where it might show up next."

"You think I'm gonna slip a gear?"

Carstairs spread his hands. "That or one of your kids might."

"You're not worried about *my* kids, you're only worried if they're her kids too."

"Do you blame me?"

Owen did, but he also understood. He didn't like it. Who would? But Carstairs was just a father trying to protect his daughter. That he was kind of an ass was irrelevant.

"I should never have agreed to let you live with us," Carstairs said.

"Why did you?" Owen never had figured that out. The guy had four kids. He didn't need another one. Especially one like Owen.

Iffy grades, fighting, mouthing off, driving fast, the incident with Emerson wasn't the only time he'd done something like that, it was merely the only time he'd been caught—with Owen it was always something. Certainly he'd been better once he lived with the Carstairs family, but he'd spent the majority of his early childhood on the edge and sometimes he behaved badly not because he wanted to but because he didn't know any other way.

"You and Becca were friends," Carstairs said.

"We were," Owen agreed. Losing Becca's friendship had hurt as much as turning his back on her love.

"She was an odd kid. You were her only friend. It didn't occur to me that you'd fall in love. You'd been pals for as long as I could remember."

For as long as Owen could remember too.

He couldn't recall where he and his mom had lived before coming to Three Harbors, or why they'd come, or how they'd somehow gotten a house. He did remember being outside, alone in the yard, digging in the dirt with a stick—his favorite toy—and he'd heard someone talking in the woods. He'd followed the sound and discovered a little red-haired girl. She'd been having a one-sided conversation with a squirrel, a chipmunk, and a rabbit. There'd been a bird perched atop her head. But that wasn't the strangest thing. The strangest thing was how the creatures seemed to be listening.

She was special and magical. A bit fey. And from the instant she'd turned and seen him there, then smiled and held out her hand, she had been his.

It had never entered Owen's head that they would become more than pals. Then one day he'd looked at her; she'd looked at him, and together they'd laughed. It had all seemed so simple.

Until it wasn't.

Her dad hadn't been blind, slow, or stupid. He'd seen the glances, the lingering touches. He'd taken Owen aside and said, "No." Only that one word, but Owen had known what he meant. And he'd tried. He really, really had.

"I'm leaving," Owen repeated.

"You sure?"

"Why wouldn't I be?"

"I saw you walk, Owen, and I'm sorry to say this, but you suck at it."

"Gee, thanks."

"Truth hurts."

So did Owen's leg, but he forced himself not to rub it, and though he really needed to sit, he didn't.

"What did Becca have to say about that?" Carstairs waved a hand in the general direction of Owen's knees.

"Not much."

"Doesn't sound like her." Becca's dad frowned. "She didn't mention it at breakfast either, and you'd think she would."

"You'd think."

Carstairs remained silent. Owen knew what the man was doing. Waiting for the silence to become so loud

Owen was compelled to fill it—a technique perfected by parents and interrogators everywhere. Despite his recognizing what Carstairs was up to, Owen still caved.

"She doesn't know."

"She isn't blind or stupid."

"No." Owen took a breath. "I didn't walk when she was watching."

"How'd you manage that?"

"Wasn't easy." And he wasn't going to be able to continue managing it if he stuck around much longer.

"Why?"

Owen shrugged. Seemed fairly obvious to him. He hadn't wanted pity, especially hers.

"If you can't go back to the Marines what will you do?"

"Well, I'm not going to hook up with Becca and let her be my sugar mama." Even if she'd let him.

"I don't remember you having a mouth like that back in the day."

"I did." Which had been half of his problem. The chip on Owen's shoulder had smoothed over a bit with Becca's friendship, attention, and love, but it had always been there, and when people poked at it, he poked back.

"I can send the boys over to fix up your mom's place. You hire a Realtor; give him my name. I'll take care of whatever needs to be taken care of. You don't have to hang around."

Owen was getting the bum's rush, and he wasn't even a bum any more.

"Until this mess with the serial-killer-in-training is solved, I think I do have to hang around town."

"They don't believe you did it, do they?"

"Not that I know of." Didn't mean they didn't.

"Then you're free to go."

As Carstairs wasn't the police chief, Owen decided not to take his word for it. Besides, he didn't think he'd be able to just leave without knowing what that mess had been doing in his house, not to mention making sure every trace of it was gone. He didn't trust anyone but himself for that job.

Reggie started up from sleep with a woof, then stared toward the front door, head tilted. Owen went to the window.

"What's wrong?" Carstairs asked.

"He heard something."

"I don't hear—" Carstairs began, then stopped as the telltale wail approached. They both stepped outside as the Three Harbors Police cruiser shot past the Stone Lake cottages.

"Speak of the police chief," Owen murmured.

The cruiser continued into town, straight down Carstairs Avenue, where it slid to a stop.

"Shit." Carstairs headed for his truck. "That's Becca's place."

"You expect me to believe there's a ghost named Henry in my apartment?"

You're the one talking to a wolf.

"Good point." I glanced at my phone, then back at Pru. Oddly it felt more right thinking of her as "Pru" than "my wolf." "You should probably lope off before I call the police."

Pru tilted her head like a dog that's heard a familiar word, but she wasn't looking at me, she was looking at Henry.

Beware the hunters.

"Okay." I pushed 9. The phone flew out of my hand and landed on the bed. I scowled at Pru. "Stop that."

I do not have the power to move objects with my mind.

"No one can."

You still believe that?

I hesitated. My phone had moved on its own twice, not to mention the aerial talents of my attempted murderer.

"You didn't do any tossing?"

I did not.

"Let me guess . . . Henry did."

Yes. Fear for your life, for mine, helped him focus, increased his power.

Something small skittered across the floor and bounced off my toe, making the same *clicky* sound I'd heard after the cuckoo hit the wall. I leaned over, tensing at the idea of discovering a tooth. Instead I saw a ring—a really big ring with some kind of crest. I started to reach for it and drew back.

The police would probably want to dust that for fingerprints. Could they dust a ring for fingerprints? I didn't know, but if they could, I certainly didn't want them to find mine.

I knelt and put my cheek on the floor. My nose nearly brushed the object. From this position I could see the likeness of a snarling wolf that had been carved into its face.

I straightened. "Did this belong to the creepy creep?"

I don't know why I continued to talk to the wolf. Maybe because she continued to answer me. Make that, I continued to answer myself. But the answers were good ones.

Give it to the authorities. Have them call the FBI.

"The FBI?" I got to my feet with a laugh. "Why would they care that some nut broke into a vet's house and tried to kill her?" I was suddenly very dizzy.

Someone had tried to kill me.

I have to go.

As I'd been trying to get her to go I didn't argue. That she actually went *after* I'd imagined her saying she would, should have freaked me out but didn't. Stuff like that happened to me all the time.

Pru descended the stairs. I retrieved my phone, called 9-1-1, and requested help. At the open back door, Pru glanced up.

Beware the Venatores Mali.

I'd taken Latin in college, but it hadn't really stuck the way it should. Besides, I was still loopy. I hadn't thought I'd had my oxygen cut off by the pillow, but apparently I had.

"Something . . . bad?" I translated.

Pru rolled her eyes. *Not bad. E—*

Her head turned sharply forward. *Oh, no! Edward!*

Then she ran.

By the time I reached the parking lot, she was gone. And if there'd been anyone named Edward there, he was gone too.

Chapter 10

A siren approached from the main highway. In the past day I'd seen more of Chief Deb than I had in the past month.

Tires screeched. I hurried from the back door to the front sidewalk as Deb leaped out of her cruiser. She'd parked kind of funky—facing the wrong way, with her left front tire nearly up on the curb and the ass end hanging into the street. If anyone else had parked like that they'd be begging for a ticket.

"Calm down," I said. "No one's here any more except me."

And maybe Henry, but I'd keep that to myself.

Deb lowered her gaze from my apartment window and her hand from her gun. "Who was it?"

"No idea. He . . . maybe she, wore a ski mask, hat, gloves."

She contemplated the street where the owners of the local businesses, as well as their patrons, had begun to spill onto the sidewalk. "Anyone see a person in a ski mask run past?"

Much head shaking ensued.

"You'd think someone like that would have been pretty obvious running down the street," Deb said.

"If he . . . ?" I tilted my head, and Deb made a "yeah,

yeah, go on" gesture to indicate she understood I'd just keep saying *he* instead of *he/she,* which had already become annoying. "If he wasn't a moron, he'd have run into the woods. And lost the ski mask."

Her gaze flicked to the shadowy tower of trees that marched right up to the edge of my parking lot then spoke into her shoulder mike. "George, I need you to go into the woods on the other side of town. Detain . . ." Her gaze flicked to mine.

"Six feet, maybe one sixty. Brown shirt." I spread my hands. "That's all I got."

Deb's eyes lifted to the heavens for help. That was the only place she was going to get it too. "Just grab anyone you find in the vicinity of six feet tall and detain them for questioning."

"Anyone?"

"Roger that. Send Billy to Doc Becca's for crowd control. Stat." She indicated the building. "Let's go."

"Front is locked." I headed around the side. My back door still gaped open.

"I'll assume it wasn't like that when you came home."

"Please do." I wasn't an idiot. My parents might not have locked their doors since the dawn of time, but I did.

"Was the door locked?"

"I used my key." I frowned. I'd just assumed I was opening it. Might it have been closed and unlocked? I had no idea.

Maybe I was an idiot.

"Don't touch anything." Deb used her shoulder mike again to ask for Ross Quinleven, Three Harbors Police Department's version of CSI.

"My prints are going to be everywhere already." It

wasn't like I dusted the doorknob or the railing on the staircase. It wasn't like I'd dusted anything in a long, long time, which Deb was going to see for herself in a minute. I should probably be more embarrassed about that than I was.

"I know, but you don't want to smudge anyone else's."

"He wore gloves," I repeated.

"We'll still follow procedure. Maybe he took them off so he could pick your lock." At my incredulous glance, she continued: "You'd be surprised what criminals do that they shouldn't."

"Like picking door locks then trying to kill people?"

"There you go."

I took the stairs to my apartment carefully. Once you were told *not* to use the handrail, suddenly the handrail seemed a lot more necessary than you realized.

The sight of the tossed bedcovers, the pillow on the floor, the table in pieces, the lamp tipped over, made me shiver. I'd always felt safe here. My mistake.

"Take me through what happened."

"Joe dropped me off."

"After Watley's?"

"Yes. No." I was so tired I was getting shaky. Or maybe my being shaky was making me more tired. "Owen dropped me at my parents' after Watley's."

"He was with you all night?"

"Yeah."

She lifted her eyebrows. I didn't elaborate. I only had so many more words left before my brain shut down. I wasn't going to waste them trying to explain something I didn't understand already.

"He dropped you at your parents' at what time?"

"Seven maybe? I had breakfast, and Joe brought me here."

"You didn't notice anything off when you came in? Anything where it shouldn't be? Doors closed when you thought you'd left them open, or vice versa?"

"You think he was already inside when I got here?"

"You tell me."

My gaze wandered the apartment. "It's a little small to hide in."

Kitchen, living, bedroom were all one. The only doors were to the outside, the bathroom, and the closet. Shit. The closet. Had he been in there watching me undress? My shiver became a shudder.

Deb set her hand on my arm, and I jumped. "Calm down. It's over."

"Is it?"

That depended on why someone had tried to kill me. Because I was there? Did that mean once I wasn't, I was safe? I didn't think so.

Deb gave me an awkward pat. "What happened next?"

"I went into the bathroom, brushed my teeth, and . . . stuff."

"Shower curtain?"

"Yes. I mean no. Yes, I have one. No, I didn't look behind it." Had the intruder been behind my shower curtain watching me pee? This just got better and better.

Did people peek behind their shower curtain every time they went into the bathroom? Paranoid much? Maybe I should be paranoid more.

"Go on," Chief Deb urged.

My attention kept drifting. From the ease with which

Deb brought me back to the topic, I wasn't the first victim to do so.

I was a victim. I didn't like it.

Deb snapped her fingers in front of my nose.

Whoops.

"I . . . uh . . . put on . . ." I indicated my scrubs. "Lay down and the next thing I knew someone was smashing a pillow on my face."

"That pillow?" She pointed.

I nodded.

"Why did he stop?"

"I—" Should I mention the wolf or shouldn't I? Probably had to.

"There's this wolf . . ." I began. "She . . . uh . . . likes me."

"A wolf likes you," the chief repeated. "Why?"

That I didn't know. "She just does. She hangs around. Follows me when I run. Stuff like that."

"And you're telling me this why?"

"She scared the guy away."

Her eyes widened. "A wolf came in the apartment?"

"The door was open."

Deb blinked. "You're sure?"

"That the door was open? Yeah. How else would she have gotten in?" I wiggled my fingers. "She doesn't have thumbs for the doorknob."

Which got me thinking—for Pru to have gotten in someone had to have left the door open and it hadn't been me. The intruder?

Or Henry.

"Very funny." Deb set her hands on her hips. "Is this wolf black, with weird eyes?"

"You saw her?"

"Not me personally. But we've had reports."

And here I'd thought I was the only one who'd seen her. I guess that was because I'd thought I was the only one who *could* see her.

"Her eyes?" Deb pressed.

"They're green."

"Which is weird, right? Most wolves have brown eyes."

"Most," I agreed. "Some might be a lighter shade, yellowish or hazel, which could appear green in certain light."

But none would ever be the green-green of Pru's eyes. Even hybrids—part dog, part wolf—would be more likely to have blue eyes than green. Pru being a hybrid would explain why she felt comfortable hanging around town, walking into apartments. It did *not* explain why I could suddenly hear her now when I hadn't before. But that was more my weirdness than Pru's.

I made a soft sound of amusement. The chief glanced at me, but I shook my head. I wasn't going to tell her the wolf's name was Pru. That would just add more weird to the weird, and how was I going to explain how I knew her name? I couldn't. Wouldn't. Definitely shouldn't.

"I need to send a report to the Department of Natural Resources," she said.

"What? Why?"

Deb jumped. I guess I had shouted.

"It's what we do when wild animals misbehave."

"She hasn't misbehaved. She saved my life."

"By walking into an apartment. Wolves don't do that.

They also don't hang around towns or follow people when they're jogging. You know that."

I did.

"She seemed harmless." At least to me. She hadn't been harmless for the intruder.

"I doubt she's harmless. She's also the only wolf that's been seen, which makes her a lone wolf and they're unpredictable at best."

Pru was definitely unpredictable. Still . . .

"What will the DNR do?"

"Send a wolf expert."

"What will he do?"

"Decide if she needs to be relocated or shot."

"I don't think you should call them."

"Thanks for the advice."

"Sarcasm?"

"You think?" I narrowed my eyes, but Deb moved on. "How did the wolf stop the masked intruder from smothering you?"

"Yanked him away by his shirt. Once the pillow was off my face, and I could breathe, I was a little harder to kill and he ran."

I'd left out how the guy had flown through the air and smacked against the wall. I was funny that way.

"If you had a pillow over your face you couldn't see exactly what happened," Deb pointed out.

"No. But I can add. The guy stopped. The wolf had a piece of his shirt in her mouth." I searched for it amid the debris. "There." I pointed to the bit of brown material peeking out from beneath the leg of what was left of my end table.

"Anything else?"

"He dropped his ring." I shifted my pointer finger to where it still lay on the floor.

Deb walked over, bent, squinted. "What is that on the face?"

"I think it's a snarling wolf."

"Weird, considering."

"Mmm," I agreed. What wasn't?

She straightened. "How did that happen?"

For a minute I thought she could tell that the ring hadn't actually fallen where it now rested. But that didn't mean she knew it had gotten there thanks to the powers of Henry, the telekinetic ghost.

I was losing my mind.

"I mean, how could his ring fall off if he was wearing gloves?"

"You think I lied about his wearing gloves?"

Her eyebrows flew up. "Did you?"

"Why would I?"

"Why would you lie about anything?" she asked. "Don't you want this guy caught before he tries it again?"

"Again?" I echoed.

"You're not dead. As he apparently wanted you that way badly enough to try it in broad daylight in the middle of town, he seems pretty motivated."

"He didn't just try to rob me, see me here, and—"

"Decide to kill you? No."

"How can you be so certain?"

"Thieves and murderers are two different types of criminals. If a thief had been inside when you got here, he would have run out instead of engaging you, especially since you were asleep. If he came in after you got here, he would have left as soon as he saw you."

She indicated the sight line from the door; my bed lay dead ahead. He couldn't have missed me. Still . . .

"You don't know that."

"You're right. I don't. So, what *did* you lie about?"

"Nothing." Everything I'd said was the truth. It was what I hadn't said that was the problem.

A chill wind seemed to ruffle my hair. I should probably shut the door, but I'd just have to open it again when Ross arrived. I hugged myself.

Chief Deb's gaze fell, narrowed. I glanced down. My fingernails were bloody.

"I scratched him!" I held out my hands as if admiring my new manicure. "You'll be able to find him now."

She reached into her pocket. "Maybe."

"You can check people's forearms."

"Because a guy who attempted murder is going to hang around in the café wearing a T-shirt and no coat? I can't just go up to people and demand they bare their forearms for my examination."

"You can't?"

She shook her head. Then she pulled two evidence bags from her pocket. "Hold 'em out."

I did, and she put the bags over my hands then secured them at my wrists with rubber bands. "What I can do is have Ross scrape your fingernails for DNA, and if this nut is in the system . . ." She clapped her hands together so loudly I started, and my plastic bags rattled. "We got 'im."

"What system?"

"The Combined DNA Index System, CODEX for short."

"FBI?"

"What was your first clue?"

"The acronym?"

Her lips twitched. "It's a federal thing."

My surprise that she knew what an acronym was must have shown on my face.

"I'm good with letters," she said. "R-E-B-O-U-N-D!"

Now my lips twitched. "I'm sure you're good with more than that."

The amusement in her iris-blue eyes faded. "Is that a 'cheerleaders are sluts' dig?"

"I didn't mean it to be."

I hadn't known that was a thing. Cheerleaders were pretty far out of my social circle in high school. I hadn't cared; I'd had Owen. I'd gone to a college with over forty thousand students. Add over twenty thousand in faculty and staff, and that was one huge campus. Cheerleaders? I'd seen a few, but I certainly didn't know them.

"I meant that I doubt you'd be the police chief just because you can spell to a beat."

"Oh. Thanks."

I suppose someone like Deb had a tough time being taken seriously as a cop. That she was the police chief at all said she wasn't as blond as she looked.

Silence descended. I tried to figure out how to suggest she send the ring to the FBI without sounding like I was telling her her business, or insinuating she was stupid.

Or explaining that the wolf had told me to.

"That ring—" I began.

"I should probably show that to the feds too."

"Couldn't hurt."

Chapter 11

Dale Carstairs had to be over twenty years older than Owen, but his legs worked a lot better. By the time Owen and Reggie climbed into the rental truck, the taillights of the man's pickup blared red several hundred yards in the distance.

"One of her patients probably freaked out," Owen said. "Or the owner of one of her patients had a stroke. Fell on the steps. Tripped on the curb."

Reggie's huff sounded disgusted. Owen had to agree. He was reaching, and he knew it. But the idea of the police chief driving that fast to Becca's place because Becca was hurt made it hard for him to breathe.

He raced down Carstairs Avenue faster than he should have. People lined the sidewalk, staring toward the clinic. The police cruiser was parked as badly as Dale Carstairs's truck. Since neither Chief Deb, Carstairs, nor Becca were anywhere to be seen, Owen parked his just as badly and climbed out.

He considered taking along the Beretta he'd removed from his backpack on the way to Stone Lake, then shoved under the driver's seat. However, while he had the requisite permits to carry and conceal the weapon, as a soldier he knew just how foolish it would be to walk into an unknown situation carrying one. Chief Deb might shoot him, and he'd deserve it. He took Reggie instead.

Considering the size of the crowd, he snapped a leash onto the dog's collar. Nevertheless, when they stepped onto the sidewalk, the gawkers inched back. Reggie was intimidating. He was supposed to be.

A second cruiser slid to a stop on the other side of the street, and Billy Gardiner climbed out. He was younger than Owen by at least three years, which made him twenty-five or less. His full beard made him appear ten years older. Always had.

When they were teenagers, Billy stopped shaving on the first day of football practice in August and didn't start again until they lost a game. In Three Harbors that meant mid-November. Owen couldn't recall the last time they hadn't won the D-3 state championship. From the number of years tacked onto the WELCOME TO THREE HARBORS—HOME OF THE STATE CHAMPION CENTURIONS sign, no one else probably remembered it either.

"What's going on, Prof?" The question came from the crowd as Billy looked both ways and hustled across Carstairs Avenue.

Out-of-towners might think "prof" was short for professor; however, Billy had earned the nickname "the Prophet," not because of his ability to predict anything, but because of the nearly chest length of his straggly black beard by the end of every football season.

He stepped onto the sidewalk next to Owen, frowning at the bizarre parking lot in front of the clinic. His fingers stroked the parking ticket booklet peeking out of his shirt pocket. However, since Chief Deb appeared to be the instigator of the parking misbehavior, he left the booklet where it was.

Billy cast a glance at Reggie, then at Owen. "Okay?"

Owen nodded. Billy's parents were well-respected breeders of Siberian huskies. He'd probably rolled around with the puppies when he was a pup, which might explain why he felt so at home wearing a face full of fur. At any rate, Billy knew dogs and could be trusted to treat this one like the weapon he was.

Billy extended his hand palm down, fingers limp— no fast, grabbing movements that might get him bitten. Reggie sniffed his knuckles, submitted to a short ear scratch, and glanced away as if bored. Billy took the hint and withdrew.

"Hey, Prof!" The same voice as before came from the crowd. "What happened?"

"Don't know yet." Billy pulled yellow tape from his pants pocket and herded the gawkers back so he could attach the tape to a building. He unrolled it across the sidewalk, then secured it around a street sign and tore the end.

"If you don't know, then why are you roping this off?"

"I was told to." Billy turned his back on the crowd, folded his arms, and stared straight ahead. The crowd began to disperse.

Folks from here knew that Billy, the Prophet, had never allowed a QB to be sacked on his watch, and he treated any police line with the same attention. Tourists were just scared at the sight of him.

Owen and Reggie stepped toward the building. Billy's dark eyes, which were nearly the shade of his beard, flicked in their direction. "No."

"But—"

"Chief said no one in until she came out."

"Becca's dad went in there."

Billy lifted an eyebrow. That *had* sounded both lame and childish.

"Is anyone hurt?"

"She's fine," Billy said.

"Promise?"

"If anyone had so much as a hangnail, the chief would have sent for Dr. D." He lifted a huge paw. "Promise."

Owen nearly asked the guy to pinky swear, but figured that was pushing it. If Becca was hurt in any way, help would have been called and Billy would know about it.

Didn't make Owen want to go inside any less, but it did make his heart stop racing. Eventually.

If he'd been quicker he'd have been there before anyone arrived to keep him out. He could make a run for it, but that would probably go as well now as it had the last time he'd tried. He didn't need to be tackled by the Prophet. It might not hurt as much as being thrown by an IED, then again it might. He'd heard Billy hit as hard as a freight train. However, the real trouble would be with Reggie.

According to those who'd been with them that day in Afghanistan, despite his own injuries, Reggie had remained conscious. He'd crawled over the bloody ground to get to Owen, who was not conscious, then protected him from everyone, including the medic. It had taken the other soldiers close to a half hour to talk Reggie down so that the two of them could be medevaced.

Reggie had been hurt and scared, and while he was the

property of the U.S. Marine Corps, and the men in their
unit were family, Owen was Reggie's person. All good
things came from him, which was the way it had to be for
them to work together the way they did. That also meant
if Owen was down, Reggie was standing over him until
he got up. He'd prefer not to have that confrontation here.

Instead, Owen stood shoulder to shoulder with Billy. It
gave him the best view of the doors to Becca's place, and
he could quiz the man without shouting.

"What's going on?" Owen asked.

Billy shrugged. Owen didn't know him well enough
to decide if he knew and wasn't telling, or he truly didn't
know.

"Chief Deb asked if anyone had seen a person wearing a mask running away from the clinic."

A young man, about the age of Becca's brothers and
far too ethnic to be from here, had bellied up to the crime
scene tape.

Owen glanced at Billy. The officer continued to stare
straight ahead as if he hadn't heard.

"Mask," Owen repeated. "*V Is for Vendetta*? Lone
Ranger? Phantom?"

"Spider-Man?" Billy deadpanned.

"Ski mask."

A ripple went through what was left of the crowd.
Someone whispered, "He speaks English."

For a minute Owen thought they were referring to
him—then the kid rolled his eyes and muttered something uncomplimentary in Spanish.

"You better hope none of them speak the language,"
Owen said.

"As if."

"Señora Mueller taught Spanish when I was here, and she was pretty fluent." Though no one in her class ever turned out to be. Señora had mostly handed out worksheets and sent them to the language lab to listen to others speak Spanish, rather than insisting they speak it themselves.

"She's still teaching," the boy said.

He did live in Three Harbors. Maybe things had changed. Except . . . Owen let his gaze wander over the people still hanging around.

The kid had the only tan in town.

"And I bet no one speaks decent Spanish but you and her."

The boy shrugged, which Owen took as a yes.

Owen had always figured Señora hadn't actively taught her classes because talking seemed to make her cough. As he recalled, breathing had made her cough.

"She still have 'allergies'?" Owen made quotation marks in the air with his forefingers.

"She coughs like it's her last day on earth," the kid said. "Considering she smells like Marlboros, I'm not sure if she's allergic to smoke or fresh air." He contemplated Reggie with interest. "Your dog is a . . ."

"Malinois," Owen supplied.

"Belgian." That was Billy, who continued to stare straight ahead as if guarding the Tomb of the Unknown Soldier rather than frayed crime scene tape hung across a sidewalk.

"I know what breed he is." The boy sounded as if he wanted to roll his eyes again. Owen had never felt so old. "He's a working dog." The kid's gaze lifted to Owen's Marines-style hair. "A military working dog."

"You know a lot about dogs."

"I work for Becca." He held out his hand. "I'm Joaquin."

Owen shook. A couple of tourists jaywalked, weaving in between the cruisers and the pickups parked willy-nilly at the curb, then strolling up the sidewalk in front of the clinic. Billy hurried over to shoo them away, then began to string yellow tape from sign to sign to prevent such a breach from occurring again.

Owen considered making a break for the back door, but Billy glanced over his shoulder as if he'd heard the thought. His glower was as threatening as it had ever been. It had never occurred to Owen that a lineman would make a great cop, but it should have. Billy's protect-and-defend instinct was well honed, and his ability to read minds, or at least eyes and faces, even better.

"Joaquin," Owen repeated. "How many people have called you Joe Quinn?"

Joaquin laughed. "You've been here before."

"I lived here once. I'm Owen—"

"McAllister?"

"Yeah." Owen considered the kid again. Maybe someone he knew had gone away and married someone who'd named their kid Joaquin. But he doubted it.

"I know you. I mean . . ." His quick grin made him appear younger than Owen had first thought. "I've heard of you."

Had Becca mentioned him to her employee? Hope fluttered.

"People talk." Joaquin's grin faded, and he shrugged. The hope died. If Becca had mentioned him, it couldn't have been anything good for the boy to go all twitchy like that.

"I was a dumb kid," he said.

"No. Well, maybe. Aren't all kids dumb?"

Joaquin got smarter by the second.

"You're a big deal now. People call you a hero."

"They do? Since when?"

Confusion flickered. "Since forever."

"Not," Owen muttered.

"I've never heard anything but how great you are."

Owen opened his mouth, shut it again, glanced at the waning crowd. Someone called his name, another waved.

"This is Three Harbors, right?"

Looked like Three Harbors, but it wasn't acting like Three Harbors.

"All day," the kid said. "Lucky us."

"Not a fan?"

"I won't complain."

"Just because you won't doesn't mean you shouldn't."

"Sir?"

"Let me guess. You're different. You don't fit in. No one wants to play with you."

"I don't wanna play with them either," Joaquin said.

"Sure you do."

"From what I heard you didn't play with anyone except—"

The kid broke off. Good choice.

However, Joaquin was frowning at Reggie and not at him.

The dog's ruff had gone razorback then he blew air through his nose, an indication that Reggie had caught the scent of something he didn't like. Not explosives.

That tell was ears up, sit down, stare at the place where the bomb was situated with the attention usually given to a five-pound steak. Razorback was for—

He took off, yanking the leash from Owen's hand. Owen stared at his empty palm for an instant before he took off too. Unfortunately Owen's version of "taking off" these days was a hop, skip, and a gimp.

Someone in the gathering behind the police tape drew in a loud, shocked breath.

"What a shame!" said another.

Then Owen could have sworn he heard a snicker.

He clenched his hands and kept going. Out of the corner of his eye, he saw movement and whirled in that direction.

Billy lifted his hands in surrender. "You get him, man. I know better."

"You need help?" Joaquin appeared at his side.

"I need a leg," Owen snapped, and the kid winced. "Sorry. No, I—"

Snarling erupted from the rear of the clinic, followed by thuds, shouts, and curses.

Owen swallowed his pride. "I'll take that help now."

He set his hand on Joaquin's shoulder and, using the kid like a crutch, moved a lot more quickly, though no more gracefully, to the back of the building.

Reggie had a man's pants leg in his mouth, and he was shaking it so hard he nearly pulled the guy off his feet.

"Aus!"

Reggie immediately let go, but he continued to stand so close, the fellow backed up until he hit the wall.

"You know him?" Owen asked.

"Not from here," Joaquin said.

When Reggie went razorback it meant "insurgent." This guy did not look like Al Qaeda. Didn't mean he wasn't. Still, Owen doubted they'd started slinking around this far north. Nevertheless, there was something about him that had set off the dog.

Was it the perfect blond hair and the well-trimmed goatee? Nah. What about the pretentious black silk shirt and slacks, or the once shiny, now dusty and slobbered-on black shoes? Doubtful. Could be the silver ring on his thumb. It certainly annoyed Owen.

"Reggie, *hier.*"

The dog appeared incredulous. But he came as he'd been told, though he paused and snatched something off the ground.

At first Owen thought Reggie had torn free a good chunk of the guy's well-pressed black pants. But when he took the item from the dog's mouth, the material was different. Heavier. Knit. With holes big enough to stick his fingers through.

A ski mask.

Owen crossed the distance, grabbed the man by his smooth silk shirt, and smacked him against the wall.

"Dude." Joaquin sounded both shocked and impressed.

"Who are you?" Owen demanded.

"Jjj— Rrr— Ga—"

"I didn't get that." Owen tightened his grip. The jerk's mouth moved, but nothing came out. He liked him better that way.

"You wanna let him go?" Becca stood in the doorway. He'd never seen her in scrubs before. He kind of liked them.

"No."

"Do it anyway."

He considered saying "Hell, no," but decided she'd understand when he didn't do it. "I hear you're searching for someone wearing a ski mask."

"He isn't."

Owen lifted his other hand, which still held the mask.

"That isn't his."

"I disagree." He loosened his grip just a little. "How about you?"

"Gar-shrul. Shll."

"See?"

Becca made a sound that was part snort, part laugh, and part cough. He wasn't sure what that meant. He was a little busy to ask. His leg had started to shake. Sweat ran down his forehead. His fingers ached. He'd known he was out of shape, but this was ridiculous.

"Owen," Becca said softly.

Owen sighed and let the man go.

Chapter 12

"Thanks for coming," I said.

"Why wouldn't I?" Owen flexed his fingers as if he wanted to grab someone again, or maybe punch them.

"I was talking to him." I pointed at the man Owen had been holding a few inches off the ground. As soon as Owen had released him, he'd slid downward, gasping.

"What happened?" Owen's gaze was on my hand, which was still encased in plastic. CSI hadn't yet arrived, though everyone else in town had. "Who is this guy?"

I stepped outside. I had to shoulder Owen out of the way to do it. He was behaving like a dog over a bone. Reggie wasn't much better, though he had the excuse that he *was* a dog. At least he stayed back far enough that I didn't have to push him out of the way. I wasn't sure I'd have had the guts to do it. Reggie appeared more annoyed than Owen, or maybe it was just the black cloth strands that hung out of his mouth.

"Jeremy?"

I went to my knees, yanking up his pants leg to see if Reggie had removed more than thread. MWDs were trained to bite, but on command. However, there wasn't a mark on him.

Jeremy rubbed his throat, eyes closed, face paler than I'd ever seen it. As he was pretty pale to begin with, that

was saying something. At this point, his blond goatee
had more color.

I touched his arm, got a shock of static electricity, and
pulled back, the plastic bag on my hand rattling with
the sudden movement.

Jeremy's eyes snapped open. He'd felt it too. It was
early for static electricity, though maybe the stupid-ass
plastic on my hand was a conductor. Who knew?

"Jeremy?" I tried again.

"Apparently, he's Jeremy."

I scowled at Billy Gardiner. "Where were you when
this was going on?" I flapped my wrist to indicate all
parties concerned, then grimaced at the annoying rustle.
I wished Deb had used smaller plastic bags.

Billy lifted a roll of yellow crime scene tape. Figured.

"What about you?" I glared at Owen. "You released
your dog on Jeremy?"

"He isn't . . ." Owen began, then frowned. "He just
took off."

"He do that a lot?"

"Never."

Reggie continued to glare at Jeremy like he wanted
to bite a lot more than his pants.

Owen picked up the dog's trailing lead. "What got
into you?"

Reggie snuffed as if he'd smelled something he didn't
like. The hair on his back was still ruffled.

Splode.

I had no idea what that meant. And I couldn't exactly
ask with all these people around. I'd never had the imaginary thoughts of animals not make sense—probably be-

cause they were my thoughts not the animal's. But, as they said, there was a first time for everything.

Jeremy continued to sit on the ground. That he hadn't gotten up or spoken was becoming worrisome.

"What's going on here?" Chief Deb didn't appear any happier about this situation than I was.

"I planned to ask him the same question," Owen said.

"Before or after you smacked him into the wall, then tried to strangle him?" I asked.

"If I'd been trying to strangle him, he'd be strangled."

"It was so cool," Joaquin said.

Where had he come from?

"Shouldn't you be in school?"

He shrugged.

I frowned. "Go to school!"

Joaquin walked off mumbling. I heard *madre* in the middle of a whole lot of *español* and decided not to try and translate. I probably didn't want to know.

"Who are you?" Deb asked.

Jeremy tried to talk and started coughing.

"Jesus," Owen muttered.

"No," Billy said. "It's Jer-e-my."

"Ha." Owen's gaze flicked to me. "I barely touched him."

"*Why* did you touch him?"

He held up the ski mask again.

"Where did you get that?" Deb demanded.

"It was on the ground next to this guy."

"Who is this guy?" Deb repeated.

"You wanted a forensic veterinarian." I swept my hand

out like a magician. "You got one. Meet Dr. Jeremy Reitman."

"Right man," Billy repeated. "That's funny."

"Hysterical." Owen's gaze remained on Jeremy.

Jeremy got to his feet, hand extended toward Deb.
The sudden movement made Reggie growl, and Jeremy
backed up to the wall.

"You're scared of a dog?" Owen asked. "What kind
of a vet are you?"

To be fair, most of Jeremy's patients were dead, or in
very bad shape, and Reggie wasn't just any dog, he was
a weapon.

"He attacked me."

"And why is that?" Owen asked.

"I don't know!"

"He doesn't like masks. I don't blame him. Anyone
in Afghanistan who's covering their face is up to no
good. Or expecting a sandstorm." Owen lifted his gaze
to the clear blue sky. "No sign of one." His eyes lowered.
"What's your excuse?"

"I wasn't wearing that mask. I didn't even see it until
you picked it up."

"I didn't see it there either," Deb said.

Neither had I, but I hadn't been looking.

My dad poked his head out the back door. I was surprised it had taken him this long. "What's going on down
here?" His gaze lit on Jeremy and he smiled, stepping
outside. "Doctor! Hey! Great to see you."

"Jesus," Owen muttered again.

Billy cast him a wry glance and returned to crowd
control.

"Dale!" Jeremy and my dad clasped hands and chest-bumped like old pals.

They'd met once when my father had stopped in Madison on the way to Milwaukee with my brothers' entries for the Wisconsin State Fair holstein competition in a trailer. He hadn't been able to stay long—cows in a trailer in August—but Jeremy had come by to loan me a textbook, and I'd introduced them. From the way they were behaving, they'd bonded like long-lost relatives.

I'd taken a single class from Jeremy in my first year of veterinary school. He was well read, interesting, a good teacher. We'd stayed in touch. I didn't have many friends, and I wasn't certain I'd even consider Jeremy one of them—more a colleague—but he'd been helpful in the past, and he had rushed over personally just on the basis of my call.

My father caught sight of Owen, and his smile faded. "What are you doing here?"

"I told you Owen was in town, Dad."

"In town is one thing, here is another."

"It isn't that big of a town."

"Don't be a smartass," he said, but he was staring at Owen.

There was something going on I didn't understand. My dad and Owen had always gotten along fine. Even that last night, when my dad had walked in on us in the barn, his face had gotten really red, but he hadn't shouted at either one of us. However, within days Owen had been gone, which seemed a lot more suspicious now than it had been then.

"Why is either one of you here?" I asked. "Dad, you

were supposed to be mending fences and you—" I switched my gaze to Owen. "I'd think you would be asleep."

"You'd think, wouldn't you?" My gaze narrowed, and Owen held up his hands. "I was on the porch, and Deb flew by. When she skidded to a stop in front of your place I certainly wasn't going to be able to sleep without finding out what was wrong."

"How did you know it was my place?"

"I can see straight down this street from my porch, and this had been the vet clinic since your father was a pup."

"Watch it," my dad murmured.

"What is up with you two?" I demanded.

"Same thing that's been up from the beginning," Owen said, and my father's hands clenched.

"Whoa!" I stepped between the two of them. "One of you want to expand on that?"

"No," they said at the same time.

"I thought you wanted me to examine a crime scene?"

Jeremy still hugged the wall. Reggie still stared at him as if he were a side of beef, or at least smelled like one. It would probably be a good idea to get Jeremy out of here.

"That's at Owen's place. I can—"

"You can go with Ross." Deb made an impatient "come here" gesture. Ross Quinleven, who had either just arrived, or been hovering out of sight around the corner, bolted forward.

Ross was of an age with my father. His own family farm had gone under while his dad owned it, leaving Ross to find other employment. He'd become a cop, and he seemed to enjoy it, though I'd never heard him speak more than a few words in my entire life.

Ross had always reminded me of a flamingo. He was tall, skinny, his hair a more unfortunate shade than my own—a faded deep pink rather than fire red. If he'd drawn himself up on one leg and stood quiet and still, I wouldn't have been surprised.

"I'll have someone take Dr. Reitman to Owen's," Deb continued.

"I can do it," Owen said.

I lifted my eyebrows. "I don't think so."

He'd already tried to kill Jeremy once. Sending the two of them into the woods, toward a place where Owen had already started digging a grave, was not the best idea.

Owen lifted one hand, palm out. "I promise not to bury him in the forest."

Jeremy rubbed his throat again.

"This shouldn't take long, right?" I asked and glanced at Deb, who shook her head. "I can drive him myself in a few minutes."

"You aren't going out there without a cop along," Deb said. "That's a crime scene."

Jeremy stiffened. "I know what to do with a crime scene. I don't need an escort."

"Fine," Deb agreed. "Becca and I will be along directly."

"He isn't going to my house without me," Owen insisted.

"Sheesh." They were acting like three-year-olds. I held out my plastic-covered hands. My palms were starting to sweat. "Just get this over with."

"Scrape her fingernails," Deb ordered. "Then get started on the rest of the room."

Ross led me away from the others, setting his box full of CSI tools on the hood of my Bronco. It resembled a tackle box, and maybe it was, but when he opened the lid I saw no evidence of lines, lures, or jigs. He removed a hooked chrome device that reminded me of something they used at the dentist's office. I hated the dentist's office. I swallowed and averted my gaze.

There were still people gathered behind the tape Billy had strung. Several waved, but my hands were occupied, so I nodded in return.

One woman sat on the bumper of a parked car and stared at me as if she knew me, though I didn't know her. Long dark hair, flowing black skirt that brushed the ground, tie-dyed T-shirt. She had her arm in a sling. She seemed a little hippie, which is something we didn't see a lot in Three Harbors.

I smiled. She didn't smile back. She seemed pissed off. Maybe her arm really hurt. Or maybe the commotion had ruined her café breakfast. She'd probably come here to get away from crime in the big city, and yet, here it was.

"What is he scraping her fingernails for?" Owen asked.

I glanced at him then back toward the crowd, still disturbed by that woman. But she was gone.

"Billy said you were searching for a guy in a ski mask. What did he do?"

"None of your—" I began, but Deb answered. "Tried to smother her with a pillow."

Reggie woofed, low and concerned. Owen smoothed his palm over the dog's head. But Reggie wasn't having it.

Scared.

He spun counterclockwise.

Angry.

He spun clockwise. Was the dog talking about himself or Owen?

"Since when do people get attacked in their own homes in Three Harbors?" Owen's face was serene, his voice completely reasonable. I wasn't buying it.

"You need to calm down," I said.

His gaze flicked to me. "Who says I'm not calm?"

"Who says I was talking to you?" I lifted my chin to indicate Reggie. The dog was still spinning—right, left, right.

Ross was still scraping my fingernails. It didn't hurt, but I certainly hoped I never had to do this again. I remembered the pillow smashing my nose, my mouth.

For more reasons than one.

"Sitz," Owen ordered.

Reggie sat, but he cast Owen a concerned glance, which Owen ignored. He was too busy glaring at me.

"I'm fine," I said. "Not a scratch on me." Although my nose felt a little bruised.

"The scratches were all on him," Deb said. "Hence the nail scrapings."

Owen grabbed Jeremy's hand and yanked on his shirt. Unfortunately the shirt was buttoned at the cuff and stuck tight about an inch above his wrist.

"Hey!" Jeremy tried to pull away.

Owen yanked the shirt so hard the button flew through the air. Reggie started barking at it.

Owen stared at Jeremy's arm for a second, then he

grabbed him by the throat and smacked him into the wall again.

Becca shouted something. Owen thought it might be his name, or maybe the doctor's. Everyone, especially Dale Carstairs, seemed to think Reitman was Three Harbors's answer to a prayer.

However, that wasn't why he put his hand around Jeremy's throat and squeezed—again. The reason for that were the scratches on the guy's arm.

Someone tried to grab Owen, probably Dale. He doubted Deb was that dumb. Reggie snarled, and the hands clutching at him disappeared.

"Let him go, Owen. Now."

That was Deb.

Owen released the guy for the second time that day, and for the second time Dr. Reitman slid to the ground like a rag doll.

"What is wrong with you?" Becca shoved past Owen and touched Jeremy's face.

"Look at his arm."

She glanced up, frowned, then lifted the shirtsleeve that had fallen back down in the upheaval.

Three scratches marred the man's skin.

Owen waited for Becca to straighten, to back away, to show them to Deb, who would then cuff the guy as Becca threw herself into Owen's arms and thanked him for seeing the truth when no one else had.

Instead her head fell forward; she shook it then stood. "Those scratches are healed over."

How had he missed that? His only excuse was that he'd been so furious at the thought of anyone hurting

Becca that he'd gone a little overboard. A world without Becca in it was not one Owen could bear.

In dog handler school they'd learned why dogs were so good at explosives detection. Not only were their noses about a thousand times more sensitive than a human's, but the size of the portion of their brain used for analyzing those scents was between twenty and forty percent larger. Which might explain why a human would smell beef stew and a dog would smell onions, potatoes, carrots, beef, flour, salt, and so on. This was how MWDs could ferret out bombs. While one explosive might be made out of different materials than another, they all needed a reason to go boom—and *that* scent set off the dogs. Owen had seen IEDs buried in dirt, covered with garbage, wrapped in Lord knows what, but still Reggie had found them.

What this meant to Owen was that even though Reggie's indication of insurgent was suspect, there was something off about Dr. "Right Man."

Certainly Carstairs's adoration of the man, so soon after he had told Owen—again—to leave Becca alone, had made Owen *want* the guy to be bad so much he'd been blinded to anything else.

He still thought it was pretty damn odd that they were searching for an intruder of the same size, wearing a ski mask, which had been found right next to a fellow who had scratches—albeit old ones—right where Becca had put some.

"Maybe he's a fast healer." Owen wasn't willing to let it go.

"Freaky fast," Deb said. "Like supernaturally woo-woo fast, even."

Becca cast Deb a curious glance, as if the chief were serious.

"Where'd those scratches come from?" Owen asked.

"What difference does it make?" Becca's dad snapped.

Owen had forgotten for a minute that the man was there.

"Jeremy didn't try to kill Becca," Carstairs continued. "Why would he?"

"Why would anyone?" Owen wondered.

"Exactly," Carstairs agreed.

"No, really. Why? You think it was random?" Owen's gaze went from Carstairs, to Becca, to Deb.

"Random is a lot more rare than people think," Deb said.

"Cat," Jeremy blurted. Reggie starting wailing.

"Lass das sein," Owen ordered.

Reggie stopped. The doctor stared at his arm so hard Owen wondered if he were trying to make the scratches disappear by wishing for it.

"What cat?" Becca asked.

Reggie let out a short yip, as if he just couldn't help it. Owen wondered how he even knew the word.

MWDs were taught to chase only what they were told to and nothing else. It wouldn't do to give a dog the command to search, then have him distracted by a rabbit or squirrel or any other furry creature and pursue it, allowing an insurgent to go merrily in another direction and AK-47 someone down the line.

"A cat scratched me here a few days ago." Jeremy tapped his forearm.

Owen frowned. The guy had tapped the wrong arm.

Chapter 13

Owen looked like he wanted to knock Jeremy over the head with his club, and drag me off by my hair. Jeremy continued to act like he'd already been hit with a club. I wondered just how much oxygen Owen had deprived him of while strangling him—twice. I didn't think it was as much as I'd lost beneath the pillow, but what did I know?

Jeremy was being loopy, and as he never had before, I had to think it was a result of today's events. I was lucky he hadn't jumped in his car and raced back to Madison without investigating the crime scene. Though it wasn't my crime scene, or even my house.

I started to stand up, teetered, reached out, and Owen caught my elbow, hauled me upright. I braced my other hand on his thigh. He caught his breath. I yanked it back. I had touched a little higher than was proper. Not that I hadn't touched even higher before.

Deb's shoulder mike squawked gibberish. She waited until it stopped then spoke into it. "Say again?"

"No one in the woods, Chief."

"No one?" Owen repeated. "On a walking trail, in the middle of the day, right after the Falling Leaves Festival?"

Deb cast him a glare, but she transmitted his question. "No one at all?"

"No one that fit the description. Six feet, one sixty."

Owen let his gaze wander over Jeremy's slim, six-foot-one frame, then lifted his eyebrows. I ignored him. Jeremy would have no reason to strangle me.

But, as Owen had pointed out, who did? People might go gonzo over losing a pet or a valuable farm animal. Though strangling your veterinarian while wearing a ski mask was well past gonzo.

Except I hadn't lost a patient since I got here. Damn good luck, or superior diagnostics, maybe both, but I wasn't complaining. Nevertheless, it meant that no one had decided to feather-pillow me to death because I'd screwed up surgery on Fido.

"Meet Doc Becca at Owen McAllister's place, will you?" Deb continued. "She's bringing a forensic specialist out. But you make sure nothing gets effed up, okay?"

"Nothing effed up. Roger that, Chief."

"I know what I'm doing," Jeremy muttered.

"Who said I was talking about you?"

"Am I going to be able to sleep in my bed tonight?" I asked. Would I even be able to close my eyes and drift off after what had happened the last time I tried it?

"You should stay with your parents," Deb said. "At least until we figure this out."

Which was going to be a major PITA for work, but lying in my apartment staring at the ceiling, jumping at every shadow, wouldn't help either.

"I need clothes." My feet were also bare. "Probably shoes."

Deb let out a growl of annoyance. "Come on."

She escorted me upstairs, stood in the living room tapping her foot while I changed into jeans and a long-sleeved shirt in the bathroom, then shoved my feet into my oldest, grungiest tennis shoes before preceding her downstairs. No one appeared to have moved since we'd left.

"We can go in my truck," Owen began. Reggie woofed; the gaze he turned on Jeremy was very cat with the canary—or cat that could almost taste the canary.

Splode.

What did that mean?

"I'll follow in my car."

Jeremy's eyes resembled those of a canary that had just caught a glimpse of the cat staring in at him from the other side of the cage. Couldn't blame him, though really, he should probably worry more about Owen. Reggie had a leash. Owen didn't.

"Becca, ride with me." Jeremy started for the trees.

"Where are you going?" my father asked.

"I parked at the head of that walking trail through the woods."

"Explains how he got back here without Billy or me or anyone but Reggie seeing him," Owen said.

"Why would you do that?" I asked. "You couldn't know that the trail wound past my parking lot."

The location of the veterinary clinic would be obvious to anyone who could read a sign, or speak English and ask a question, but knowing where the hiking trail led wasn't.

"I didn't."

"You were supposed to call me when you arrived."

"I tried. You didn't answer."

I'd probably been busy gasping for breath, and I hadn't had time to check my phone since.

"Then I saw you at the head of the trail." His forehead creased. "Or I thought I saw you. You never told me you had a twin."

"She doesn't," Owen said.

"There was a woman who looked exactly like you." Jeremy's gaze flickered over my face. "Except she had dark eyes, black hair and it was shorter."

"We need to discuss your definition of *exactly*," Owen said.

Jeremy cast Owen an evil glare, which caused Reggie to growl.

"Hush," Owen murmured. Reggie hushed, at least out loud. In my mind he continued to grumble.

Stink. Bad. And the inevitable: *Splode.*

"You talked to her?" I asked.

Jeremy shook his head. "I pulled over, called your name. She kept walking onto the trail, so I followed. She was pretty far ahead, then she stopped and stared north. Trail wound around. I lost sight of her, but when I got to the place she'd been, I stopped." He waved at my Bronco. "I saw your car and the VET sign. The door was open, so I figured you'd gone in. I started to follow then—" He jerked his thumb at Reggie. "That grabbed me."

Reggie lifted his lip and showed teeth. *Asshole.*

I turned my inappropriate desire to laugh into a cough-type throat clearing. I was very good at it. "You really thought she was me?"

"You could have dyed your hair. You also said you had a sister."

"She doesn't look anything like me."

He shrugged. "They say everyone has a twin some-where."

They did say that. But how weird was it that my dop-pelgänger had shown up in my teeny-tiny hometown and walked down a forest path, then stared at the place where I lived right after a masked person had tried to kill me?

Superweird, but today what wasn't? It also made me wonder if the woman who'd sat on the car and stared at me had been doing so because she'd seen my twin too.

"Did *you* see a woman who looked like me?" I glanced at Owen.

"There was a pretty big crowd out front but I'd have noticed that. She probably continued down the trail."

"And straight out of Three Harbors," I said. "Damn. I would have liked to see how much she looks like me."

"Probably not that much," Owen said.

"I'm not blind," Jeremy snapped.

Owen ignored him.

"I need to get home to your mother." My dad started for the street.

"What's the rush?" I asked.

He continued to walk, throwing his answer over his shoulder. "Someone will have called her about this. She'll be worried."

"Call and unworry her."

"Forgot my phone."

"I can call h—"

"Things to do, Becca."

He disappeared around the building. An instant later I caught sight of him pulling a U-turn before he gunned it out of town.

"I'll drive you around on the street to Reitman's car." Owen pulled out his keys. "It's on the way to my house."

"I'm not getting in an enclosed space with that dog," Jeremy said.

Woof!

Reggie stared at the trees. Was Pru watching? Or was Edward still chasing her?

Who was Edward? Another wolf? Pru hadn't sounded glad to see him.

"Becca's not walking through the woods with you," Owen said.

"I thought we'd determined I wasn't the one who tried to kill her."

Owen crossed his arms. "I'm unconvinced."

His biceps bulged against the sleeves of his khaki T-shirt. Jeremy seemed almost as entranced by them as I was. I suppose he was the one being threatened by them.

"We'll take Owen's truck." At Jeremy's flash of annoyance, I lifted a hand. "The sooner we arrive at the crime scene, the sooner we can all go back to our lives. I'm sure you need to get on the road, Jeremy."

"I made a reservation at a hotel for the night. I hated to drive all this way and not spend some time with you."

"Fabulous," Owen muttered.

I cast him a glance. What did he care?

"Let's get this over with," Owen continued. "I'll drive. Don't worry about Reggie. He won't hurt you."

"He won't, because I'm not going with you." Jeremy started for the trees.

While I didn't think Jeremy had tried to smother me, I also wasn't keen on walking into the forest where whoever had done so had run. Just because George hadn't found the culprit, didn't mean he wasn't still in there. And Jeremy wouldn't be much protection at all.

He glanced over his shoulder. "You coming, Becca?"

Owen took my arm. "No."

"Honestly." I took my arm back. "Put Reggie in the truck bed. I'll sit between you two so I don't have to listen to a litany of 'he's touching me'!"

Owen's lips twitched. "You sound like a kindergarten teacher."

"I had little brothers and a little sister." Who'd burned me out on little kids long before puberty. Too bad. If I'd gone into teaching I could have saved myself a shit ton of time and money on college.

While it would have taken ten minutes to walk through the woods, it took less than three to drive to Jeremy's car. Owen didn't even argue when I got out too, though he did roll his eyes at the bright yellow Jaguar.

"You know a car like that just shouts small penis?"

I slammed the door and walked away.

Owen knew he was behaving like the child she'd accused him of being. He couldn't help it. The guy was annoying.

He became even more so once they got to the house. Owen hadn't expected anything less. Stupid might be as stupid does, but annoying was the same damn way.

Reitman took one step onto the porch and at the resulting creak stepped off. He eyed the roof, the cracked windows, the rickety railing Deb had kicked into what had once been a flower bed. "This place appears ready to come down on my head."

"If only," Owen said.

"How can you live here?" Reitman wrinkled his nose. "I suppose it's all in what you're used to."

"Owen doesn't live here any more." Becca took the steps, ignoring the creak and the sway. "If he did, I doubt there'd be animal sacrifices in his living room." She opened the door and went inside.

"I don't." Reitman followed.

Owen glanced at Reggie, who still sat in the bed of the pickup as ordered. "I see why you don't like him."

Reggie tilted his head.

"Well, I see why I don't like him." Owen scrubbed a hand through his hair. "But you not liking him . . ." Owen walked toward the house. "That's a mystery."

A mystery he wanted to solve. Reggie didn't take a dislike to people unless he had a good reason. For instance, they smelled like C-4. Owen doubted Reitman did, but he smelled like something that bothered the dog. And that a veterinarian—forensic or not—was so uncomfortable around an animal was troublesome.

Owen caught sight of a police cruiser parked near the collapsed barn on the far side of the house, but no George. He was probably in the house, though why he'd parked way over there was anyone's guess. Maybe he was taking a leak. There wasn't a working bathroom for close to a mile.

Owen told Reggie to stay. He could imagine what the dog would do if a stranger came out of the woods and approached the house. Though Reggie had been trained not to bite those in uniform, he'd also been trained not to "fetch" unless he was told to, and he'd fetched the hell out of Reitman.

The smell of death hit Owen just over the threshold. Why hadn't he smelled it that first night? Then again, he'd smelled death so much in the past ten years he should be more surprised that he *had* noticed now than that he *hadn't* then.

The forensic veterinarian bent over the mess in the living room, poking with a plastic gloved hand at what had been left behind.

"What's that?" Becca pointed.

Reitman peered closer. "Hard to say."

"There's another one here." Becca moved to the opposite side of the table, leaned in, frowned. "Is that a brand?"

"What kind of brand?" Owen asked.

"Isn't a brand a brand?" Reitman kept poking and peering.

Ghoul.

"Hot metal pressed against flesh with the purpose of leaving a mark," Reitman continued.

"For identification," Owen agreed. "Which means all brands are different, and whatever those are might be important. Might be a clue, a lead, a smoking gun, a neon sign."

Reitman cast him an annoyed glance. Owen found it interesting that Becca had seen the marks and not the "specialist," though this was her second view of the crime scene.

"The evidence is too badly burned and decayed to identify much without a microscope. I'll need to take everything to my lab." Reitman looked around. "Did the officer show up yet?"

"His car's here. I'm sure he will be soon."

"You think if you find out what the brand is, it could point to whoever did this?" Becca asked.

"Could." The professor had gone back to poking.

Becca lifted her gaze to the five-pointed star on the wall. "Why would someone draw a symbol for a group that harms none directly above so much harm?"

"That isn't a Wiccan symbol." Reitman straightened.

"Isn't it a pentagram?"

"Yes. The Wiccan pentagram is usually drawn with a circle connecting the points. Some call it a pentacle. The Wiccan symbol has an ascendant point." He jerked his thumb upward. "To represent spirit and the Wiccan belief that spirit is more important than earthly concerns. The four other points on either side and to the bottom represent the four elements—fire, air, water and earth."

Owen contemplated the five-pointed star on the wall. The single point faced downward not upward. "What is that?"

"Point descendant favors earthly over spirit concerns." Reitman chewed the inside of his lip. "Satanism."

Considering what the thing had been drawn over, Owen wasn't surprised.

"I asked around to see if there've been any whispers of kids messing with that." At Owen's incredulous glance, she continued. "Black animals. Halloween. Sacrifices. Weird star." Becca pointed at the wall. "It added up."

"Then what did you need him for?" Owen wondered. They both ignored him.

"What did you find out?" Reitman asked.

"Nothing."

"Even if kids were screwing around," Owen said, "they wouldn't admit it."

"No." Reitman's gaze returned to the table. "But I don't think this is kids."

"Why not?"

"I've investigated this kind of thing before."

"Hence our need for him." Becca didn't stick out her tongue, but Owen could tell she wanted to.

"Kids go about things half-assed," Reitman continued. "Dead animals are one thing. The pentagram, the fire, the brands." He chewed his lip some more. "This is serious stuff."

"Someone was trying to raise Satan?" Owen felt like laughing, and then again he didn't.

"You aren't going to get Satan with the souls of animals. Most people don't believe animals have souls."

"Bullshit," Owen said.

"I concur."

Becca's lips twitched. Owen's wanted to. The guy had a stick up his butt that he couldn't quite seem to yank out.

"If you aren't going to get Satan with this"—Owen waved at the table—"what are you going to get?"

"Practice."

Becca and Owen exchanged a glance before Becca asked, "Practice for what?"

"People."

Owen blinked. "Say what?"

"Raising Satan would require people." At their continued blank expressions, he elaborated. "Human sacrifice."

"Deb did think someone was gearing up to be a serial killer," Becca said. "I just thought she'd read too much Tami Hoag."

"I'm not following."

"Serial killers usually start with animals. I never considered someone was practicing. I didn't like to consider what was going on here at all."

"Witches. Serial killers. Satanists. Sacrifice." Owen threw up his hands. "How do you know all this stuff?"

"It's my job." Reitman straightened as if the stick had suddenly been jabbed in farther. "Also a hobby and a calling and a birthright."

"How is being a forensic veterinarian a birthright?"

"It isn't. Being a witch is."

Owen laughed. Reitman didn't. Owen glanced at Becca. "Did you know that he thinks he's a witch?"

"I *am* a witch. My mother was one too."

People had called Owen's mother a witch. Sometimes, when she was really, really high, or off her meds, or both, she believed it. Once she'd used their broom to try and fly off the roof.

Becca set her hand on his arm. She remembered too. They'd been eight, playing at the creek, building a mud castle. The screaming had brought them back to the house. Becca had run to her parents and gotten help. Owen had stayed here and tried to keep his mother from walking on a compound fracture.

That wasn't the first time Owen had spent a few weeks in foster care. But it was the last. After that, when his mom went away, Owen stayed at the Carstairs' place.

"Are there a lot of witches in Wisconsin?" Owen asked.

Becca coughed, then cleared her throat, which meant she was smothering a laugh. Witches in Wisconsin *was* kind of funny.

"What's a lot?" Reitman asked.

"Two," Owen muttered.

"Then, yes. I belong to a coven in Madison. There's one in Eau Claire. There might be another hereabouts. I'm not sure."

"How can you not be sure?"

"We don't advertise in the Yellow Pages or have a Web site. That's just asking for trouble."

"What kind of trouble?"

"You think there's discrimination against minorities? Try being a witch."

"No, thank you," Owen murmured. "If there isn't a way to find a coven, how do covens get found?"

"Wiccan shops. Word of mouth. I'd ask my high priestess if there was a coven this far north, but . . ." Reitman's gaze went back to the animals. "She was murdered last week."

"How?" Owen blurted.

"Arm hacked off. She was—"

Something creaked upstairs, and they lifted their eyes to the ceiling. The creak continued down the staircase with the measured beat of steps.

"George?" Owen called.

The creaking stopped.

"What the heck was he doing up there?" Owen asked no one in particular.

"What was who doing up where?" George walked through the front door.

"If you're here then who—"

A figure flew out of the shadows. Long, tangled hair obscured the face. A sacklike, tan jumpsuit shrouded the body. The sunlight through the open front door glinted off a knife.

"Bringen," Owen said, but Reggie wasn't there.

"Die," the apparition shouted, and rushed into the living room.

Owen dived for Becca.

"You witch, huh—"

George plowed into the intruder, cutting off the rest, managing to grasp the descending forearm before the knife plunged into Reitman's chest.

Becca and Owen crashed to the ground. The knife clattered to the floor. The subsequent thuds and grunts, followed by the jingle then snap of handcuffs, told Owen that George had subdued the attacker.

Beneath Owen, Becca caught her breath. Was there more than one psycho with a knife? Considering what had been going on here lately, why wouldn't there be?

Owen turned his head. Nope, only one psycho with a knife.

"Hi, Mom," he said.

Chapter 14

Owen hadn't seen his mother since he'd left on his previous tour. He probably should have felt worse about that. Except the last time he'd seen her, she hadn't remembered who he was.

He'd told himself it didn't matter. As long as he was paying for her care, reading whatever they sent him to read, and returning any phone calls made to him about her, then he was doing his duty.

It wasn't true, but out of sight was out of mind. And Afghanistan was just about far away enough for him to forget for maybe a day at a time that his mother was cuckoo for Cocoa Puffs.

"You told me they weren't ever going to let her out." Becca pushed at his chest, making Owen realize he still shielded her from the rest of the room.

"Considering her outfit"—Owen rolled free and stood, then offered Becca a hand—"they didn't."

She placed her palm against his and static leaped, the spark making both of them jerk back. It was kind of early in the season for that much of a static shock, wasn't it? It had been so long since Owen had been in Wisconsin, he wasn't sure, but the way Becca frowned at her hand, then rubbed it on her pants and got to her feet on her own, made him think she'd been as shocked—ha-ha—by the spark as he'd been. That his hand continued to feel oddly warm and tingly had to be his imagination. There was no other explanation for it. Unless it was witchcraft.

Owen used his nontingly hand to rub his eyes. Talk about cuckoo for Cocoa Puffs.

"You think she escaped?" Becca asked.

"Yeah." He dropped his hand. "I do."

"Th-th-that's your mother?"

Reitman crouched in the tiny corner formed between the stone fireplace and the wall. Owen couldn't bring himself to answer. He didn't have to.

"Mrs. McAllister?" George shouted, and she flinched.

"She isn't deaf," Becca said.

"She also isn't Mrs. McAllister." Owen's parents had never been married. Owen wasn't sure his mom even knew who his dad was.

"Mary?" George said in a normal voice. "What are you doing here?"

"Baby boy," she cooed. "Come to Mama, sweetheart."

Becca glanced at Owen.

"She isn't talking to me." His mom wasn't even looking at him but at the empty hallway, and she'd never once called him "baby" or "sweetheart."

Reggie appeared in the entryway, and Reitman cursed. "Keep him out of here!"

"Talk about a baby boy," Owen muttered.

"His hair will contaminate the crime scene." Reitman's prissy voice reminded Owen of Miss Belinda, the ancient librarian who'd never allowed him and Becca to sit on the same side of the table in school. Had Belinda been her first name or her last?

"The crime scene is three ways from fucked already," Owen said.

However, he did tell Reggie to *"bly'b,"* though the dog had ignored the order to stay already or he wouldn't be in the house. They were going to have to do some retraining before they went back to Afghanistan.

"Baby boy," Owen's mother murmured again, and Reggie inched a little closer.

"Seriously?" Owen asked the dog.

Reggie hung his head as if he understood, even as he scooted ever nearer, as though he couldn't help himself.

Animals liked Owen's mom, and they, in turn, calmed her, as she was calmed by little else but heavy medication. Becca had always had a dog or a cat or two, which had followed her everywhere, including to Owen's house. They'd usually wound up on Mary's lap, or curled next to her wherever she'd passed out. Too bad they'd never been able to afford pets. Might have helped more than therapy ever had.

"Go on." Owen flapped his hand in his mom's direction, and Reggie's head tilted. "You know you want to."

Reggie promptly sprawled across Mary McAllister's filthy crazy-house slippers. From their worn appearance she'd walked here, which was a pretty damn long walk. The Northern Wisconsin Mental Health Facility was a half-hour drive from Three Harbors.

"You think he smelled the blood on her?" Reitman asked.

Owen stiffened as if he'd inherited Reitman's stick. "Excuse me?"

"I suppose she's washed up since she did this."

The doctor indicated the pentagram and everything beneath it.

"She didn't do that."

"She's got a knife."

"So does three quarters of the town."

"She's here."

"So are we."

"She's obviously off her rocker."

"So are you." The guy *did* believe he was a witch. "She's barely able to function. She certainly didn't have the capacity to snatch all those animals without someone seeing her."

Although she had escaped a secure mental institution, and Owen really needed to find out how. When? And why he didn't know about it.

"These are domestic animals," Reitman continued.

"Your point?"

"They wouldn't be hard to snatch. They'd probably come right to her." His gaze went to Reggie. "He did."

"She's not a killer, especially of animals."

Becca cast Owen a quick glance, which he ignored. His mom hadn't killed anyone. Yet. Apparently she hadn't given up trying.

"Consider the dog," he continued. "He's trained to know what a killer smells like."

"Can he smell a witch?" George asked.

"What does that have to do with anything?" Owen demanded.

George shrugged.

"She's a witch?" Reitman glanced at Becca.

Becca shook her head. "They called this the witch's house when we were kids."

"Still do," George offered.

Becca gave George a dirty look before returning her attention to Reitman. "You know how small towns are."

"Not really," he said.

"What difference does it make if she is a witch or if she isn't?" Owen blurted. "You said this wasn't witchcraft."

"I said it wasn't Wicca."

"What's the difference?"

"Wicca is a religion. Witchcraft is a skill set."

Owen blinked. "Huh?"

"Witchcraft is a craft. Spells and magic."

"Magic," Owen repeated. "You think this is magic?" He waved at the mess nearby.

"I don't know what it is, but that"—Reitman pointed to the inverted star—"hints at Satanism."

Owen thought it did more than "hint" but he wasn't the expert. Didn't want to be.

"My mother definitely isn't a Satanist."

Reitman eyed Mary. "You sure?"

"Fuck you."

"That's helpful."

Owen let out a breath. "She worships narcotics not the devil. She'd rather drink vodka than blood."

"Who said anything about drinking blood?"

Owen considered giving the guy the finger, but that would be redundant.

"She was the local crazy, who lived in a broken-down house in the forest," Owen said. "Hence the name 'witch's house.'"

Reitman's forehead crinkled. "I don't get it."

"Where are you from?"

"L.A., originally."

"They don't have witches there?" Owen asked.

"They call them something else. Starts with a *b*."

"You can say *bitch*. No one will wash out your mouth with soap." Though it might be fun to try.

"*Bruja*." Reitman's lips tightened. "In L.A. they call them *brujas*."

"What. Ever." Owen's lips tightened too. "My mother isn't one."

"We still don't know that she didn't kill these animals."

"I do. You're the one who doesn't believe it."

"Convince me."

Owen toyed with another bout of "fuck you." Then Becca touched his arm. "You should probably call the mental health facility."

"You should probably call a lawyer," George said. "Attempted murder is pretty serious."

"Good luck with that," Owen returned. "She's certifiable."

A judge had said so—although in more legal-type terms—and one continued to say so every year when the order to keep Owen's mother in the mental facility came up for renewal.

"She's also committed," Becca said. "She didn't check herself out, especially dressed like that. You need to find out what she's doing here."

"They won't know the reason." Owen considered his mom, who was still whispering to Reggie. At least she was occupied. "I doubt she does."

"I meant when did she escape? Why don't you know about it?"

"Right." He'd already wondered that and gotten distracted by . . . everything. He pulled out his cell, pushed the contact number for the mental health facility before he remembered. "No service."

Becca pointed upward. Owen headed for the stairs. He hadn't taken two steps when Becca cried out. Reggie woofed. Owen spun, hands up, expecting his mom to barrel into him and body-slam him to the ground. Wouldn't be the first time. When she was lit up, she'd thought Owen was all sorts of strange things.

However, his mom remained right where he'd left her. The dog stared at Becca. Becca, Reitman, and George all stared at Owen's leg.

Owen glanced down. Considering their expressions, he half expected to see blood darkening his pants. But everything looked normal, or as normal as it had looked since he'd gotten out of the hospital in D.C.

Ah, hell. He was walking like a peg-legged pirate. All he needed was a parrot and an eye patch.

Becca stepped toward him, hand outstretched, concern all over her face. "You're limping."

"I've been limping for months. Limping is pretty much why I'm here."

"You said . . . I thought . . . You haven't . . ."

"I know."

"I never saw you limp until now," Reitman said.

"And don't think I don't appreciate it."

"How have you avoided walking without my seeing?" Becca asked.

"Wasn't easy."

"It's impossible."

"Not."

"You weren't limping when you grabbed me behind Becca's place," Reitman pointed out.

Owen doubted that. He also doubted the guy had been noticing anything besides Owen's hands around his throat.

"You walked from my parking lot to your truck before, and I'd have noticed if you were doing that." She jabbed a finger at Owen's leg.

Owen's hand fell to his thigh, and he rubbed at the ache. The movement made him remember Becca's palm landing in the same place only an hour before when he'd helped her stand. An accident, but he'd enjoyed it.

In times past the simple brush of her fingers would have made most of his blood pool north of his thigh, leaving none in his leg to pulse and pain him. That hadn't happened today, but he liked to remember the days when it had. Maybe the memories, the distraction, the shock— who knew—had caused him to forget the pain for a few minutes. It was back.

It didn't matter why he hadn't limped before, he'd done so now and Becca had seen. She pitied him. So did Reitman and George. If his mom had any brain cells left, she might as well.

Owen had to get out of this room—recoup, regroup, recon.

"I'll make that call." He gimped his way into the hall. Becca followed. "I could do it."

"They aren't going to tell you anything. Privacy rules." Her gaze flicked to the stairs, then back to him.

"I can manage the stairs, Becca. If I was that bad off don't you think you'd have noticed I had a limp before now? In a few weeks I'll be good as new. I just need more rest."

"You aren't getting any here."

"Not today," he agreed.

Thankfully the stairs wound upward, disappearing from view of the hallway after Owen had climbed the first three. Then he could start taking them with his good leg, pull the bad one up, use his good leg, pull the bad one up. Rather than alternating right, left, right, like the rest of the world.

Two miserable minutes later he reached the porch, wiped the sweat that had sprouted during the stair-climbing portion of the program from his brow, and called the mental health facility. He asked for Peggy Dalberg, his mother's caseworker.

"Missing anyone?" he asked when she picked up the phone.

"How do you know?"

"Starin' right at her." Or close enough.

"Where?"

"Her house in Three Harbors."

"She's never gone there before."

"What do you mean 'before'?"

He had the presence of mind to lower his voice, rather than shouting like he wanted to. He didn't need anyone else knowing about this.

"She's escaped two times. Three if you count today."

"And no one called me?"

"I thought you were in Afghanistan."

"The phones still work."

"What would you have done from there?"

"I still should have been told."

"You would have been if we hadn't found her fairly quickly. We always have."

"How long has she been AWOL this time?"

"Late last night."

"You're sure?"

Peggy drew in a long breath. "Since she got all the way there, yes. Unless someone gave her a ride. We post signs on the highway that people shouldn't, but no one reads as well as they should. Or maybe they don't comprehend as well as we hope."

Owen grunted. Preaching to the choir there. "From the looks of what's left of her shoes, she walked."

"She was definitely here at lights out."

"Okay." His mom was clear for the animal sacrifices, as Owen had found them yesterday afternoon. And, according to Peggy, she'd never come here before.

That they knew of.

"When was the last time she escaped?"

Papers rustled. "A month ago. Or near enough. Not unusual. The full moon is like that."

"You lost me."

"The full moon sets some people off."

"Werewolves?"

She laughed. "Good one. Ask any nurse, psychiatric worker, cop, waitress about the full moon. Makes normal people twitchy. Makes twitchy people a lot twitchier."

Owen would take her word for it.

"Has she always escaped on or near the full moon?"

Papers rustled again. "Yeah."

"Where's she gone the other times?"

"Small towns nearby. No rhyme or reason to them that we can tell. If she lived in any of them before, it isn't in her record."

"What are they?"

She ran through the names.

"Never heard of them."

"We thought she was just running, trying to get as far away as she could. There were some issues with the voices, telling her things. You know how she is. But maybe she was trying to get home all the time and never made it until now."

"How has she been escaping?"

"If we knew that, she wouldn't be able to keep doing it. It's like she's being beamed out."

Owen pulled the phone away from his ear, frowned at it, put it back. "Who is this?"

"Not funny," she muttered.

"Neither are you. My mom is a danger to others, which is why she's incarcerated."

"I know why she's incarcerated. I just don't know how she's getting out. It's a little hard to get good information from people who think tinfoil hats are more than a shiny fashion statement."

"What have they said?"

"Where do you think I got the 'Beam me up, Scotty' explanation?"

"Fair enough."

There was still the issue of his mom trying to kill Reitman. That she'd called him a witch could not be an accident considering what was going on here, there, everywhere, not to mention that he was one, or thought he was. How had Mary McAllister known

that? He doubted asking her would lead to a worth-
while answer.

"Anyone gibbering about witches?"

Silence fell. He could almost see Peggy gaping.

"Have you had someone check up on us?"

"Should I?"

"Feel free," she said, unconcerned. Which went a long
way toward his being the same. "Your mom made a new
friend."

"She has friends?"

"One. They share a common interest."

"My mom was never interested in witches before."

Except those few times she'd thought she was one. But
she'd also thought she was a bird and a dragon and a
jet plane. Which meant her obsession was flying. Or at
least it had been. Why had that changed? Because her
"friend" had been whispering sweet nothings, or maybe
bad somethings?

"If this person upsets my mom maybe they shouldn't
be together."

Kindergarten basic—separate the troublemakers.
Probably worked pretty well in mental health facilities
too. And prisons. And life. Like the book said: *Everything I Need to Know I Learned in Kindergarten.*

"Your mom gets even more upset when they're separated."

"Who is it?" Owen asked. His mom had hooked up
with some real losers in the past. Why should now be
any different?

"A young woman with problems."

"That narrows it down."

"I can't tell you more than that. If your mother does, that's her prerogative."

"My mom's a little 'blah-blah, die, witch' right now."

Shocked silence descended. Owen couldn't blame her.

"That doesn't sound like your mother."

From what Owen could recall, the words might be different but the sentiment was the same.

"She was interested in witches," Peggy continued. "As it's a peaceful religion, and we're a peaceful people, I didn't see the harm in teaching her."

"Teaching her? You?"

"I follow the tenets of Wicca."

Now the stunned silence came from Owen.

"You're sure she said 'die, witch'?" Peggy asked.

"That was the gist," Owen said. "The real kicker was when she tried to kill one."

This time the silence pulsed for three ticks of the clock.

"I'll be right there."

Owen's voice lifted several times—anger? fear? both?—but I couldn't hear what he was saying.

Mary seemed content with Reggie. Reggie was content with her. You'd think animals would sense crazy, and an animal like Reggie better than most. Maybe he did, but Mary's kind of crazy wasn't the kind that bothered him. She didn't smell like explosives and . . . whatever else a terrorist smelled like.

"Hush," Mary said, and stroked his head.

Hush.

Reggie pressed closer, either cuddling, or making sure

she couldn't get away without stepping over or around him. Who knew?

"You changed your hair."

For a minute I thought Mary was still talking to the dog. Then I lifted my gaze and her eyes were on me. She seemed to recognize me, so I smiled, shook my head. "Not really."

I either braided it or I didn't. That was the extent of any changes in my hair.

"You colored it," Mary insisted.

Ouch!

Mary's fingers no longer stroked Reggie's fur, but clenched it. She was getting agitated. I decided not to argue with her about the color of my hair.

"Huh," Jeremy said.

Mary's eyes flicked toward him, and her nostrils flared as if she'd smelled something bad. Reggie growled.

"George," I said. "Maybe you should take Mary to the squad car."

"Why?"

"Because she tried to kill Dr. Reitman once already. I don't want to give her another chance."

"She's handcuffed."

Mary bolted in Jeremy's direction. If Reggie hadn't been lying on her feet, she would have gotten him too. Jeremy scrambled back. Reggie started barking—at him, not her.

As George hauled Mary outside, she mumbled a lot of words, very few of which sounded like English. That was new.

"Nein!" I ordered Reggie. He cast me a surprised glance.

Sprechen Sie Deutsch?

I ignored that. I had to. I certainly couldn't answer him. Especially in *Deutsch*.

"She must have seen the same woman I did." At my blank expression, Jeremy waved at my hair. "Looks like you but different color."

"Must have," I echoed. How could I have forgotten about the woman who looked like me but not quite?

Apparently Mary had seen her too.

Chapter 15

Owen returned to the first floor to discover his mother in the back of the squad car banging her head against the window and screaming in tongues.

Just another day at the McAllisters'.

"What happened?"

Reitman glanced up from bagging the evidence. He must have received permission to take it. Fine with Owen. He wanted every last bit of it out of here.

"She lunged at me."

"She's handcuffed."

"Legs still work." He let his gaze lower to Owen's. The comment "unlike yours" was left unsaid. Owen heard it anyway and his hands clenched. Reitman quickly went back to work.

George came in. "I'm taking your mom to the station."

"Her caseworker is on the way to get her."

"She can get her at the station." George held up his hand. "There's gonna be paperwork."

"I'll call her back," Owen said, though the idea of climbing the stairs to make another call made his leg ache worse.

George frowned at Reitman. "I didn't say you could take that."

The doctor didn't pause in what he was doing. "You said you'd call."

"Calling isn't okaying."

"I don't have the okay?"

"You do," George said. "But what if the chief had said no? It's not like you could put it back the way it was."

"I could. I took a photo and I'm sure someone here did too." Reitman set the final bag on the ground next to the others. "But the FBI uses me, why wouldn't you? I work at the UW, which has ridiculously well-funded lab facilities. If it didn't, I wouldn't still be there. I'm the best forensic veterinarian in the state. Probably in the Midwest. Ask Becca."

George glanced at Becca, who nodded.

"I was trying to be polite by asking, but the okay for me to take the evidence was a given. Why waste time?"

George blew air out his nose, sounding like the Carstairses' prize bull on his way to a pawing, charging tantrum. Owen knew the feeling. Reitman was beyond annoying.

"You'd better be as good as you think you are," Owen said.

"I am." Reitman turned his gaze to Becca. "I'm not going to be able to stay like I planned." He motioned to the plastic bags. "This shouldn't sit in my trunk over-night. I'll head back now and get right on it."

"I understand." Becca moved forward as Reitman drew off his plastic gloves and tossed them onto the now empty table like a surgeon who knew the peons would be cleaning up after him later.

Owen turned away. He wasn't going to watch them

say good-bye. There'd be hugging and kissing. He just knew it.

He found it odd that Reitman had planned to stay in the first place. The man had known he was coming here to examine animal sacrifices. Had he thought the scene would be so cut-and-dry that no further forensics would be needed? Or maybe so messed up further forensics would be inconclusive? Owen should be happy that Reitman believed there was evidence still to be had.

He was, but he was even gladder the guy was going. Not just because he was a pain in the ass, but he obviously knew Becca a lot better than she'd let on. They didn't seem to be romantically involved, but that didn't mean they couldn't be. Wouldn't be. Hell, shouldn't be. They were an ideal couple. They'd have perfect, pretty children, with brilliant brains. In the evenings they could sit around drinking fancy wine and discussing their common interests. Her dad would be in heaven if she married that dick.

"I'll let you know if I find anything," Reitman said.

Owen turned, relieved that the two weren't locked in each other's arms. If they had been, it hadn't been for long.

"No you won't." George jabbed a finger at the bags clutched in Reitman's hands. "That's evidence. This is a case. You'll let the chief know, then she'll decide who else gets to hear it afterward, if anyone." He shuffled his feet. "Sorry, Becca. Owen. But that's just the way it is."

Reitman looked as if he'd sucked on a lime, lips disappearing into his prissy facial hair before he left without another word. Owen's mom's shouts increased in volume at the sight of him, though Owen couldn't understand a word she was saying. George headed for the door.

"I can clean this up, right?" Owen asked.

"You need to wait for an all clear from Chief Deb." The officer paused. "You should probably leave now too."

"Swell," Owen muttered, gaze on the ick.

"We won't touch anything," Becca said. "You go ahead. We're right behind you." She lifted her hand, palm up. "Promise."

As the bangs and shouts from his squad car continued unabated, George fled. A door slammed, an engine growled, tires crunched, then blessed silence.

"I'm not going to be able to clean this place up, put it on the market, and boogie, am I?"

"Do you really want to leave now?"

"I want to leave yesterday." Before he'd kissed her and remembered how much he missed it. Before she'd told him she didn't want to see him any more while he was here. He'd deserved that, but still, it had hurt.

"Your mother needs you."

"Did my mother even say my name? Ask how I was? Wonder why I was here? She doesn't remember me, which means she doesn't need *me*." She never had. All she'd ever needed was a bottle, a needle, a snort, or a pill.

"I doubt she's forgotten she has a son."

"I don't."

"You're just going to leave without finding out why she escaped, what that whole 'die, witch' thing was about?"

"No." He might want to, but he couldn't. "According

to her caseworker, Mom's escaped three times, and they have no idea how."

"That's crazy."

"What isn't?" Owen waved at the pentagram. "It's a damn horror show."

Reggie kept looking back and forth between the two of them, as if following the conversation. Owen rubbed the dog's head and received a lick on his wrist in return.

"I can't believe she had anything to do with this," Becca said. "Animals love her. She loves them. She wouldn't—"

"I have no idea what she'd do." He never had. "Except she didn't escape until *after* I found this mess. But she came here this time, and she never did before. Why?"

"Why not? It's home. Or at least the last home she had." Becca cast a glance toward the front door. "Let's go back to town." When Owen hesitated, she took his hand and tugged. "I told George we wouldn't stay."

Owen didn't want to hang around. Even though the sacrifices were gone, their memory remained. So he whistled to Reggie and they followed Becca onto the porch. He was surprised to see the sun was straight up noon. With all that had happened so far today, it should be tumbling down by now.

"I'll drop you at your parents'."

"Again?"

"Deb said you couldn't stay at your place." Any more than he could stay here. "Both yours and mine are crime scenes."

"For completely different reasons."

"I doubt that."

Reggie cast puppy-dog eyes in Owen's direction.

"Geth voraus," Owen said. *Go ahead.*

The dog trotted into the underbrush—to do his business, chase squirrels, or maybe, right now, his business was chasing squirrels.

"You think Satanism has something to do with the pillow over my face?"

"I think a budding serial killer and an attempted murder are too similar to ignore. Especially in a town that previously had only my mother for entertainment."

"Nothing connects these two crimes," she insisted.

"Nothing," he agreed, and started down the steps. "Except you."

Owen's words surprised me so much I stood dumbfounded on the porch as he headed for the pickup. Then I became distracted by the obvious glitch in his gait. How had he hid that from me for so long? That he'd hidden it from me at all made me nearly as sad as his having it in the first place.

Once, we'd shared everything. Those days were as gone as he'd been.

I watched Owen move, observing him like a doctor, not a lover. He wasn't my lover, hadn't been for a very long time. So why did I remember every dip of muscle, every swirl of his hair, the very taste of his skin?

I didn't. Not really.

His muscles were huge where once they'd been . . . quite adequate. His hair was buzzed—not enough there to swirl—with flecks of gray that had not been there before. His skin was wind worn, sun touched—older, like him, like me. Would it taste differently?

I should lick him and find out.

He turned; I yanked my eyes from their perusal of points south and up to his face. Had he noticed? I hoped not.

What was wrong with me? Nothing a good roll in the hay wouldn't cure.

I cleared my throat. "How long is your leave?"

His gaze flicked to the trees where the dog had disappeared. "It's open-ended."

Right. Because the military was so easygoing. I decided not to press the issue. Owen had never been the kind of person who yielded to pressure, and I doubted ten years in the Marines had changed that. However, despite his words to the contrary, he wasn't going back to active duty limping like that.

"I should let Reggie run a bit before we go back to town, okay?" Owen set his hand on the truck as he moved to the rear, then put down the tailgate and hitched his butt onto it.

"Sure." I sat close enough to touch, but not touching, then swung my legs above the ground like I used to way back when.

He'd had a pickup then too—a POS that he'd tinkered with constantly just to keep it running. He'd worked at the café nearly every night after school when it wasn't football season. I'd seen him handing money to my dad more than once. My dad hadn't taken it, but he'd never stopped offering.

"I don't have any appointments until later," I continued.

And no one had called all day with an emergency— real or imagined—which was so strange I took out my phone.

No service. No wonder. When we got back to the town limits, the thing would no doubt start buzzing like a bee-hive with missed calls and messages. Oddly, the idea that I'd missed calls didn't bother me the way that it should. For just a minute or two, I wanted to sit in the warm autumn air with the only man I'd ever loved.

"How bad is it?" I asked.

He stared straight ahead. "How bad is what?"

"This." I laid my hand on his thigh.

The whole world stilled. I swore neither one of us breathed. But he didn't move away. He didn't take my hand and push it off. So I left it right where it was.

Beneath my palm his jeans felt on fire, even though the trees shaded the sun and the bulk of the rays shone on the house and not here. I flexed my fingers, my short nails scritching on the fabric. Static snapped, and he tensed.

"Shh." I continued to stroke.

Had he told me where his injuries had been? I didn't think so. But I'd watched him limp; I could figure it out. When I closed my eyes, I could see the bones like an X-ray. I traced the femur with my index finger, brushed the dark line of the fracture, halfway down, with my thumb. There was more wrong here than just that. Nerves. Tendons. Maybe both.

There'd been a few times in the past when I'd known something was off with a patient, despite all indications to the contrary. I'd close my eyes and "see" a bleeder, or a tumor, or a hairline break that didn't pop on an X-ray. Once, during surgery, I'd found a golf ball in a Labrador's stomach after I'd already located the half of a tennis ball I'd gone in there for.

There'd been occasions where an animal had just gone south. No matter what had been tried, nothing worked. Then the owner brought them to me, I acted on what I "heard" from them, or sensed myself, and they got better.

Not right away. It wasn't magic. I was a fantastic diagnostician. Nothing more.

But the sparks, the warmth? That was new.

Either I was crazier than before or . . .

I had no idea.

"Don't," Owen said.

I stopped stroking, but I didn't lift my hand. "Am I hurting you?"

He gave a garbled, strangled laugh-sob, and my gaze flew to his. Then I couldn't look away.

"There's hurt," he said, "then there's agony."

I yanked back as if I'd been burned. My palm continued to pulse with heat so intense my skin tingled. The breeze kicked up and stirred the damp tendrils on my brow. Our lips met. It was inevitable.

The kiss was harsh, desperate, greedy, needy—everything that roiled within me reflected in him. My mouth opened, tongues warred. I licked his teeth; he nipped my lip. I returned the favor along his gloriously stubbled jaw.

My hand was on his leg again, but higher up. The heat remained. If I rubbed my thumb across his tip as I'd rubbed it along the imaginary line of his break would sparks fly? I had to find out.

I traced where I had a dozen times before, about half an inch below his belt, right where an erection should end.

It didn't. He was as soft as Reggie's ears.

What was going on? He wasn't kissing me like an un-interested man. He was kissing me like a man drown-ing in desire, one who couldn't wait to bury himself inside of me.

But there'd be no burying anywhere with a shovel like that.

He lifted his mouth. I wanted it back. He tasted like sex and love and life—three things I'd had precious little of since he'd left.

"I haven't been able to—" His lips, full and wet and inviting, tightened. "Since the accident." His head drooped, and he let out a laugh that was anything but amused. "I think it's broken too."

The idea of him trying to mend "it" with anyone but me made my fingers clench. They were still close enough to his nonerection to brush against it. A single spark made him jump. That jump pressed him to my wrist. My hand cupped him and warmth spread. I stroked, and the warmth flared into heat. Something else jumped. I ran my thumb where I'd felt movement and was rewarded with a growing pressure from the other side of his jeans.

"Huh," he murmured, face full of the same wonder it had held the very first time I'd touched him like this.

"Doesn't feel broken." I yanked on the snap, pulled down the zipper. "Let's make sure."

I dipped my fingers inside, curled them around him. He went so hard he seemed to fill my hand in an instant. I pumped him once, and he groaned, closed his eyes, arched.

Nope, not broken at all.

"This is . . . This is . . ."

"Amazing." I continued my movements. He got harder, larger, even more so.

"It is. You are." He looked down, and his eyes widened. "Apparently I am."

"Yes," I agreed, and he kissed me again.

The desperation remained, a definite need for speed. I understood. Any man who'd thought "it" was broken, then found that it wasn't, would be frantic to use it before it broke again.

He fumbled with my shirt, the button on my jeans, the actions both sweet and disturbing. I didn't want it broken before I used it either.

I pulled back, and he set his forehead to mine. "Sorry. This is nuts. We can't—"

"We can. We will. We *are*." I circled his wrists, met his eyes. "But let's just lose our clothes and save some time. Okay?"

His lips curved. He yanked his T-shirt over his head, kicked off his shoes, shucked his already open pants and everything else.

Next he busied himself spreading the blankets from the corner—Reggie's, but I was pretty sure the dog would share—across the truck bed. I was glad, not only because I'd rather get naked unobserved but because I was momentarily distracted—and distressed—by the scars on his body that hadn't been there before.

By the time he'd made our bed, I'd managed to not only drag my gaze from the criss-cross slashes of pink and white, some worse than others, the one on his thigh really bad—but toss my shirt, jeans, shoes, socks, and panties in a pile of their own.

I joined him on the makeshift bed, thrilled to observe that he remained "unbroken." Even more thrilled that the truck shielded us from view on three sides. He yanked the tailgate up—make that four sides. We'd hear any cars approaching on the dirt path from a long way off, and Reggie would make sure nothing and no one else approached in any other direction.

Privacy was nice, but right now I didn't much care. I might have balked at doing him on the fifty-yard line at Lambeau Field during halftime. Maybe.

I set my hand on his chest, following the trail of my fingertips with my lips, tasting his skin, testing those larger, tighter, better muscles. His stomach rippled. I licked his ribs then traced the gooseflesh with my thumb.

"Becca, I can't—"

"Can," I insisted, and used my teeth on his tip.

The next instant I was on my back, his wide shoulders blocking out the sprinkle of sun through the tree limbs. Our legs tangled together; the hair on his tickled. Thank goodness there wasn't any hair on mine. I certainly hadn't planned on having sex today—or any day, week, month, year.

Hell.

"Protection."

He kissed me quick, then set his forehead on mine again and just breathed. The ebb and flow of his chest brushed his skin along mine, making my nipples tighten and ache.

I cupped his cheek. "We don't have to."

"Oh, we have to. Just give me a sec."

"Does your leg hurt?"

"I'll manage."

He rolled free, hunted down his jeans, rustled around, and came back with a condom. Should I be thrilled that he had one or—

The snap of latex brought my gaze back where it belonged. I was definitely thrilled that he had one, a bit sad that he didn't have two.

He winced, just a little, as he crawled to the blankets, but he covered it well, no doubt because he'd been covering it for a while. Nevertheless, I worried.

"I could go on top."

His gaze flicked to mine. "That obvious?"

"I just—"

He lay back and held out his arms. "First time for everything, right?"

"It isn't—" I began, then snapped my mouth shut.

He wasn't talking about me in general but us in particular, and in that, he was right.

We'd been kids—eager and fumbling—in the dark, in the cab of his truck, the woods, his closet, then that haymow. We had not had the time, the experience, or the inclination for experimentation. It had been missionary all the way.

He cupped my hips. I took him in slow. Had he always been this big? Or had my lady parts shrunk from lack of use?

The sensation of stretching, filling, oh, so full was glorious. His tip struck something deep inside that sent a thrum of need all the way to my toes and I arched, thrusting my hips against his, and then . . .

Then I rode.

This was a lot better than riding a horse. I rubbed my

inside against his outside. I never wanted to stop. The breeze stirred my hair, cooled my skin; the sun flickered across my face; the leaves above sang and danced.

I stifled inappropriate laughter at the mental images, which played through my brain like a pornographic version of *Fantasia*.

"You're so beautiful." He watched me through half-open eyes. The sun dappled his skin, highlighting every ripple and curve. The shadows played across cheeks and chin, giving me glimpses of the boy I'd loved in the face of this man.

"Touch me," I said.

Never stop.

The last two words drifted through my mind but I managed to keep them there. I wanted nothing to slow this, end this, ruin this.

His large hands brushed upward and I shivered, the movement pushing us together in such a new and interesting way, I gasped. He pulled away.

"I scratched you."

"Do it again." I pulled him back. "Higher this time."

His eyebrows lifted, so did his lips, then those gloriously rough palms scraped my breasts. I liked that so much, I pressed my own hands to his and helped.

I watched his throat work and leaned down to lick his Adam's apple, my nipples peaked, pressing into his chest. "Becca, I have to—"

I sat up and rode some more.

Time passed. It seemed both forever and just a day.

He moaned. A prayer, my name.

"Soon," I promised.

He curled upward, took my breast in his mouth, worried my nipple with his teeth.

"All right," I agreed, then tightened around him and whispered . . .

Chapter 16

"Now," Becca said, and Owen exploded, there was no other word for it. He knew explosions.

Everything went bright and silent, perched on the edge of brilliance in that instant before the whole world changed.

He lifted his lips from her breast, wanting to drink her gasps, her sighs, her moans, and met hers coming down. Then he did to her mouth what he was doing to her body—claiming it, possessing it, making it his.

He'd been afraid he would never be able to do this again—not just with Becca but with anyone, even himself. He should have known if there was anyone on this earth who could get him hard, keep him that way, then make him come as if the world was ending—or maybe beginning—it would be her.

He ended the kiss, gazed into her face, which was slightly above his and just a bit dazed. He felt that same.

"That was epic," he said. He hoped he hadn't broken the condom.

"Epic," she echoed, a tiny wrinkle appearing between her eyebrows.

That wrinkle always meant she was thinking. Which always led to trouble.

Speaking of trouble. Now that he'd thought about

breaking the condom, he was terrified that he had. Wouldn't that just be great? Knocking her up at twenty-eight after managing not to at eighteen?

Would her father gloat about being right that Owen had finally managed to ruin her life? Or just kill him and be done with it? Owen thought he'd prefer the latter. He was certain Dale would too

Reggie barked, out in the woods still, but Becca's head spun toward the sound. Her movement caused a slow slide down low and Owen grabbed his dick and the condom before disaster happened. He cast a silent thank-you to the dog for the distraction, which allowed him to dispose of the evidence in an old plastic bag before Becca even realized what was going on.

Having sex in the back of a pickup had never been ideal, even when they were young enough for it to make sense.

"We should probably go." She reached for her shirt.

"We should probably talk." He reached for his.

"What about?" The question was muffled as she pulled the garment over her face.

He did the same. "What do you think?"

"We had sex, Owen. It wasn't the first time."

He didn't want it to be the last, but he wasn't quite sure how to say that without screwing up so badly he would assure that it would be.

"I hope it isn't the last."

He blinked as his words came out of her mouth.

"You aren't leaving."

"I am," he insisted.

"I meant—" She reached for her panties and pants. "Not right away."

"No," he agreed.

"Then we don't have to stop."

He almost asked what had changed since that morning, when she'd said she didn't want to see him any more while he was here. But, really . . . He didn't want to know why. He was just glad that it had.

"Unless you want to," she continued when he remained silent.

"Hell, no," he said. In fact, his penis, which had been unresponsive, to say the least, for months, now twitched at the sight of her bare bottom in the twinkle of the early afternoon sunshine. Apparently it didn't want to stop either. And that was so fantastic, he didn't notice at first that she'd stilled, head tilting, forehead crinkling, listening to—

The long, low, not distant enough howl of a wolf.

"Shit." He grabbed his own underwear and jeans. "Reggie!" He whistled.

"She won't hurt him."

"She already did."

"Not on purpose."

"How do you know?"

She bit her lip and didn't answer.

The idea of that wolf, or any wolf, and his still injured dog tangling out there where he couldn't stop them had Owen's heart pounding nearly as hard as it had not so long ago, but for a much less pleasurable reason.

A gunshot sounded.

The two of them scrambled out of the truck and ran for the trees.

* * *

The howl that rose before we'd gone more than fifty yards was distinctly different from the original.

Dog howl, not wolf howl. That couldn't be good.

"Go," Owen said. "Don't wait for me."

I didn't have to be told twice. I went.

I glanced back once; he was doing amazingly well. His gimp seemed a lot better. Which made no damn sense at all. But what did lately?

In a copse of birch trees, the sun glancing off their autumn-yellow leaves, the wind rustling them and making the sound of ghostly whispers, Reggie sat next to a prostrate Pru, nose tilted upward, howl vibrating his throat. They were alone. No one with a gun, at least that I could see. I probably shouldn't blaze into the open, but I didn't have much choice.

"Hush," I ordered as I did just that.

Reggie lowered his snout. *Hurt.*

I went to my knees next to Pru. My fingers fluttered over her blue-black fur. I didn't see anything, not even blood. "Where were you shot?"

Pru lifted her head, but almost immediately it fell back down. Her "voice" was weak.

New Bergin.

"That's a hundred and fifty miles from here."

Her chest heaved faster than it should, even for a wolf. *Wasn't today.*

"I heard a shot."

Wasn't at me.

"I don't understand."

Reggie yipped and trotted into the trees. From the rustles, Owen was almost here. I'd have to stop talking to Pru soon.

I went to New Bergin.

Wolves didn't usually wander that far. They had a territory and they stuck to it. Of course, Pru wasn't your average wolf.

"Why?"

He shot at me before he knew.

I opened my mouth to ask "He who?" or maybe "Knew what?" but she kept going.

Just grazed my flank. Burned like fire, but it proved I wasn't . . . She panted several times very fast.

"Wasn't what?"

Dangerous? Rabid? How could a bullet prove that? How could a bullet "prove" anything?

I thought it was healed, but—

Pru's rear leg jogged as if she were running in place, and I caught a whiff of something foul. I set my hand lightly on her flank, and she whimpered. A section of fur was damp, a little oily. I pushed it to the side.

"This is infected."

Pru didn't answer. She'd passed out. Which was all to the good. It allowed me to probe what did not look anything like a graze.

"That's a bullet hole."

"Since we heard a gunshot"—Owen emerged from the trees—"that makes sense, though why is she unconscious from a bullet to the butt?"

"This isn't fresh, and it's festering." I needed to get her to the clinic where I had antibiotics and alcohol and anesthetic and other great things that didn't start with A. I started to slide my arms beneath her.

"Whoa." Owen set a hand on my shoulder. "That's a wolf."

"No moss on you."

"You can't take a wild animal into your clinic."

"Can. Will. Am." I didn't mention that she'd already been there.

"What if she wakes up while you're walking to the truck? Or in the truck? Did you ever see that YouTube video of the guy who put what he thought was a dead deer in his backseat?"

I had. It wasn't as funny as everyone seemed to think it was.

"I'll put her in the truck bed," I said. "Then sit back there with her." All I'd need would be for her to regain consciousness, jump out, and disappear into the forest. She'd die. I couldn't, wouldn't let that happen. She'd saved my life.

"What if she wakes up on the way to the truck and eats my face?"

"Your face?"

Owen scooped up the unconscious wolf and started back the way we'd come. "You don't think I'm going to let her eat your face, do you?"

Twenty minutes later Owen parked the truck in my lot then carried a still unconscious Pru inside. Reggie padded behind him as if Pru were a long-lost friend. I had to wonder what had taken place out in those woods and changed things.

The crime scene tape cordoned off the stairs to my apartment, but my clinic was clear. I motioned for Owen to set the wolf on the exam table as I washed my hands, then started to assemble what I'd need, moving past the

As and into the wonderful world of S—scalpel, scissors, sutures. Med school *Sesame Street*.

"You need help?" Joaquin stood in the doorway.

"Thought I told you to go to school."

"Did." He stepped inside. "Done." I narrowed my eyes, and he held up one hand. "Swear."

"Scrub in."

Reggie whined and set his front paws on the operating table, then licked Pru's chin. A stainless steel bowl fell off the counter, clattering against the floor as loudly as an alarm clock. Owen jumped, then squatted, hunching his shoulders and lowering his head as if to avoid a projectile.

"Sorry!" Had I shifted the bowl too close to the edge when I was grabbing supplies? I could swear I'd actually moved it farther back to avoid just this problem.

My next thought was "Henry" though I couldn't figure out why Pru's ghostly cohort would toss a steel bowl.

Owen lifted his head, then straightened. "Sudden noises." He gave a sheepish shrug.

Reggie kept his gaze on the shiny silver bowl in the corner as if he expected it to fly through the air and smack him in the head.

"You're gonna need to get him out of here," I said. "And you told your mom's caseworker you'd meet her at the police station."

Owen had made the call as soon as the truck hit the highway and cell service resumed. I was impressed he'd remembered. My mind was befuddled enough with the sex, let alone the unconscious wolf in my lap.

"Your mom's in jail?" Joaquin appeared at my side.

"Kind of."

"What did she do?"

"What didn't she?" Owen hooked a lead to Reggie's collar and practically dragged him out the door.

The dog still stared at the steel bowl, or perhaps at the empty corner behind it. I couldn't decide. Which made me think that corner wasn't as empty as it seemed.

I picked up the anesthetic and slipped the needle into Pru's leg. Cleaning out an infected wound was going to hurt. Pru didn't need to be awake for it any more than I wanted her to be.

Joaquin strapped her down without being asked, then removed the matted fur from the area. Cotton pads soaked in alcohol came next. Pru's leg jerked even in her sleep, and the flesh rippled as if cold, despite being far too hot to the touch.

With the matted fur gone and the dried blood and weepy pus cleaned off, the wound seemed less like a graze than ever before.

Tweezers clattered onto the exam table. I turned my head to ask if Joaquin had seen something in the wound that needed extracting. His eyes were better than mine. But he stood on a step stool at the counter, reaching for more gauze on an upper shelf.

Now *my* skin rippled as if cold.

I should probably do an X-ray to make sure there was something in there before I opened it up again but . . .

I set my hand on her flank. I could feel an object in there—foreign, festering.

"Doc Becca?" Joaquin had returned.

I lifted my hand, frowned at the wound. It seemed to

have healed more in the few minutes we'd been here. Which was impossible.

I blinked a few times. The wound still looked less open. Probably because I needed to open it more.

"Scalpel, please."

I planned to make an incision, clean the wound thoroughly, perhaps insert a drain for the infection, inject antibiotics. My hands had other ideas.

I cut deeper. A whole lot of nasty flowed out. Joaquin handed me some of the gauze he'd retrieved and I blotted, swiped, then touched her flank again. Something shifted beneath the skin as though alive.

"What's wrong?" Joaquin leaned in close.

Probably just her muscles fluttering. But I'd learned to follow my instincts. They'd never steered me wrong.

The police station wasn't far from Becca's office. Nevertheless, Owen got into his pickup and drove there.

Reggie wasn't a service dog, and could therefore not waltz into any building that he wanted to. Owen would have to leave him in the truck, and he'd prefer to keep the truck, and Reggie, nearby.

Inside the Three Harbors police station a phone was ringing, ringing, ringing. He waited for someone to answer it, except he didn't see anyone in the room *to* answer it.

The chief's office was empty, as was the bullpen and the dispatcher's desk. Owen stood on tiptoe and checked the floor behind the reception area. Nobody.

He settled back on his heels as the phone stopped ringing. He listened for distant talk and laughter. Maybe it was doughnut day and they were all in the break room.

Or maybe his mom had slipped her leash and—

"Hello?" he shouted.

"Yeah!"

All the pent-up air in Owen's lungs rushed out. At least one person was left alive.

Candy Tarley shot out of a doorway and hustled in his direction. She was of an age with his mother, though she appeared fifteen years younger, perhaps because she possessed hair the shade of cherry Kool-Aid. Or perhaps because she hadn't touched anything harder *than* Kool-Aid all her life.

"You waiting long?"

"No, I just—" What? Been worried that his mom had gone *Walking Dead* on the entire police force?

"Owen!" Candy's polite expression went positively cheery, or maybe that was cherry. She came around the reception desk and took his hand, but instead of shaking it she sandwiched it between hers and squeezed. "Thank you so much."

"For?" He tried to pull back, but she held on and patted him a few times for good measure.

"For all you've done."

He racked his brain, came up with nothing. He hadn't been in Three Harbors for ten years, so he hadn't done anything. Maybe that was what she was thanking him for. When he'd been in town, he'd done plenty. A lot of it was probably recorded around here somewhere.

Candy released him with a final pat. "Your service, Owen. Thank you for your service."

"Oh—uh—yeah."

He still hadn't gotten accustomed to people not only thanking him with words but with deeds. In the airport

someone had paid for his Starbucks. On the flight someone had bought him a beer. When he'd rented the pickup,
a woman in line behind him had insisted he use her
Triple A discount, and the woman at the counter had
let him.

What he was accustomed to was being cursed at, shot
at, blown up. Being fawned over was a new and not altogether pleasant experience. He felt like an imposter because the true hero was Reggie not Owen. But whenever
he tried to explain that, folks just laughed and bought
him something else.

"Your mom got off just fine." Candy returned to the
chair behind the reception desk.

"She what?"

"She's on her way to the mental health facility."

"I was supposed to meet her caseworker here."

"Your mom was . . . agitated."

"Still banging her head?" Owen asked.

Candy lifted a shoulder, which was answer enough.
"Peggy wanted to get her back to the environment she's
used to. She said you could come out there, or give her
a call in a few hours." Candy patted his arm again. "You
okay with that?"

He wasn't sure why he was disappointed that he
hadn't gotten to say good-bye. He doubted his mom
would remember him any better here than she had at
the house.

The phone started ringing again. This time Candy answered right away. "Three Harbors Police Department."

Owen started for the door.

"What was that?" The cheery in her voice fled,
leaving something behind that made Owen turn. "All

right. Someone's on the way." She disconnected. "It's your mom."

"What happened?"

Candy lifted one finger as she used the radio. "George, we've got 417A on Route GG."

"Roger that. I'm on the other side of the lake but I'm on my way."

"What's a 417A?" Owen asked.

"That was Peggy who called." Candy used the radio again. "Need an ambulance to Route GG. Assault with a knife."

Static nattered through the mike. Since Candy let go of the transmit button, he figured the ambulance was on the way.

"Is my mom—"

"Gone."

His heart gave such a lurch that he grabbed the edge of the reception desk.

"Sorry! Not dead gone, but actually gone, as in run off again."

The joy that Owen felt that his mom wasn't dead and gone fled as he came to the conclusion that she'd been the one doing the assaulting, rather than the assaultee.

Only one thing surprised him about that.

How in hell had she gotten a knife?

Chapter 17

The tweezers slid over the edges of the object, then I pulled, slowly and gently, until it slid free. Joaquin shoved the steel bowl that had previously been on the floor in front of me. The tinny clatter echoed in a silence broken only by Pru's drugged breathing and the distant wail of a siren.

"Is that a silver bullet?" he asked.

"I'm not sure." I'd never seen one before.

"Why would someone think she was a werewolf?"

In the process of flushing the wound, I bobbled the tool. "A what?"

"Silver bullet," he repeated in the same tone my brothers often said. "Duh!"

I refrained from cuffing him in the head only because he wasn't my brother.

"She isn't a werewolf."

"If she were, a silver bullet would have killed her on contact." Joaquin handed me the antibiotic syringe.

"That's insane."

"Hey, I'm not the one who shot her with a silver bullet."

Who had? Deb had mentioned calling the DNR to report Pru's odd behavior. I'd asked her not to. I doubted she'd listened, but I also doubted the DNR had had time to send anyone yet, let alone someone who carried silver bullets.

And while we'd heard a gunshot earlier, that bullet had not been the one I'd found inside the wolf. Even if I ignored Pru's statement that she'd been shot a hundred and fifty miles from here, she would not have an infection from a wound inflicted today.

A lot of questions I had no answers to. Along with the tiny problem that the answers I did have had come from listening to a wolf and believing what she'd "said."

I finished cleaning, injecting, stitching, bandaging, then picked up a cone of shame.

"You're going to put that on a wolf?" Joaquin asked. "She'll bang it against every tree in the forest."

"I'm not letting her go until the stitches are out." I doubted she'd come back in seven to ten days for their removal. And leaving them in would only cause another infection.

"You going to keep a wolf in the kennel?"

"Where else?"

"The dogs will go ballistic, and the guinea pig might have a stroke."

I wished he'd stop making good points. "I'll have to keep her here."

"Isn't that kind of dangerous?"

Less dangerous than keeping her at my parents'.

"You have office hours tomorrow," he continued. "I doubt she'll lie in the corner nicely. She's more likely to eat the customers."

"She's not a normal wolf."

"Which might be why she got shot."

"Abnormal doesn't make her a werewolf."

"What does it make her?"

Pru's paw jerked. I heard a single word.

Not.

Not what? Not a werewolf? Or not, not a werewolf? I needed some sleep.

"If you're going to put that cone on her you'd better do it," Joaquin said. "She's coming around."

I slipped the blue papery plastic apparatus over Pru's head and tied it securely. "Can you go into the kennel and get some bedding, dog food, and dishes?"

Joaquin frowned, but he did it. As soon as the door shut behind him, I spoke. "I know you're awake."

Pru sat up. She turned left, right. The cone followed. *Get this off.*

"It'll keep you from licking or biting your stitches."

I'm not an idiot.

"You're not a werewolf either."

No, she agreed.

"Who thought you were?"

Edward.

"Who's he?"

That's almost as long and complicated a story as who I am.

The door to the kennel opened, barking flowed out, the door closed, steps approached, and I lowered my voice so that only she could hear.

"As soon as I get rid of the kid, I got nothin' but time."

Owen had no trouble finding Peggy's car. Not only was the bronze SUV parked sideways across the eastbound lane of Route GG. But it was on fire.

How had Peggy neglected to mention that? To be fair, being stabbed might make her a bit forgetful. It also might make her BBQ.

He parked the pickup on the shoulder about a hundred yards back, leaped out, ordered Reggie to stay. The dog did, but he started barking, gaze on the fire. Infernos always had that effect on him.

Owen approached the flaming car, hoping to yank out Peggy and then get far enough away that neither one of them would be incinerated when the gas tank blew. He was about ten steps away when his gaze was drawn to a body in the ditch on the other side of the road.

He was nearly there when he heard the telltale *whoosh*. He dived, covering the woman as pieces of SUV fell all around them. Reggie barked louder. The distant wail of sirens wasn't helping.

Beneath him, the body stirred, and Owen rolled free to reveal a plump, grandmotherly woman with short hair fading from gold to silver. She wore an ID badge around her neck that confirmed she was Peggy Dalberg.

Her eyelids fluttered, opened. Her eyes were light blue and full of pain. One pale, veined hand clutched at her stomach. Blood pulsed between her fingers to the beat of her heart. The other she held to her neck.

Owen was half afraid his mom had gone for the jugular too, but the only blood on Peggy's neck were a few drying streaks in the shape of fingers.

"Help will come soon."

Owen yanked off his jacket and pressed it to her stomach. She winced.

"Sorry. We gotta keep pressure on this."

She lowered her hand from her neck. She'd been

branded with the head of a snarling wolf. That wasn't his mother's MO.

Neither was fire. Didn't mean she hadn't done it.

"Mary," Peggy whispered, and blood bubbled on her lips.

Owen had seen injuries like this in the field. If he wanted to find out what had happened, he needed to do so pretty damn fast.

"Mary McAllister did this?"

"No."

"Who did?"

"Woman ran into the road, had to stop."

"You know her?"

Peggy shook her head.

"Did my mom?"

"Seemed to. Mary called her—"

Peggy coughed. Blood sprayed. Owen should urge her to rest, but he didn't.

"Called her what?"

"Bitch-whore."

That was his mother's MO.

"What did she look like?"

"Tall. Solid."

A tall, solid woman would be about . . .

"Six feet?"

Nod.

"One sixty?"

Nod—shrug.

"What else?"

"Brown hair past her . . ." She closed her eyes.

"Ears? Chin? Neck? Shoulders?"

"But," Peggy blurted.

"But what?"

"Hair past her butt," she clarified. "Stabbed me w-w-with an athame."

"I don't—"

"Knife." She made a *Z* in the air with her finger. He had no idea what that meant. "Carved handle. Matched the ring."

"What ring?"

She turned the trembling finger toward the livid brand on her neck. "She used the ring to make this."

"What does that mean?" he asked.

"Venatores Mali," she whispered.

And then she died.

"You should meet your mom at the café," I said.

"It's not even close to the end of her shift." Joaquin's gaze remained on the wolf curled atop a dog bed in the corner of the exam room.

"I'm sure you have homework."

"I'm sure you're trying to get rid of me."

The kid always had been too smart.

"Then why won't you be gotten rid of?"

"Where are you going to sleep?"

"I'll figure it out."

I'd planned on sleeping with Owen.

Bing! The light went on. I'd take Pru to the cottages, sneak her in after dark. Krazy Kyle might be amenable to hunting dogs, but wolves were another matter.

I glanced at the clock. Speaking of Owen . . . where was he?

"Go." I urged Joaquin to, then out, the door. Before he could say anything more, I shut the door, flipped the lock. After a few seconds a muttering shadow passed the window. The mutters faded. So did Joaquin.

"Thought he'd never leave."

Pru didn't comment. She was still pouting about the cone of shame. I was still refusing to take it off.

I drew a chair next to the dog bed and collapsed into it. It had been a helluva day. Had it only been this morning that someone tried to kill me?

I pulled out my phone—I'd had a few calls from an "unknown" number, but no messages—I dialed Owen. It went directly to voice mail. Had he driven out to the house, where cell service was terrible? Or was he ignoring me?

I waited for the beep to leave a message. I didn't have much choice. I couldn't exactly go searching for him and leave a wolf alone in the office. Wild animals trapped inside . . . It never went well.

"Where'd you go?" I asked. "Little worried. Call me."

I pressed *end,* then contemplated the wolf. "You wanna tell me the story now?"

Take it off. I look ridiculous.

"You'll look more ridiculous dead."

If I haven't died in over four hundred years, I doubt I'm going to die now.

Four hundred years? I guess she was the same wolf I'd been seeing since childhood. Or maybe "wolf" wasn't quite the right word.

"You sure you're not a werewolf?"

She stiffened, appearing very regal despite the cone of shame. *I am not.*

"Why are you so offended?"

Besides this ridiculous ruff?

She shook and the plastic-paper rattled like distant thunder.

"Don't whine to me if you give in to an irresistible urge to chew open your stitches." I yanked the string and drew the cone over her head. She dipped her snout toward her paws in thanks.

Werewolves are evil. Insane, murdering beasts.

I'd expected her to say werewolves didn't exist. Silly me. "So there *are* werewolves?"

Have been since the beginning of time. A lot more since World War Two.

"You're making that up."

Why are you so amazed? You're speaking to a wolf.

"Am I? Or am I just imagining that I am?"

What do you think?

I had no idea any more. Once I'd believed I was special. I'd had to give that up or risk everything—my family, my future, my sanity. However, deciding that the thoughts of animals were only the projections of my own hadn't stopped them from coming. Hadn't stopped them from being spot-on accurate either.

"I think I have bigger things to worry about at the moment. Someone tried to kill me." I frowned. "And someone tried to kill you. Which has to be related somehow."

Not really. Edward thought I was a werewolf. They tried to tell him I wasn't, but he didn't get the memo in time.

I managed not to ask how a four-hundred-year-old wolf knew about memos. At the moment, I needed to keep my questions confined to the really important ones, like—

"Who is Edward?"

Mandenauer. He's the leader of a group of monster hunters known as the Jäger-Suchers. That's German for "hunter-searchers."

"And what does World War Two have to do with anything?"

With this? Nothing. With werewolves, more than I have time to explain right now. Suffice it to say, Hitler was a lot busier than anyone thought. The Jäger-Suchers are still cleaning up his mess.

"If Edward is such a werewolf expert, why didn't he know you weren't one even without the memo?" Or the silver bullet to the ass.

Werewolves have human eyes. Pru lifted her bright green, not-at-all-wolf eyes to mine.

"Ah," I said. "Then what's your excuse?"

I'm a witch.

Chapter 18

Little worried. Call me.

Owen's thumb hovered above the *delete* button, then he put the phone back in his pocket without touching it. He might want to listen to that message again on a dark night in Afghanistan. There'd been many times in the past when he'd wished he could hear Becca's voice anywhere other than in his imagination.

She did sound worried. He should call her. But what he really wanted was to see her, touch her, kiss her, hold her.

His gaze wandered over the circus on Route GG. From the looks of this, that wasn't going to happen for a while.

George had pulled up less than a minute after Peggy died. The two of them commenced CPR, only stopping when the EMTs arrived and commenced it for themselves. They didn't have any better luck. They were loading the body into the now silent ambulance when George took out his notebook and pen. "What happened?"

Owen took a deep breath, opened his mouth, and let both breath and words out.

"A break," the officer murmured when Owen finished.

"Stabbed," Owen said. "Not broken."

George cast him a disgusted glance. "A break in the case."

"Which one? You seem to have a crime spree right now."

"We thought so, but you just proved it's all one case."

"Didn't mean to."

"Well, not you personally. But the ring. The brands." George lifted his hand and tapped the air. "Bing. Bang." Then pointed at the car. "Boom."

Owen tried to follow. Gave up. "Huh?"

"I read the file. I was at the house when Becca and the out-of-town doc found the brands on the animals. Now this lady has one too."

Owen saw a trickle of light in the pitch-black darkness. "Whoever killed the pets killed Peggy?"

Owen vaguely remembered Reitman saying the pets were practice for humans. But that didn't explain . . .

"Why Becca? Nothing connects her case to either of the others."

"The ring does." At Owen's blank expression, George frowned. "Becca's attacker dropped a ring just like the one that branded Peggy."

This was the first Owen had heard of it. But things had been a little busy.

"There were brands on the animals too, but Reitman couldn't see what they were."

"Doubtful there's a crazy or two running around killing, burning, and branding with different brands," George said. "But you never can tell."

Chief Deb's cruiser skidded to a stop about six inches from the rear bumper of Owen's rental. At least Reggie had stopped barking at the flaming car, even though the car was still flaming.

She crossed the road. "What happened here?"

George pointed at Owen and walked away. Someone had to help Billy with traffic control. Where there had been no cars on the highway before, there were dozens now. The tower of smoke seemed to have drawn them like flies.

Owen repeated what he'd told George, including George's conclusions about the connections in the crime spree. Deb didn't look any happier about it than Owen was.

"Where is it?" he asked.

"Huh?" Deb stared at the car, chewing the inside of her lip.

"The ring."

"Locked in the evidence room waiting for the FBI to come and get it."

"Why would the FBI want it?"

"Your guess is as good as mine. Ross called VICAP— Violent Criminal Apprehension Program. I thought it was too soon with one attempted murder, but . . ." She shrugged. "He got antsy. He mentioned the ring and the FBI said they'd send an agent."

"Sounds like it wasn't too soon," Owen said. For the FBI to dispatch someone, they'd seen this or something similar before. "When's the agent supposed to arrive?"

"Anytime. Conveniently, they had one nearby."

"*Convenient* isn't the word I'd use."

"Coincidence?"

"How about conspiracy?"

"Conspiracy suggests more than one person."

"Exactly."

It was Deb's turn to appear confused.

"If Becca's attacker dropped a ring, which you have locked up, that makes the ring that branded Peggy another ring entirely."

"Doesn't mean another person attacked Peggy," Deb pointed out. "Might be one person with a boxful of rings."

"You believe that?"

"I'd like to," she said. "Otherwise we've got at least two people running around killing folks and then branding them."

"Considering the FBI is in the neighborhood, and they're interested in the ring," Owen said, "I think there's more than two."

"Is that why I can hear you?" I asked. "Because you're a witch?"

You hear more voices than mine.

"What does that mean?"

What do you think it means?

I used to think it meant I was nuts. I'd settled on it meaning I had an overactive imagination. But I didn't think either of those choices was what Pru was getting at.

"Are you saying I'm a witch? Because I'm not."

How can you be so certain?

I didn't know much—anything—about witches, but Jeremy did. And he'd said—

"Witchcraft is a birthright."

True magic, the kind you have, is *passed through the blood. Blood magic is the most powerful kind.*

"No one in my family is a witch."

"That's because your family isn't your family."

The voice was real. Not in my head. Not Pru's.

I leaped to my feet, spun, blinked, then blinked again at the woman standing in the entryway to the exam room.

Jeremy had been right. Except for the color of her hair and eyes, she did look exactly like me.

"Hi, Pru." She nodded to the empty corner. "Henry."

"Y-y-you see him?"

"Always have."

"You hear her?"

She shook her head. "That's your gift, not mine."

"Who are you?"

"Raye Larsen. Kindergarten teacher from New Bergin and—" She glanced at the corner, shrugged, turned back. "Your sister."

"My sister's name is Melanie."

"She's not really your sister." Raye waved between the two of us. "You can see that now, right?"

"Everyone has a twin," I said desperately.

I felt like the earth had shifted beneath my feet. I was dizzy and hot, yet I shivered. Everything was changing. My fingers clenched and unclenched. I wanted to hold on to something but I was afraid that no matter what I grasped it would crumble to dust just like my world.

"We aren't twins."

At last she spoke sense.

"We're triplets. Just haven't located sis number three yet."

"How—how—"

"I was found on the side of Interstate Ninety-four,

halfway between Madison and Eau Claire. Naked, without even a blanket. At least it was July, otherwise I'd have been dead."

I'd been born in July. Didn't mean anything.

"I saw ghosts. Still do. From the moment I could talk, I spoke to them. Freaked my parents out." I must have made a movement because she lifted an eyebrow. "You too?"

"No." I hadn't seen ghosts. I'd heard animals. But it had freaked my parents out.

"How—" I began again.

"How'd I find you? Magic."

"I was going to ask how you got in here." I'd locked the door.

"Same thing." She wiggled her fingers, and the surgical instruments I'd cleaned and set out to dry lifted into the air and hung there, then settled back where they'd been.

I sat down. I had to.

"You're crazy." Or I was.

"I thought the same." Raye tilted her head as if listening. "Okay." She crossed to the wolf.

"You probably shouldn't—"

"You have magic too, Becca, and I can prove it to you." She knelt next to Pru and beckoned. "Touch her wound."

"It's an open wound. Nothing and no one should touch it. Including her."

"Afraid I'm right?"

"About what?"

"Your touch can heal."

I had a sudden flash of what I'd thought I'd seen during the surgery—Pru's wound seeming to mend faster than it possibly could have.

But that hadn't been real. Had it?

"Why do you think your patients get better faster than any others?" Raye asked. "That you've never lost one yet?"

My gaze narrowed. "How long have you been in town?"

"Long enough to hear a reputation that's nothing short of mythic."

"I'm good at what I do."

"You're that good for a reason."

"I am not magic."

"Prove it." Raye yanked the gauze off Pru's flank. The wolf didn't even snarl. Magic right there. "Touch her wound."

"If I do and nothing happens, then what?"

"When you do and something happens, I'll tell you."

"Right." I laid my palm over the raw, angry-looking injury. A spark jumped, heat pulsed. Had the infection spread?

Beneath my hand her flesh moved, and not because she had. The creepy-crawly feeling reminded me of worms or snakes, and I yanked back, expecting to see just that. Instead, the redness was gone. The raw edges had sealed together.

"You should probably take out those stitches," Raye said.

"I just put them in." Nevertheless, I went to the sink, washed my hands, and retrieved the instruments I needed.

The air around me seemed to whoosh with a sound like wind or rushing water. My hands shook a bit. My legs felt wobbly. My head spun, my thoughts too.

Was I dreaming? Maybe.

A suture needle floated up, hanging in the air right in front of me. "Stop that!"

"What?" Raye turned, frowned. "Henry!"

The needle dropped to the counter and lay still. I snatched it and poked my arm. I didn't wake up, but I did bleed. I set my thumb atop the tiny wound and when I wiped off the drop of blood, it didn't well again.

I gloved up, then returned to Pru's side. Nothing had changed since I left it. I snipped the first stitch and waited for blood to well there as well. None did.

Pru shifted, huffed. *Finish.*

Snip. Clip. Snip. Only a fine, pink line remained. Curious, I set my hand on top of it—spark, heat, movement. When I lifted it again, the line had faded from pink to white.

"I—I've never done that before." My head spun faster.

Yes, I was good at my job, but I didn't heal animals on contact. "If it's real and true, how could I not have noticed?"

Raye lifted one finger and listened to the corner. "Henry says that there's power in three. Always has been."

"Why?"

"Who knows? There's a reason for the Trinity—Father, Son, Holy Ghost."

"What does that have to do with this?"

"I'm just giving an example of a famous power of three."

"Even if I did believe you were my sister—" She rolled her eyes. I couldn't blame her. The visual evidence was pretty damning. "One and one does not make three."

"We're more powerful together than apart." Raye stood, closed her eyes, set her hands to the side, and slowly her feet lifted from the ground. Pru yipped. I wanted to.

When Raye's head brushed the ceiling, her eyes opened and met mine. "Couldn't do that yesterday."

She turned her hands palms down, then floated back to the floor. "Once we find our third we'll be able to stop them."

"Stop who? From doing what?"

"Stop the *Venatores Mali* from raising their leader."

"Wait." I glanced at Pru. "She told me to beware the *Venatores Mali.*"

"Hunters of evil."

"But . . ." I was so confused. "The werewolf hunters are Jäger-Suchers."

"Two different evils," Raye said. "Evil werewolves and other assorted creepy-crawlies are hunted by Edward and clan. The *Venatores Mali* hunt witches."

Several puzzle pieces came together in my head with a click so loud I started. "Let me guess, they wear rings with a snarling wolf on the face."

"You met one of them already?"

"Henry tossed him or her into a wall."

"I love it when that happens."

I had too. "Why did this person come after me?"

Raye pointed at Pru's now nonexistent wound. "People have noticed your talent."

"Just because I'm good at my job doesn't make me a witch. Especially around here."

Had I accepted that I was? Not completely. But I couldn't deny something weird was going on. Always had been.

"We don't know how they know what they do. I've always been seen as strange, but to leap from weird kid to witch is a stretch. Someone did, because they came to New Bergin first."

I glanced at Pru, but she'd fallen asleep. "Is that why she was there?"

"Yes. I've seen her and Henry all my life. For a long time I thought she was a ghost too."

So had I. "No one else ever saw her but me. Until Owen."

Raye's eyebrows rose. "Boyfriend?"

I lifted one shoulder.

"Interesting. No one saw her in New Bergin until Bobby."

"Boyfriend?"

She lifted her shoulder. "Fiancé. He was a New Orleans homicide detective."

"How'd you meet a New Orleans cop?"

"He came to New Bergin following what he thought was a serial killer."

"It wasn't?"

"Technically it was. Mistress June killed at least a dozen witches."

My eyes widened. "A dozen?"

The world was a great big mess. But when hadn't it been?

"Who is this woman?"

"All we have is her first name. No one seems to ever have heard her last. Her fingerprints weren't in the system, neither was her DNA."

"How could she kill all those people and yet no one knows anything about her?"

"She's very good at being bad. She didn't kill in the same way or in the same place. Made it look random, which is really hard to connect. But now that they know what to look for . . ."

"What?"

"Brands. Burning. Witches."

"Who's looking?"

"FBI."

"The FBI is looking for witch killers," I repeated.

"Yes. Well, no. The FBI, per se, is looking for a serial killer. But the agent on this case, Nic Franklin, is also a Jäger-Sucher."

"You just said the Jäger-Suchers hunt werewolves."

"And assorted evil creepy-crawlies," she repeated. "The *Venatores Mali* are very creepy-crawly. And evil. They have been from the get-go, which was about four hundred years ago."

"Four hundred years?" My gaze went to Pru again. Still asleep.

"She told you?"

"That she was four hundred years old? Yeah." I found it a lot less crazy now than I had when she'd brought it up.

"What else did she say?"

"That she was a witch, and so is Henry. Are they related?"

"Married."

"Wolves can get married?"

"Henry isn't a wolf. Neither was Pru at the time."

My head spun again. "Maybe you should start at the beginning."

"Maybe I should."

She went to the counter, snatched up a brown paper bag that she must have brought but I hadn't noticed, then returned to the exam table and started pulling things out.

Two white candles. A clear crystal. A hand mirror. A gorgeous wand with a cherrywood handle. One of those books you can write in yourself. Her journal?

"I'm going to take us back to the beginning."

She picked up a candle and, using the pointed tip of the quartz, carved *Scotland* into it, then she carved *1612* into the other.

"You think we're going to Scotland in 1612?"

"Not going, no." Raye opened the book, paged through, found what she wanted, and set the book in front of her.

"What is that?"

"Book of Shadows." She lit a match, held it to the candles. "Every witch has his or her own."

I didn't.

"You will," she said.

Had I said that out loud? I didn't think so.

"Witches born to the craft are elemental and each has their particular item of power. I'm an air witch so this . . ." She lifted the wand and waved it. I could swear sparks flew through the air in the wake of the tip. "Is my item. We can use other items. For instance, this pentacle"—she reached inside her shirt and withdrew a necklace with a star surrounded by a circle—"helps me to focus and call spirits, though traditionally it's the item of an earth witch."

She dropped the necklace and lifted the book, turning it so I could see inside. Handwriting filled the page. At the top I read: *Spell to See into the Past.*

She positioned the book so she could see the spell, tapped it once with the wand. Did it glow? Then she lifted the mirror, reflective side facing away, took my hand, and pulled me close.

"Together we look into it, okay?"

"Am I gonna fall through the looking glass?"

"Let's find out," she said, and flipped it over.

Chapter 19

"They come," Raye whispered.

We stood in the shadowy corner of a one-room cottage—thatch roof, stone walls, rough-hewn furniture, fireplace that doubled as a stove. If this wasn't 1612, it was doing a damn good imitation. In the distance, wolves howled.

"They'll never get here in time," Raye continued.

"In time for what?"

She pointed to the room's inhabitants. A man, all in black—clothes, hair, even his eyes—stared into the darkness beyond the slightly cloudy pane of a single window.

"Darling," he murmured.

"Sweetheart," the woman answered.

Her equally dark hair spread over the blue and orange tartan clasped around the shoulders of the gray dress. She held the large skirt wide, as if she were about to curtsy. Perhaps it was the orange streaks in that tartan that made her eyes shine like emeralds. I'd only seen eyes like that once before.

"Pru," I whispered.

"Yes," Raye agreed with equal softness. Though Pru didn't hear us and neither did—

"Henry?"

Raye nodded.

The door burst open, and men clothed in black filled the room. A tall, pale, angry fellow strode in after them. The flames reflected at the center of his eyes lent him a satanic appearance.

"Roland McHugh," Raye said. "Chief witch hunter of King James."

He jabbed a bony finger at Pru and she spun toward the three cradles that had been shielded by her skirt. Three men snatched the children within and carried them out the still-open door.

"No!" Pru cried, and a crockery bowl fell off the table, shattering against the floor. She ran after the children, but before she reached the door, two minions snatched her arms and escorted her out. Several more led Henry along behind.

The next thing I knew Raye and I were in the yard. My ears whistled as if a sharp wind had blown by. Those not occupied hauling the inhabitants from their home had been busy building a pyre. From the looks of it, they'd done so before.

"More than one soul in a womb is Satan's work." McHugh's lip curled as he contemplated the infants. I could only see the tops of their heads—one blond, one red, one dark. "How many lives did you sacrifice so your devil's spawn might be born?"

Henry and Pru remained silent as their captors lashed them back-to-back against the stake, then formed a circle around them. Two lackeys appeared with torches.

The witch hunter removed a ring from his finger and a pincher from his wool doublet then held the circlet within the flame until it glowed. He pressed the red-hot metal to Henry's neck.

I choked on the scent of burning flesh, flinched at the horrifying hiss. Raye took my hand, lacing our fingers together and squeezing tight.

The livid image of a snarling wolf remained behind on Henry's flesh. "Are you mad?" he asked.

"Sometimes the brand brings forth a confession."

"Shocking how pain and torture makes people say anything."

"It did not make you." McHugh jabbed his ring back into the flames; his gaze slid to Pru.

"I did it," Henry blurted. "I sold to Satan the lives of your wife and child to bring forth our own."

"Of course you did," McHugh agreed.

"What's he talking about?" I asked.

"Pru is a midwife," Raye said. "One of the best. She'd never lost a patient. Until she lost McHugh's wife and child."

"How did that happen? I thought she was a witch."

"Some things can't be healed. By the time that jerkwad fetched her, his wife had lost far too much blood, and the child was already dead."

McHugh pressed his ring to Pru's neck. She stiffened until the stake creaked. I tightened my fingers on Raye's until they crackled.

"White ring of fur," I whispered, thinking of Pru the wolf.

"Yes."

Lightning flashed, and somewhere deep in the woods a tree toppled over. The wolves howled, louder, closer—I swore there were more of them—and the circle of hunters shifted.

"I confessed, you swine," Henry shouted.

"You thought that would save her?" McHugh tut-tutted, then snatched the blazing torches and tossed them onto the pyre. The dry, ancient wood flared.

Henry reached for Pru's hands. They were just close enough to touch palm to palm. "Imagine a safe place," he said. "Where no one believes in witches any more."

"Uh-oh," I murmured.

The forest shimmered. Clouds skittered over the moon. Flames shot so high they seemed to touch the sky. Several hunters standing too close stumbled back, lifting their arms to shield their faces. The fire died with a whoosh, leaving nothing behind but ashes and smoke.

No Henry. No Pru.

A cry went up. The men who'd held the children now held empty blankets.

Between one blink and the next, four hundred years fell away. My eyes registered a silver-tinged, chilly Scottish night, the smoking pyre, those fluttering binkies. Then I stood beneath fluorescent lights. The candles on the exam table winked out in a wind that wasn't. I swayed, slapping my palms on the cool, silver surface as Pru yipped.

"What *was* that?" My voice shook as badly as my legs.

Raye clapped her hands, making me start. I was jumpier than the proverbial cat in a roomful of rocking chairs. Could you blame me?

"It worked!"

"You had doubts?"

"I never tried this spell before."

"So we could have ended up in limbo?"

"We didn't actually go anywhere, Becca."

"Something went to Scotland." I paused. "Didn't it?"

"Our minds? Spirits? Souls?" She shrugged. "A little of all three?"

As the Scotland of 1612 no longer existed, that made sense. Or at least it made as much sense as anything did lately.

"You said the *Book of Shadows* was yours."

"It is."

"Then why don't you know more about the spell?"

She began to return the articles she'd set out to the sack. "I should have said that it's mine now."

I rubbed my head. There were so many things I wanted to ask. Where to start, where to start? She didn't give me a chance.

"I'm an air witch. We rule the crossover between this world and the next. We can communicate with the dead." She spread her hands. "Air witches can bring the dead across—either to this plane as ghosts, or we can send a ghost on to the next."

She waited for me to comment, but what was I supposed to say to that?

"This book belonged to another air witch," she continued. "She had the power to alleviate pain, an air witch gift that I don't have. At least not yet. She left her book to me when she died." Her eyes met mine. "The *Venatores Mali* killed her."

"How can a witch-hunting society from the seventeenth century still be active today?"

"They've been revived."

"Why?"

"To raise Roland."

"The asshole we just saw?"

Raye nodded.

"That doesn't make any sense."

"If you want sense, you came to the wrong place."

"How do you raise a dead witch hunter?"

"Sacrifice of a witch by a *Venatores Mali* who's killed the most witches, while the worthy believers chant, sky-clad, or naked, beneath the moon."

"Tell me you're kidding."

"Unfortunately, I've seen it. I was nearly the witch du jour."

"Someone tried to kill you?"

"It's the world's new favorite pastime."

"Join the club," I said. "Why us?"

"Apparently the crazies get points for every witch they kill. Then they're supposed to brand the victim with their secret decoder rings and burn the bodies. Initiation to the freak zone."

"You have no idea how they knew we were witches before we knew ourselves?" I wasn't even sure I believed it now.

"If I ever get my hands on one of them for more than a minute, I plan to beat a lot of things out of them. That's on the list."

"What happens when they raise this dude?"

"I don't want to find out. We're going to stop them before they succeed."

Sounded like a really good plan. I'd only had one glimpse of Roland McHugh, and I didn't want another. Especially if he'd been dead for the last four hundred years.

"But why would a bunch of witches go to all this trouble to raise a man who hates them?"

"The *Venatores Mali* aren't witches. They're witch *hunters*."

"Who chant and perform spells, naked, beneath the moon. What isn't witchy about that?"

"Murder is not witchcraft. Those who practice Wicca, and those born to the craft, true witches, harm none. Harm is all the *Venatores Mali* do."

I remembered the upside-down pentagram at Owen's place. "Satanism?"

"Maybe. All I know is that they mean to bring Roland back, and they've got a rocking head start."

"Why does he want to come back?"

"Wouldn't you? Hell can't be much of a picnic."

"What does he hope to accomplish? His family's gone."

"But the family he blames for that isn't."

"Henry's a ghost. That's pretty gone. Pru's a wolf." I wasn't sure *what* that was.

"Roland wants to end the Taggart line, as his was ended."

"By Taggarts you mean Pru and Henry?"

"And their three daughters."

"The amazing, disappearing babies who were born four hundred years ago. I doubt they're still around."

"Henry and Pru are still around."

"Not the way they once were. And why is that?"

"We don't know for sure. They performed a spell that sent the girls to a place where no one believes in witches any more. The sacrifice of their lives fueled the magic. But the spell was to save their children not themselves."

"Yet here they are." Kind of.

"Maybe once the *Venatores Mali* were revived, so were Henry and Pru."

"Why are the *Venatores Mali* revived now?" I asked. "Why not go after the Taggart descendants ASAP? The longer they waited the more of them there would be. By now, there are probably hundreds. Thousands even."

"Not quite," Raye said. "What he's really after, and has been from that night in the woods, is us."

I blinked. "Us?"

"Triplet girls," she said. "One dark." She fingered her hair. "One redhead." Her gaze touched on my braid. "One blond." She spread her hands. "Sent through time to a place that doesn't believe in witches any more."

"You're saying we're those babies?"

"You didn't see that coming?"

I hadn't, and here's why.

"I'm not adopted."

The door to the clinic was open when Owen arrived. Light spilled into the gravel parking lot, pushing against the threat of night.

Two voices rose from within. One was Becca's. She didn't sound angry or frightened. She didn't sound thrilled either.

At least Owen had had the sense to bring his gun. Before he could pull it out of the holster, Reggie nosed open the door and trotted inside.

"Whoa!" Becca ordered, as the wolf growled. "She's not ready for prime time yet."

Owen stepped inside just as Reggie slid back toward him as if he'd run across the slick tile floor and lost traction.

"Henry!" someone—not Becca—exclaimed.

The dog bumped against the wall and scrambled to his feet, ruff lifted.

"Bly'b," Owen ordered. Reggie stayed, but he didn't look happy about it.

When Becca and the other woman turned toward him, Owen had to lean against the wall as the weird washed over him. He'd made fun of Reitman for saying they looked exactly alike except for their hair and eyes, but the man had been right. They were almost twins.

"Who are you?" he asked.

The dark-haired Becca clone offered her hand. "Raye Larsen. You must be Owen. I didn't catch your last name."

The only way she could have "caught" his first name was from Becca. That Becca was still alive and not stabbed, strangled, smothered, or branded meant this woman wasn't her attacker. Not to mention that while she had dark hair, it only brushed her shoulders and she wasn't anywhere near six feet tall.

"Owen McAllister." They shook. "This is Reggie."

"Hello, Reggie."

She didn't try to pet him. Good choice. The dog appeared both spooked and annoyed. For some reason he stared at the empty corner next to the wolf as if an invisible pork chop danced the tango there.

"Why did you call him Henry?"

"I didn't."

Owen opened his mouth, then snapped it shut. Not an argument he needed to have at the moment.

"The wolf seems fine now." Or as fine as a wolf got. Her eerie green eyes flicked from person to person as if she were listening.

"I took out a bullet," Becca said. "Considering the infection, it had been in there a while."

"About a week," Raye said. "Give or take."

"You shot her?" Owen asked.

"No!" She sounded horrified. "She's my—" Her lips tightened.

"Pet?" That would explain her constant proximity to people. An explanation Owen liked much more than rabies.

"Wolves aren't pets."

"Okay." He waited for her to explain *what* the wolf was, but she didn't. From the silence that followed she wasn't going to.

"Is your mom all right?" Becca asked.

"She's in the wind again."

Quickly he explained what had happened, not even caring that a stranger was hearing the details. She looked so much like Becca she didn't seem like a stranger at all.

"This Peggy was attacked and branded?" Raye asked.

"Just like the animals."

"What animals?"

Becca explained.

"Animals won't raise the dead," Raye said. "Only people do."

Owen flicked a glance at Becca. Reitman had said something similar, though he'd said human sacrifice brought forth Satan. Owen wasn't buying either one.

"You think killing people brings the dead back to life?" he asked.

"It doesn't matter what I think. It matters what they think."

"Who's 'they'?"

"The *Venatores Mali*."

"Shit," Owen muttered.

"You've heard of them?"

"Peggy said that right before she died."

"Was Peggy a witch?"

Owen blinked. "How'd you know that?"

"You'd better tell him," Becca said.

Raye connected the dots. The revival of an ancient witch-hunting society, their purpose to raise their leader from beyond, with a recipe that involved dead witches, branding, fire, blood, sacrifice.

"Peggy was attacked," Owen continued, "then branded, but she wasn't burned."

"The car was on fire," Becca said. "Whoever attacked her probably lit it up and took off, then Peggy crawled out."

"Fat lot of good it did her. She should have run over the long-haired bitch instead."

"Brown hair?" Raye asked. "Down to her hips? Big woman—six feet, solid?"

Owen nodded.

"Mistress June."

"Wait a second," Becca murmured. "Did she have her arm in a sling?"

"Peggy didn't mention it," Owen said. "I doubt she'd have been much good at the killing with one arm. Why?"

"A woman with long, dark hair was watching me from the crowd after someone tried to kill me."

"You weren't suspicious of a woman that size?" Owen asked.

Becca shrugged. "She was sitting on a car and had her arm in a sling. So no."

"She's probably been here since she ran out of New Bergin," Raye said. "I'd hoped she crawled under a bush and died, but that almost never happens."

"Why would she?"

"My fiancé shot Mistress June."

"Why?"

"She was trying to kill me."

"She thinks you're a witch too?" Owen asked.

"That's one way of putting it."

"How badly was she shot?"

"Not badly enough," Raye muttered. "She's here. She's still killing people."

Raye plucked a paper sack from the exam table. "I'm staying at the Harborside Motel." She pulled a card from her pocket and set it on the table. "Here's my number." She paused in the doorway. "If you see Mistress June again, run." Then she was gone.

"You stay." Becca pointed at the wolf. "I gotta go talk to my parents."

"Now?" Owen was almost as amazed at that as the idea of her telling a wolf to stay. Except the animal did, sticking her nose under her tail and closing her eyes.

"Right now." She shooed Owen and Reggie out the door. "If you want, I can come to the cottages afterward."

Owen led her toward his pickup. "Your name is on the witch-watch list." Beneath his palm she tensed. "I'm not letting you out of my sight until this is over."

"Just because someone tried to kill me doesn't mean—"

"I heard about the ring."

She didn't respond.

"The crazies think you're a witch. There'll be no convincing them otherwise. I learned that much from my mom."

Once in the pickup and on the way to the farm, I wrestled with what to say. There wasn't much I could tell Owen without sounding as insane as his mother.

"Who is she?" he asked.

Reggie sat between us, his huge head and solid body a comforting barrier. I leaned into him, and he nuzzled my hair.

Love her.

"Who?" I asked, one question for both guys.

"Raye," Owen said.

Pru. That was Reggie.

Hell. That was me. I didn't have time for puppy love. Which might actually produce puppies. Cubs. Cub-puppies.

"Raye Larsen. From New Bergin."

"I know what her name is, and that she's involved in this mess somehow. But who is she, Becca? It can't be a coincidence that she's your clone."

"Maybe it's witchcraft."

"Ha-ha."

I scrubbed my fingers behind Reggie's ears.

Good. More. Yes.

I had to tell Owen something. I chose the best option from a whole lot of bad ones.

"She says she's my sister."

Owen frowned into the setting sun. "She explain how that could be possible?"

She'd intimated that the spell of two witches, cast four hundred years ago, fueled with sacrifice, fire, and magic, had sent my sisters and me to this time—where no one believes in witches any more. Or at least not the kind they'd believed in then.

"Not really," I hedged.

"Why should you believe her?"

"You saw her, right?"

"Right." He reached over and laid his hand atop mine where it rested on Reggie's bony head. "What are you going to do?"

"Ask my parents if I'm adopted."

Despite all the childhood conjecture, I never had before.

"What if they deny it?"

"There's always DNA."

Owen turned into the lane that led to my parents' farm. "This is gonna be swell."

Chapter 20

Moose brayed like a banshee, and Reggie tried to climb over me while doing the same. As soon as the truck stopped, I reached for the handle.

"Reggie should stay here," Owen said.

"He doesn't play well with others?"

"His idea of play is work and vice versa."

"What does that mean?"

"He lives to play with his ball after he finds deadly explosives. Got a grenade you could hide for him?"

Reggie stared out the window, panting. *Play. Run. Chase.*

"He wants to play," I said.

"He tell you that?"

Instead of answering, I opened the door. Reggie vaulted out of the truck and chased Moose into the high grass. I listened for growling, yelping, or snarling. When none came I cast Owen a glance, but kept the "told you so" to myself. I had bigger fish to fry.

Both of whom stood on the porch, having been alerted to our arrival by the security system known as Moose.

"Should I stay in the truck?" Owen asked.

"No need."

I certainly wasn't going to bring up witchcraft, time travel, spells, and the like to my parents. All I wanted was the truth about my past, and I didn't mind Owen hearing it too.

We crossed the yard. My mother hurried down the steps and threw her arms around him as if he were a long-lost child who had at last come home. He kind of was.

"Owen," she said, the same way she always had.

In contrast, my father's scowl seemed completely out of place. Though Owen's arms had gone around my mom and held her close, his gaze had gone to my dad. He wasn't smiling either.

"What's up with you two?" I'd asked before, but neither one of them had answered. I was pretty sick of it.

"You tell me," my father said, eyes still on Owen, who'd released my mom, though she'd taken his hand as though afraid he'd disappear if she didn't hold on to him tight. I understood the feeling. "He broke your heart. Now he's back and that's just fine and dandy?"

I certainly didn't want to discuss how broken my heart had been, how long it had taken me to get over Owen—the truth being that I never had—in front of my parents.

In front of anyone, ever, not even him.

"I'm not here to talk about Owen."

"Then feel free to run along," my father said to him.

"No." I took the hand my mom wasn't clinging to and clung a bit myself. "He stays."

"You afraid he's going to disappear if you don't keep an eye on him?"

"A little."

"He's going back wherever he's been, Becca. You shouldn't get too attached."

I'd started for the house, but his words made me stop. "How do you know that?"

My father's mouth tightened, as if he didn't want more damning words to flow free.

I glanced at Owen. "How did he know that?"

"We ran into each other."

"You've been here a day."

"He stopped by the cottages this morning."

My gaze narrowed. "You said you had to mend fences. That was a euphemism for talking to Owen?" Didn't appear like they'd mended much. More like they'd broken things even more.

"Dale?" My mother released Owen's hand. "What did you do?"

He took a step back; his face flushed, and I knew.

"You told him to leave," I said. "Not just today but ten years ago."

It wasn't a question, so neither one of them answered.

"Mom, did you know about this?"

"No." She stared at my dad. I knew that expression. He was in so much trouble.

"Why?" I asked.

"You were my little girl," my father said.

"Was I?"

His gaze flicked to my mother's. Owen's fingers tightened around mine, and I knew that truth too.

I wasn't.

Though Dale cast Owen a withering "go away" glare, Owen followed everyone into the house. He might be leaving eventually, but he wasn't going to leave now. He owed Becca that.

Besides, she was holding on to his hand as if she really needed it. He couldn't take it back and walk away.

As he climbed the porch steps, Becca pointed at his leg. "You aren't limping."

He rubbed at the ache. Still there, but a lot better than when he'd arrived. Had that only been yesterday?

"It's a good day," he said.

The doctor had told him some would be better than others. Until today, none of them had been. He'd enjoy the reprieve while it lasted. Tomorrow would be worse. Had to be. It wasn't as if he could heal overnight, even though it felt like he had.

Come to think of it, Reggie had run off with Moose like a puppy, when the dog had been gimping just last night. Owen never would have thought a Wisconsin autumn was conducive to healing. Usually the cool, damp air made aches worse. Or so he'd heard from anyone who'd had aches the last time he'd been in town.

In the living room, Becca sat on the same couch that had been here all those years ago. Owen sank into it so far he worried he wouldn't be able to climb back out. Either the springs were shot, or he weighed a lot more than he had at eighteen. Probably both.

"Where are the boys?" Becca asked.

"Team dinner after football practice," Pam Carstairs said. "They won't be home for another hour at least."

Becca pointed at the chairs on the other side of the coffee table, and her parents sat in them as if they were the kids and Owen and Becca the parents. He kind of liked it.

"What makes you think that you aren't our daughter?" Pam asked.

"I'm the redheaded stepchild."

Her mom stiffened. "You are not!"

"Mom, I don't look like any of you."

"That doesn't mean anything."

"I met a woman today who could be my twin."

Her mother blinked, then all the air seemed to leak out of her like a balloon punctured with a pin. "What did she say?"

"That we're sisters." Becca peered at her hands, which were twisting in her lap. She separated them, laid her palms on her thighs, and lifted her gaze. "Is it true?"

"I don't know."

"Wouldn't the adoption agency tell you if I had sisters?"

"Sisters?" Owen asked. Plural? Where had that come from?

"Whatever." Becca kept her eyes on her parents.

"You weren't adopted," Dale said.

"Dad, come on."

"You've seen your birth certificate."

"What does it say?" Owen asked.

"It lists Dale and Pamela as my birth father and mother." She tilted her head. "How'd you do that?"

"Wasn't easy," Pam muttered, and Dale snapped, "Honey!"

Becca's mom threw up her hands. "She knows. I'm not going to keep lying about it."

"Why did you lie in the first place?" Becca asked.

Pam's eyes filled with tears. "I didn't want to lose you."

"Why would you lose me?"

"Maybe you better start from the beginning," Owen said.

"I lost several babies." My mom's voice was so broken I ached. "Over and over, they died."

"You never said," I began.

"I couldn't. I . . . I . . ."

My father set his hand on her arm. "Don't."

"She needs to know. It's time." She drew in a breath and laced her fingers with his. "I was only a few weeks from delivering. I'd never gotten that far along, so I didn't realize. How could I? The baby didn't move like babies do."

I didn't like the way this story was headed, but I had to know. As she'd said, it was time.

"I went into labor at home. It was hard, fast. I had her here. She was—" Her voice broke.

"Stillborn," my father said. "I suppose we should have called the doctor, the hospital. I don't know. We didn't. I . . . couldn't. We buried her near the others."

I didn't realize I'd taken Owen's hand again until his fingers tightened around mine, and I clung. "And then?"

"I would visit the grave every day," my mom said. "Then one morning I heard a baby crying."

She paled and her lips trembled. I understood. She'd thought she was crazy. Who wouldn't?

"I followed the sound and—" She swallowed, smiled. "There you were. Naked, without even a blanket. It was July, but still."

Raye's words—almost exactly.

"You were in the woods alone. No note. Nothing."

"They didn't deserve you," my father said. "So we made you ours."

I saw how it had happened. My mother had been expecting, then she had a baby. Why would anyone doubt that the child Pam Carstairs presented to the world as hers wasn't?

"No one ever came asking questions? No news reports of a missing baby?"

"No," my mother said.

In a normal world, someone should have been searching for me. But if I'd time-traveled from the past, not so much.

"It never occurred to me that you were a twin," my mother continued.

Triplet, but who was counting?

"Where was the other girl . . . ?" Mom tilted her head. "What's her name?"

"Raye."

"Where was Raye found?"

"Side of the interstate between Madison and Eau Claire. Near New Bergin."

"That's a hundred and fifty miles from here. Why would they separate you like that?"

"The farther apart the babies were left, the less likely anyone would connect them," Owen said. "It's a lot harder to find two separate mothers of unrelated children than it is to find one mother of twins. Even harder to find a dumped baby that was never reported as dumped."

"So how did Raye find us?" my father asked.

I wasn't touching that question. Not now. Hopefully not ever.

"Why didn't you tell me?" I glanced between the two of them. "I was teased all my life for being adopted."

"Would it have made things better if I'd told you that you were?" my mother asked. "You didn't feel as though you belonged already."

"Because I didn't."

"You did," she insisted. "You do. You're my child. My firstborn. I waited years for you."

Had my mother kept the truth from me because she couldn't accept it herself? Had she replaced that dead child in her heart and mind with me and in so doing made what had happened fade away?

"I'm not her," I said softly. "You buried her in the woods."

"I know who you are. Just because I didn't give birth to you myself doesn't make you any less mine. Once I had you, I was . . ." She made a motion with her hands, looking for a word to describe that feeling. "Whole. Healed. You used to pat my stomach and call for a brother or sister. Every pregnancy after you came to live with us went to term. It was a miracle."

Or magic.

What could I say? Maybe I had healed her.

"You still should have told me."

"Why?" My father spread his big, hard hands wide. "Someone tossed you away to die in the forest."

"That makes it all right to lie, commit fraud, and kidnap a child?" Owen asked.

"I told you he shouldn't hear this," my father said.

"Owen won't tell anyone." I squeezed his hand. "Right?"

"Don't you want to know who your real parents are?"

I already did, but I wasn't going to share.

"That's a problem for another day. I'm a little preoccupied with figuring out who tried to kill me."

"Shouldn't the police be doing that?" my mother asked.

"Deb has a lot on her plate."

Animal mutilations. Peggy's murder. Owen's mom running amok.

"How is it that your twin sister shows up in town the same day someone tries to kill you?" my dad asked.

"It wasn't her."

"You're sure?"

"Raye is the same height and weight as me. Whoever put the pillow over my face was a lot bigger."

Mistress June size.

"Still wouldn't trust her. Just because she's your blood doesn't make her blood."

That might sound like gibberish, but I knew what he meant. There was a bond in a family that went beyond DNA. I'd shared everything with the Carstairs, and I loved them. But, oddly, or maybe not now that I knew the truth, I'd never felt related to them. Yet the instant I'd seen Raye Larsen, I'd known we shared more than the same nose and mouth. We shared parents and a past.

"I have to go."

"Don't," my mother said. "Not yet. Please."

"Mom, I have to think."

Her eyes filled. "You called me 'Mom.'"

"You are my mom. Nothing will change that. But I have to go back to town."

"With him?" My dad's gaze was on Owen.

"He brought me," I pointed out. "I don't have much choice."

"You do, Becca. You always had a choice."

I was starting to think I'd never really had much choice at all. I'd been born a witch. Just because I hadn't known it hadn't made the magic go away.

My parents claiming me as theirs hadn't changed who I was. My name might be Carstairs on paper, and in my heart because of my love for them, but deep down, where blood boiled and the soul lived, I was a Taggart.

In the same way, Owen's leaving hadn't changed a thing. I still loved him. Always had, always would. Couldn't stop. There was such a thing as destiny, and I had found mine. Or maybe it had found me.

"I'll call you."

The tears in my mother's eyes spilled over. I felt awful. I didn't want to hurt her. There were far greater crimes than love. But right now, I had to go.

Outside, Owen whistled and Reggie came running. I opened the car door; he jumped in. It wasn't until I followed that I saw a tuft of fur hanging out the side of his mouth.

"He's got something," I said as Owen slid behind the wheel.

Before I could open the door and bail, Owen ordered, *"Aus."*

Reggie opened his mouth. I let out a tiny squeak as what I really hoped was not a rodent fell into my lap. It had been thoroughly drooled upon and would have resembled a drowned rat if it hadn't been calico.

"Kitten," I said.

Mine.

I glanced at Reggie. He didn't seem the type to have a pet or a pal.

"Did he hurt it?"

I picked her up. "Not a mark on her except for the drool. He was carrying her very gently, almost as if he were afraid she might explode."

Splode.

Aha.

"She is about the size of a grenade," Owen said. "She kind of looks like a camo cat too."

Soaking wet, she kind of did.

"I should put her back with her mom." I got out of the car. Reggie went wild.

No! Mine! Granate!

My father stepped onto the porch. "What in blue blazes is going on out here?"

"Reggie had a kitten in his mouth." I held her out.

"Ah, her. That one's mama died. There were only two in the litter and another cat took in the brother. This one . . ." He shrugged. "She's weaned and on her own. Haven't seen her in a while. Thought she might be hawk food. She will be if she keeps wanderin' off."

This was usually the way I ended up with fosters. It was me—or the hawk.

I took her with me to the car. Reggie immediately stopped barking and nosed the kitten. Instead of lifting her back like a Halloween cat, she licked his nose.

Mama.

I bit back my laughter as Reggie preened.

Mine. Granate.

"What does *granate* mean?"

Owen cast me an odd glance. "Where'd you hear that?"

I glanced at Reggie, who was now licking the kitten like any good mama would. "Around. Why?"

"*Granate* is German for grenade."

Chapter 21

Owen wasn't sure what to say to Becca. It wasn't every day you discovered you were abandoned in the forest.

"Is that your cat now?" he asked.

"I think she's Reggie's."

The dog did appear obsessed. Or in love.

"He isn't going to be able to keep her." Owen couldn't imagine trying to smuggle a cat into Afghanistan. It would probably be easier to bring in some dope.

"You tell him," Becca said. "I don't have the heart."

"Are you sure you don't want to stay at your parents'?"

"I'm sure." She cast him a sideways glance. "I'd rather stay with you."

He'd rather she stayed with him too.

The crazies were still out there. A lot of them, his mom included. He hadn't been kidding when he said he didn't want to let Becca out of his sight.

Owen started the truck, drove up to the main road, paused. "Do you want to stop at your place first?"

"For pajamas?"

He snorted, and he could have sworn she blushed, but it was hard to tell in the blue-gray of approaching twilight. He pulled onto the road and drove toward town.

"What about the wolf?"

"Pru."

"Pru," he repeated, and Reggie sat up and looked out the window with interest. The kitten tumbled off Becca's lap and began to chew on the dog's foot. Reggie didn't seem to mind. "What does that mean?"

"Short for Prudence." She shrugged. "Gotta call her something."

"So you chose Prudence?"

Of all the names to choose for a wolf, that would not have been one of them. Then again, the kitten appeared to be named Grenade.

Reggie woofed, low, a bit startled.

"Deer," Becca said, but she was staring at the dog and not the road.

Owen followed Reggie's gaze and hit the brakes as a deer bolted in front of the truck.

He hated it when Becca did stuff like that. Sometimes he swore she was psychic, would have believed it too, if he were the sort to believe in things like that.

"Do you need to check on Pru?"

"No." Becca peered out the passenger window. "The anesthesia should make her dopey enough to knock her out for the rest of the night."

"And in the morning?"

"In the morning, we'll see."

"What about your sister?"

"Which one?"

He didn't answer. She knew which one.

Instead of taking Carstairs Avenue through town, Owen skirted Three Harbors altogether. Lights blazed in the tavern; the scent of food made his stomach rumble. When was the last time he'd eaten?

He parked in front of his cottage and handed Becca

his key. "You go in. I'll get us some dinner." He contemplated the kitten. "What about her?"

"Order me a chicken sandwich. She can have some of that."

"Any other requests?"

"Wine," she said. "Bring the bottle."

I juggled Grenade as I opened the door. At least she wouldn't explode if I dropped her.

Reggie pushed past me and I let him. If anyone or anything waited within that shouldn't, he'd know about it.

Something creaked. I flicked on the light. Reggie stood on the bed. He twirled once and lay down. I deposited his kitten next to him, and she crawled between his paws. Within seconds the two of them had crashed.

I wished I could. When was the last time I'd slept? Would I be able to sleep tonight with all that swirled in my head?

My parents weren't my parents. My brothers weren't my brothers. My sister wasn't my sister. My name wasn't my name. I should be more upset about that than I was.

I'd always known I didn't belong. Having it confirmed made me kind of Zen for the first time in a lifetime.

Eventually I'd have to decide what to do, what to say, if anything, to the rest of the world. For now, I had to let it all settle in.

A fire had been laid in the fireplace. The idea of sitting on the faux-fur rug, staring into the dancing flames with Owen, had me striking a match. I went in search of wine glasses, had to settle for juice glasses instead.

By the time he returned with the food and that wine, I was dozing. The sound of the door, the rush of cool air brought me back.

I accepted the bag of food and the bottle of wine. We didn't even have to search for a corkscrew. Kyle, or whoever was working tonight, had already done the honors. He'd also provided a litter box and litter.

"Cat lover?" I asked.

"He said he had all sorts of things that people had left behind."

Owen joined me on the rug, held the glasses so I could pour. "This is homey." We tapped rims, drank.

He smelled like chill wind and the fresh outdoors. I scooted closer so I could lean my head on his shoulder. We stared into the fire and sipped. Grenade purred a contented serenade. I wanted to stay here forever. With him.

"Hungry?" he asked.

"Not really."

"You want to talk about it?"

I wasn't sure which "it" he meant. Didn't matter.

"No." I drained my wine.

"More?"

I set my glass on the end table, turned back, took his, and set it aside too. "Yes." I pulled off my shirt.

His gaze went to my breasts. "Becca," he began.

"Shh," I said, and kissed him.

He tasted like red wine and winter wind. I sucked on his lip. His hands, still cold from outside, felt glorious in contrast to the heat pouring from the fireplace.

I lifted my mouth just long enough to yank off his shirt. Then I traced the patterns the flames made across his chest with my tongue and my teeth.

He pulled the band from the end of my braid, worked his fingers through my hair. The drift of the strands on my shoulders made me shiver. Or maybe it was the flick of his thumbs on my nipples. The heat had softened them; his touch changed that. I puckered, pebbled, and he pulled me into his lap, guiding my legs on either side of his hips.

"Wait." I reached for my zipper.

He stayed my hand. "Not yet."

Then he took my breast into his mouth, suckling, teasing, tormenting—first one, then the other—as he hardened against me. I had to steady myself with my hands on his shoulders, then I became fascinated by the play of muscles beneath my palms, the spike of his collarbone beneath my thumbs.

His hands tightened on my hips, pulling me against him. Through several layers of clothing I felt his heat, the beat of his pulse, or maybe that was mine.

"Please," I whispered, dizzy with desire.

He lifted his head then became captivated by the flicker of flame too. His tongue chased the shadows across my neck, my collarbone, my shoulder. The dampness left by his mouth cooled despite the heat, and I shivered.

He scooped me into his arms, rose to his knees, tilted, and laid me on the fur. It was warm and soft. I shimmied against it, and he cursed, stood, and lost his pants.

"Wait." He was so beautiful—naked and rippling and damn near perfect. Even the scar that marred his leg was smooth and sleek.

He clenched his hands, released them, and clenched them again. "You're killing me."

I beckoned, and he dropped to the ground and reached for my jeans. I'd forgotten I still had them on.

He drew them down my legs, removed my socks, then kissed and stroked his way back up. A peck on my toes, his thumbs against the arch of my foot, tongue behind each knee, teeth on the inside of my thigh.

His breath brushed my core, and my hips lifted from the fur. His mouth pushed me back down. With fingers and tongue he made me come, gasping, biting back the scream. I didn't want to wake the animals. Though the animal in me, in him, had awoken shrieking.

He slid into me while I was still quaking. Stroked once, twice, a third time—harder, deeper, better. I hadn't thought it was possible, but what the hell? I came again.

I saw the storm in his eyes, felt the pulse radiating from him, through me. My fingers chased the firelight across his face. He turned his head and kissed my palm. My eyes prickled. I tightened my lips so I wouldn't beg him not to go.

He kissed me until we were both shaking, spent, a little cold. He moved to the couch, snatched up an afghan, strode back. Instead of covering us both, he draped it around my shoulders then added wood to the fire. I reached for my clothes.

"No," he said, not even turning around. "I'm not done."

I pulled the afghan tighter and enjoyed the play of muscles in his back as he fed the flames. The room brightened, warmed. He straightened, turned, and the wide, jagged scar running the length of his right thigh captured my gaze.

I rose onto my knees, ran my thumb down the mark.

When I reached the middle, where the scar seemed the deepest, a spark sprang, so bright it looked like a shooting star in the night.

He hissed, took a step back, and rubbed the place I'd touched. "I think I'm done," he said, in direct contrast to his last sentence.

"I can wait."

He shoved the same hand through his hair. "Done in the service. I can't go back like this."

"You're getting better," I protested.

Why? I had no idea. I certainly didn't want him to leave.

"Not better enough. I can't run like I used to, like I need to. Can't jump out of a plane on my own, let alone with Reggie strapped to me. When I hit the ground on this leg, it'll give out and we'll both wind up dead."

"You jumped out of a plane with a seventy-pound dog strapped to you?"

"How else do you think we got on the ground?"

I hadn't thought. Hadn't wanted to. But I certainly wouldn't have imagined that.

"Reggie's almost full strength."

I curled my fingers in on themselves. Was that my fault? I hadn't meant to heal him; at the time I hadn't even known that I was. I couldn't take it back. I wouldn't. I shouldn't.

"I don't know what I'll do," he said. "All I've ever had was that."

"You had me."

Same argument, different year.

"Don't," he began.

"I love you," I said. "I never stopped."

"I hurt you."

"You didn't mean to."

"Of course I did. I had to make you forget me."

"Did you forget me?"

"No."

"Then how could you think I would ever forget you?" I laid my lips on his scar, and his hand fell to my hair. I licked the length of it, and he shuddered. "Did that hurt?"

"Yes. No." He rubbed it again. "It's better since I've been here."

Of course it was. If I touched him enough, he would heal, just like Reggie, like Pru, like my human mother, like any number of people and animals I'd made as good as new.

And then he would go.

Chapter 22

They'd made love again as the fire danced. Becca avoided touching Owen's scar, when before she'd done a lot more than touch it.

Had he flinched? Probably.

She'd seemed sad, and he wasn't sure why. Owen did his best to make that sadness go away, kissing her as he moved inside of her. "Smile for me," he whispered.

She did, but there was still something wrong. Of course, someone *had* tried to kill her. But he didn't think that was it.

He led her to the bed, but it was occupied. "Beat it."

Reggie lifted his head, then his lip. Grenade lay draped across his paws, dead to the world.

"It's all right," Becca said. "We can fit."

As she curled against one side, and the dog against his other, with the kitten's purr tickling his skin, Owen's chest shifted with longing.

"What did my father say to make you go?"

His contentment fled. He'd known this conversation was coming.

"The truth," he said. "You deserved better."

"There's no one better for me than you."

"I saw what it would have been like."

"You're clairvoyant?"

"Huh?"

"You see the future?"

"It was pretty clear." He began to play with her hair. "You would have gone to college; I'd have stayed here. I would have visited you one weekend a month if I could get off work at the café, or the gas station, or the grocery store."

Which would have been the extent of his options back then. Still might be.

"You'd have come home to see me too at first. Things would have been fine. Then the visits would have become fewer and farther apart."

"I don't believe that."

"If you'd spent all your free time with me—whether it was there or here—you would have missed out on all the things you could have done, the people you could have met, the experiences you should have had."

Just like in the Marines, the training was important, but the camaraderie was even more so. What Owen had gone through with his fellow Marines had made him who he was.

"You'd have been giving all that up for me," Owen continued. "You deserved better, and your father was right to make sure you got it any way that he could."

"What way?"

"It doesn't matter."

"You fought for your mother. You fought for this country. You never would have left without fighting for me, unless there was a damn good reason. What did he say? Do?"

Owen didn't answer. He wasn't going to tattle at this late date. In the end, he didn't have to. Becca was smart;

she figured it out. He was surprised it had taken her this long. Of course, until today, she hadn't realized her father was capable of great, big, life altering lies.

"He threatened you with something." Her brilliant mind clicked along so quickly, so loudly, he could practically hear it. "Theft? No. Anyone who knew you knew better."

"Tell it to Emerson."

"Kid stuff."

"I still stole his beer."

"Owen," she said, exasperated.

"I was underage. Not only is stealing illegal, but so was drinking it."

She caught her breath, and he wished he'd kept his big mouth shut. "You were eighteen. I wasn't." She shifted so she could see his face. "So were a lot of people who dated senior year. It wasn't like I was fifteen. I don't think that counts."

"It doesn't. Didn't." He thought about denying it but why? It was over, done with. Like a lot of things. "Your father made the threat sound good. I was a kid. I didn't want you to go through that."

"You think my father would have put me through that? You don't know my father."

"I realized that pretty quickly, but I was mortified that he'd caught us. Caught me, touching you."

"You loved me."

"The one thing he asked of me was that I leave you alone. But I couldn't."

"He what?"

Reggie woofed, low and startled, and Grenade made a surprised kitten-cat sound.

"Shh," Owen said, to the dog, the cat, the woman.

"You agreed to that?" She sounded pretty mad.

He could relate. He'd been angry for a long time. He'd been angry right up until he'd seen her again and realized that she'd become all that she'd dreamed of becoming.

And that she'd done so without him should have made him madder, or at least sadder. But, instead, it had made him glad. Or at least as happy as he got these days with his own life such a mess.

"I didn't think it would be that hard," he said.

"Gee, thanks."

"You were my friend. Your family was my family." Or as close to a family as he'd ever had. "But I was wrong."

About so many things.

"I *wasn't* your friend? They *weren't* your family?" If possible, she sounded angrier.

"You became more than my friend, and because of that they couldn't be my family. I have no one to blame but myself. I wasn't honorable. I didn't keep my word."

"It was more honorable to break my heart?"

"If I'd stayed, you would have wound up hating me."

He would have wound up hating himself. And who needed that?

"I hated you anyway," she said, but her voice had gone thick; her body had relaxed against him. It *was* after midnight, and neither one of them had slept since . . . who knew?

Owen pressed his lips to her hair, matched his breath-

ing to hers, and for the first time in their lifetime they
slept together.

I heard a distant beelike buzz, swatted at it, but the *brr-brr* continued.

My phone.

My eyes opened. I blinked at the expanse of male
chest.

Owen.

He hadn't even moved. I wanted to sink back into the
same oblivion, but I couldn't. Emergencies happened. All
the time.

I slipped out of bed. Reggie opened one eye, closed it
again. Grenade continued to snore. I gathered my clothes,
snatched up my phone, and went into the bathroom. I
discovered a text from Joaquin.

There's something weird about this wolf.

"You think?" I muttered then texted back: *Be right
there.*

I found a piece of stationery imprinted with the words
Stone Lake Cottages, and scribbled a note.

Had to check on Pru. Back soon. I'll bring coffee.

That should smooth over any crankiness Owen might
experience upon waking and finding me gone. With his
truck.

I stepped into the early morning chill of a northern
Wisconsin autumn. As Three Harbors was both a farming community and a tourist hub, there were plenty of
cars on the road at just before seven A.M. I parked in my
lot, opened the back door, and Pru shot out.

He saw.

She raced across the gravel and disappeared into the trees an instant before Joaquin appeared.

"Where'd she go?"

I pointed at the forest, grabbed his arm before he could run off too. "You aren't going to catch her."

"No," he agreed. "She's completely healed."

Ah, hell! How was I going to explain a perfectly fine rump that had not been fine only yesterday?

Now that Pru was gone, I didn't have to.

"Sure she is."

"You should have seen her wound. Except there wasn't one any more."

"Joaquin, that's—"

"I swear." He lifted one hand. "I'd have thought I imagined the whole thing, but the hair was still shaved, there just wasn't . . . anything. No stitches, no scar. Poof."

"Poof," I repeated.

"Then you opened the door and she took off." He shook his head. "She shouldn't have been able to run like that either."

"You'd be surprised what wild animals can do. Deer heal so quickly that blood trails seem to disappear less than a mile from impact." Much to the chagrin of deer hunters everywhere. Deer didn't actually heal *that* quickly, but within a week, yeah. "They wouldn't survive out there if they didn't heal fast."

"This was freaky fast."

I spread my hands. "Whatever you say."

His face flushed, and his fingers curled tight in frustration, but without the evidence, he had nothing.

"Don't you have school?" I urged him out the door. "I'll see you later."

"Later," he repeated, as if in a daze.

"Office hours."

"Oh, right. Sure." He left.

"Phew!" I threw the lock on the back door, ducked the crime scene tape, and ran upstairs. I probably shouldn't have until I was given the all clear, but tough. I jumped into the shower, rustled up new clothes, and returned to the pickup.

The best coffee in town, after my mother's, could be found at Bean and Gone. No Starbucks in Three Harbors. Yet.

I parked just as Raye and a gorgeous man who must be her fiancé exited the coffee shop and headed for the Harborside Motel, conveniently located right next door.

"Raye!"

She turned, in her hands a tray with four cups. The man, Bobby she'd called him, had four cups too. At the sight of me, he bobbled them.

"Wow. She really does look like you, *cher*." His accent was both Southern and foreign. His skin was the shade of summer sand, his hair as black as Raye's. Both those things only made his eyes shine more blue.

"This is Bobby Doucet," Raye said.

I nodded, smiled. He did too.

"You spoke to your parents?"

"Yeah."

"You were adopted?"

"No."

Now she bobbled her tray. If this continued, there wouldn't be any coffee left, though neither of them had spilled a drop from what I could see. Magic or luck?

"That's impossible," Raye said.

"Not really."

I hadn't been adopted, I'd been . . . substituted. Quickly I explained all I'd learned.

Raye glanced at her fiancé. "That explains why you didn't find any record of another abandoned baby in the area."

"You're a New Orleans detective?"

"I was. I accepted the job of chief of police in New Bergin when the last chief retired recently."

"Convenient."

"The town hadn't had a murder in eons. Chief Johnson wasn't equipped to handle several in a week."

"Who is?"

"Me," Bobby said. "New Orleans isn't exactly a murder-free zone."

"You'd know." I didn't. The farthest away I'd ever been—unless I counted Scotland—was Milwaukee. Also not a murder-free zone, though probably not as hopping in that area—or any other—as New Orleans.

"Your parents' story explains why there was no mention of your being found," Bobby said. "But where is your other sister?"

"Don't ask me. I'm still getting used to her." I pointed at Raye. "You mentioned you found me by magic. How'd that work?"

"I cast a spell to find Henry once, saw you. He filled me in on the rest."

"Couldn't you do the same to find her?"

"I tried, but I got nothing. Maybe the two of us together—"

"We have murderers to catch first," Bobby interrupted.

"Homicide cops," Raye said. "Always about the murders."

"We're funny that way."

My lips twitched. I liked him. I liked her. I felt like I'd known them both a lot longer than I had.

"Want some coffee?" Bobby asked.

"God, yes."

"We've got extras. Join us."

"Eight cups for two people?"

"A few more than two," he said.

The door opened without either one of them touching it, and for an instant I thought Raye had done it—she'd opened mine—then I caught sight of three figures inside.

"It's time you met the gang," Raye said.

"I don't—" I suddenly took several quick steps forward, as if pushed or pulled, over the threshold and into the room. I hadn't meant to.

"Raye." Bobby shut the door.

"Sorry." I didn't know if she was talking to him or to me. "This is my sister, Becca." She set her tray of coffee on the dresser.

A tall man, with salt-and-pepper hair and a dark, crisp suit, led with his hand. "I'm Nic Franklin."

"FBI," Raye said. "Though I'm sure you could tell."

I shook his hand. "Why would I be able to tell?"

"No one dresses like that on purpose," said the tiny woman just behind. If not for the white streak in her dark hair, and the crinkles at the corners of her eyes I'd have thought she was a teenager.

"I'm Cassandra," she said.

"Are you in the FBI too?"

"I'm a voodoo priestess."

I laughed. No one else did.

"Anyone want to explain why we need a voodoo priestess?" I glanced at Cassandra. "No offense."

"None taken. I'm a witch expert."

"Sure you are."

"I employ only the best of the best," said the ancient fellow sitting stiffly in a desk chair in the most shadowed corner of the room.

"Edward Mandenauer," I said.

"How do you know?"

"Your German accent kind of gave it away."

Even though he was sitting I could tell that he was over six feet tall and far too thin. His eyes were a faded blue and his white hair had the muted hue of the once blond.

"In this neighborhood I am not the only one with such an accent."

Germans did love Wisconsin more than the next immigrant. Might be because the deep, dark, Grimm-like forests reminded them of home.

"Probably not," I agreed. "But you are the only one wearing bullets like a fashion statement before eight in the morning."

Raye coughed to cover a laugh, and Edward shot her a glare.

Franklin handed him a cup of coffee. "She has a point, sir."

"Is there a reason you shot Pru with a silver bullet?"

"She is a wolf with human eyes. That is reason enough."

"Don't do it again."

"Why would I? She did not explode; she is clean."

"She almost died."

"Yet still she lives."

"How can you be so certain?"

"According to your lovely sister, your mother the wolf is fine. You have healed her." He indicated the nearest corner. "And your ghostly papa tells us that she is free."

"Henry's here?"

Raye tilted her head. "He says you're beautiful. He's sorry. He loves you."

I wasn't sure what to say back. I couldn't see him. I didn't love him. I didn't even know him.

"Don't worry about it," Raye said. "He understands. He's just glad we're okay."

"You will not be okay for much longer." Edward took a sip of coffee and made a face, set the cup on the dresser, swallowed. "You must stop the crazy woman before she raises the equally insane hunter of witches."

"Works for me," I said. "How?"

"Let's discuss." Nic Franklin waved at an empty chair. I took it and the nearest coffee.

"Mistress June must be staying somewhere, and a woman that tall is a little hard to miss."

"It's a tourist town," I said. "There are probably a hundred rooms she could be holed up in."

"I'll start canvassing."

"That doesn't even take into account the privately rented cabins in the forest where I'd think she would be more likely to lurk."

Franklin cursed.

"It's a waste of time to search for her," Cassandra said.

"She's not dumb. She won't make it easy. Eventually, she's going to come to us." She glanced at Raye, then at me. "Or probably to one of you."

"She knows about us?"

"We're not sure what she knows," Franklin said. "She tried to kill Raye, on an altar, beneath the moon in order to raise Roland. But she didn't indicate that she knew Raye was one of the Taggart sisters. Now . . ." He waved a hand up and down to indicate me. "She's probably figured it out."

Dizziness washed over me, whether at the acceptance that one of the triplets born four hundred years ago was me, or the idea of being killed because of it, I had no idea.

"Wouldn't Roland want to kill us himself?" I asked.

"As he's a serial killer, and an asshole, probably." Raye spread her hands. "Though I don't know how, or even if, he's communicating with his minions."

"What should we do?"

"I vote we find Mistress June, then beat all the answers out of her," Bobby said.

I smiled at the man who would become my brother-in-law. "I like how you think."

Chapter 23

"The full moon is tomorrow night," Cassandra said. "I think she'll try again then."

"What does the full moon have to do with it?" I asked.

"What doesn't it?" Edward muttered.

I waited for him to elaborate, but he didn't.

"If the full moon can exert power over the tides," Cassandra said, "it can exert power over a lot of things. As long as there's been magic, that magic has been best performed under the full moon."

"How long has there been magic?" I asked.

"In the beginning, God created the heavens and the earth."

"Wasn't that a miracle?"

She shrugged. "Semantics."

"June wasn't able to raise Roland the last time she tried," Raye said.

"Why not?"

"She took too long to kill me. I doubt she'll make the same mistake twice."

"If she needed a full moon why didn't she use one?" I asked.

"She needs the moon, a sacrifice, believers," Cassandra clarified. "A full moon should speed things up, give her more juice. Since she's failed once, she's gonna want both."

"If she fails again?"

"There's always All Hallows' Eve. It's one of the most powerful nights of the year."

"For magic and witchcraft, right?" I asked. "But the *Venatores Mali* hate witches."

"They do, but power is power, and raising the dead is magic. Dark magic, but still magic."

"That makes no sense."

"You expect them to make sense?" Raye shook her head. "Don't."

"She's going to move soon." Cassandra noticed I'd finished my coffee and handed me another. "The longer she waits, the more chance there is that someone else will kill more witches than she has." At my bemused expression, she continued. "The nut job with the most witch kills is considered the leader of the *Venatores Mali* and is the one who raises Roland. The longer she waits to bring him back, the less chance she has of being the one to do it."

"If she raises him, what does she get?"

"Whatever's behind door number three." Cassandra shrugged. "It's a mystery."

"We should set a trap."

Everyone looked at the FBI agent.

"We know Mistress June is here. We think she'll try and raise Roland again tomorrow night. She'll need a witch to kill." Franklin's forehead creased. "As the two of you will be ultravigilant, and a lot harder to snatch than your run-of-the-mill witch, I think she'll look elsewhere for her sacrifice."

"How are we going to keep an eye on every witch in town?" Cassandra asked.

I burst out laughing. "Every witch in town? This is Three Harbors. There aren't any."

"That's what I thought about New Bergin," Raye said. "I couldn't have been more wrong."

"How'd you find out who was a witch?"

"They turned up dead and branded."

"We need a better way."

"You think?" Raye asked, with the exact inflection I would have.

How strange. Or maybe not very strange at all.

"Is there a coven here?" Cassandra asked.

"If there were, I wouldn't know about it." I paused. "Jeremy was going to check on that."

"Jeremy?" the priestess repeated.

"Reitman. He's a forensic veterinarian. He came here to examine the animal sacrifices at Owen's house. He also happens to be a witch."

"Coincidence?" Franklin murmured. "I don't think so."

"He's the best forensic veterinarian in the state," I protested.

"Which means if there were animal sacrifices, he'd be called. I don't suppose anyone tried to kill him while he was here."

"Owen's mom, but she's schizophrenic."

"Did she try to kill him because a voice told her to?"

"Maybe?"

"That voice could very well be Roland's," Edward said.

"Are you trying to tell me that Owen's mom isn't

crazy? That the voices she's been hearing for most of her life are real?"

"Is the voice of a dead man real?" Edward wondered.

"Yes," Raye said. "Although I doubt that Roland's been whispering to Owen's mom since she was young. We weren't even born then."

"According to you we were born four hundred years ago, which means we were."

"Time travel gives me a great big headache," she said.

I couldn't argue there.

"Has Owen's mother tried to kill anyone before?" Cassandra asked.

"Owen."

"Because?"

"She was never very forthcoming on that."

"Does she hate witches?"

I shook my head. "There were times she thought she was one."

"Is she?"

"I . . ." I paused. "I don't know. Until a few days ago, believing you were a witch was nutty. Although, if she is, why did she try to kill one of her own?"

Which only brought us back to nutty, unless . . .

"She's been in a mental health facility for a long time. According to her now-dead caseworker, she's escaped several times in the past few months, and no one knows how."

Had it been magic? Maybe.

"A crazy woman on a mission would be the perfect weapon." Edward lifted one bushy white eyebrow. "I have seen such things before."

"You've seen everything before," Cassandra said. "Is Dr. Reitman still in town?"

"He took the evidence back to Madison."

"He's from Madison?" Raye asked.

"The UW has the largest veterinary college in Wisconsin."

"Did he say if he belonged to the coven there?"

"He does, and he was going to ask about a coven near here, but his priestess had been—" I paused, blinked. "She was killed. Did you know about that?"

Raye and Bobby exchanged glances with Franklin and Cassandra. Together, they nodded.

"Can you call him?" Franklin asked.

I was already dialing my phone. It was early yet. Jeremy shouldn't be in class, but the phone rang so many times I was expecting voice mail when he answered.

"Becca! I was just going to call you."

"Great." My voice sounded both too cheery and kind of stiff.

"Something wrong?"

"Beyond the animal mutilations?" My lips were poised to say "yes." But Raye started shaking her head like Moose after he'd gone for a swim, and instead I said, "I was wondering if you'd found anything yet?"

"I haven't. The evidence is not in good shape."

"Do you have any idea who might brand and burn sacrifices?"

Now Raye nodded, encouragingly. I must be on the right track.

"I don't," Jeremy said. "I've never seen anything like this."

Raye waved to get my attention, then mouthed: "Coven."

"Were you able to find out if there's a coven in my area?"

"I wasn't."

I shook my head, and everyone frowned.

"My coven has been thrown into a bit of an uproar," Jeremy continued.

"I can imagine."

Franklin held up a sheet of paper, on which he'd written: *Is there a natural altar near here?*

I repeated the question into the phone.

"Not that I know of."

I shook my head again, and the FBI agent crumpled the paper in his fist.

"That's the kind of thing local witches would know," Jeremy continued.

"I suppose so. Well, thanks."

I disconnected. It wasn't until Raye said my name that I realized I was standing there frowning at the phone in my hand.

"What's wrong?" she asked.

I shoved the phone into my back pocket. "He said he'd never heard of branding and burning sacrifices. But being a witch, wouldn't he know about the *Venatores Mali*?"

"Considering Roland died in the seventeenth century, not necessarily," Raye said.

"Wasn't his high priestess branded?"

"Those details aren't common knowledge," Bobby said. "Which was why it took me so long to connect the dots among all the cases. I thought I was tracking a serial killer—"

"It *was* a serial killer," Raye interrupted. "Witches are people too."

He laced their fingers together. "The brand and the burnings were the only link between the bodies. And a lot of the bodies were burned so badly, the brand wasn't a certainty. We didn't find the connection until we started searching for burned witches. Not easy since being a witch still isn't something people advertise."

"How did you figure it out?" I asked.

"One of the victims didn't die right away." He swallowed, and Raye's fingers tightened around his. "She told me about the *Venatores Mali*. From there it was all downhill."

"How did the FBI get involved?" I asked.

"It's a long story," Franklin said. "Short version, anything weird gets passed by me."

"Weird is awful wide."

"I've become pretty good at separating normal-weird from weird-weird."

Sadly, that made sense.

"It bugs me that whoever attacked you tried to smother you," Raye said.

"Me too," I muttered.

"Mistress June's weapon of choice is the athame of Roland McHugh," Bobby said. "I've never known her to use anything else."

"What's an athame?" I asked.

"Double-edged ritual knife," Raye answered. "Used by a fire witch to cut herbs, draw the sacred circle.

Roland's is squiggly." She made the sign of an S in the air. "He carved his snarling-wolf symbol into the hilt."

"If an athame is a witch's instrument, why did McHugh have one?"

"Because he could?" Bobby asked. "The way it was explained to me is that Christians often appropriated pagan holidays and symbols. In that way they blurred the lines between pagan and Christian. People weren't even aware they'd been converted until they were."

"There's a reason the sabbats fall next to the Christian holidays," Raye continued. "Christians put the holidays next to the sabbats."

"Apparently Jesus wasn't even born on December twenty-fifth." Bobby seemed a little upset about that.

"You think McHugh snatched the ritual knife of a fire witch then carved his symbol into it?"

"I think McHugh snatched a fire witch," Bobby said, "but close enough."

"And now his chief minion has it?"

"Yes." Raye lifted a hand to her upper arm and rubbed. "She stabbed me with the thing."

Fury washed over me at the thought. "Does it still hurt?"

She dropped her hand, colored a bit. "It's only been a week. It'll heal."

I pressed my fingers where she had. A spark jumped. Her skin shifted and warmed. She sucked in a sharp breath, and I drew back.

Raye went to the mirror, pulled her shirt down, baring her shoulder to just above her breast, then leaned in. I wasn't sure what she was looking at until she drew a finger over a thin, red line. She spun, threw her arms around my neck, and pulled me in close. "Thanks."

"If I'd known you were hurt, I'd have done it right away."

Although, until yesterday, I hadn't realized I could.

"She has the powers of a fire witch?" Cassandra asked.

Raye considered me. "Healing? Check. Destruction of disease and illness? Check and check. What else?"

"The ancients considered a fire witch a djinn," Cassandra continued. "With fire in the veins instead of blood."

"I bleed." Though I'd rather not have to prove it.

"Probably not a literal interpretation," Cassandra said. "But you never can tell. A fire spirit also has the power to shape-shift into animals."

"I do not!" I protested.

"Maybe not yet," Raye put in. "I couldn't levitate until I met you. Heaven knows what we'll be able to do once we find our other sister."

I didn't mind healing people and animals. But turning from one to the other? Not a fan.

From the way Edward was stroking his rifle and staring at me, he wasn't either. The man was spooky squared.

"Shape-shifting might explain Pru's present form." Raye's gaze flicked to Henry's corner, and she tilted her head. "Or not. He says that Pru could call wolves, control them, but she wasn't one of them."

"At least not then," I said.

"She's not really one of them now. She can think like a human. She can communicate with you and with Henry. She's different and they know it. Wolves avoid her."

"Lonely," I observed. Pru couldn't hang out with the humans. They'd run, screaming, "Rabies!" And the wolves didn't want her around either.

"Henry says loneliness was a small price to pay to keep their children safe."

I saw again the pyre flaring to the sky and the empty stake left behind. "Loneliness wasn't the only cost."

Silence descended. The FBI agent stood. "I need to get the ring to Elise."

"I will take it." Edward held out his hand, and Franklin placed a plastic evidence bag into it.

"I'm not an expert," I said, "but isn't the FBI going to throw a hissy fit if you give evidence to just anyone?"

When the old man's eyes narrowed on me again, I wished I'd kept my mouth shut.

"Edward isn't just anyone," Franklin answered. "The Jäger-Suchers have been secretly funded by the U.S. government for decades."

If it was such a secret I had to wonder why he was telling me. I decided not to ask in case the realization that he had might require Edward to kill me, or at the least cut out my tongue. He seemed capable of it.

"Besides," Franklin continued. "The Jäger-Sucher lab has equipment the FBI isn't even aware of yet."

"How'd that happen?"

"Ask him." Franklin pointed at Edward, who was already striding for the door.

"I'll take your word for it."

"My wife, Elise, is in charge of the lab. She's a virologist by trade, but she's the most brilliant woman I've ever met."

"She hasn't cured herself yet," Edward said, and slammed the door behind him.

"What's he so mad about?" I asked.

"Elise is his granddaughter," Franklin said.

"What's wrong with her?"

"Nothing," Franklin snapped, at the same time Cassandra said, "Werewolf."

"The greatest werewolf hunter of all time has a granddaughter who is one?"

"Life's just full of little ironies, isn't it?" Cassandra murmured.

Chapter 24

I sensed a long story there, but I didn't have the time. If I didn't get back to Owen soon, with coffee, he was going to start searching for me. I didn't want to explain . . .

I glanced around the motel room.

Any of this.

"Where do we go from here?" I asked.

"We'll see if we can get info on a coven, witches, or an altar in the area." Franklin indicated himself and the voodoo priestess. "Between the two of us we should be able to uncover something."

"I hope before someone else dies," Cassandra said.

"I need to go." I moved toward the door, and Raye followed, stopping me with a hand on my arm.

"Watch yourself."

"Mistress June is going to be pretty easy to spot."

"There's more than one killer," Bobby said. "Again."

"You sure?"

"The animals." He lifted one shoulder, the movement both smooth and slightly foreign. "They're the work of an amateur."

"Practice," I murmured.

"Oui," he agreed, and my gaze flicked to Raye's.

Her lips quirked and while she didn't say anything, I

could almost hear her thoughts. *How could I resist a man who speaks French?*

It would be pretty damn hard.

"Mistress June is a pro," Bobby continued.

"Therefore the animal sacrifices were practice and that equals two killers."

"At least," Raye agreed.

"I'll be careful." I opened the door.

Owen stood on the other side.

Owen had awoken when what he thought was Becca's fingernails scratched his chest. He'd reached for her and gotten a fistful of Grenade instead.

He sat up, the kitten tumbled off, Reggie *woofed*, and the two of them started running around the cabin.

Owen rubbed his eyes. He was used to waking up much earlier, with a lot more noise. Real grenades going off in a completely different way for instance. Yet still he had a headache.

"Becca?"

No answer. A trickle of unease had him inching to the edge of the bed and calling her name again a little louder.

She'd probably had an emergency or an appointment. Except he hadn't heard her phone, hadn't heard her leave. Which made the unease deepen for more reasons than one.

A few months out of the field and he slept right through noises and movement? If he'd been in Afghanistan he'd be dead.

Owen put on some pants and stepped onto the porch.

Reggie nosed the kitten back inside when she would have followed. Owen shut the door.

"What's your excuse?" he asked, but the dog trotted into the high grass at the edge of the lake. At this rate, they were both going to have to do some retraining before they returned to work.

Owen's hand fell to his thigh, rubbed where the stiff morning ache usually lived. It was faint today. Amazingly so.

His gaze zeroed in on Carstairs Avenue. From here he couldn't tell if Becca was at the clinic or not. She could have walked back since he'd driven—

His eyes narrowed on the empty space where his rental had been. "Huh."

Reggie smacked his head against the door. Grenade mewed from the other side, and the dog started barking.

"Shh." Owen opened it, and the two tumbled across the floor like puppies. He hadn't seen Reggie behave like this . . . ever. Work was play, hence his reward of the rubber ball whenever he found what he was sent to find. Since they'd been here, Owen had used the ball so little, he wasn't sure exactly where it was.

As he pulled the spare from his duffel and shoved it in his pocket, he caught sight of a piece of paper where one hadn't been last night, and crossed the room, read Becca's note, then glanced at the clock. Eight A.M.

The time meant nothing, as he'd no idea when she'd left. He retrieved his phone, texted her, waited. Waited some more. Gave the animals some water, a little food. Checked his phone, peered out the window. Twitched. Twitched again.

Finally he put on shirt and shoes, grabbed Reggie's

leash, snapped it onto the dog's collar, and they left. It didn't take long to find her. Finding things was what both he and Reggie did best.

The pickup sat in front of the coffee shop like a blazing white flag. However, he could see through the windows that she wasn't inside. Which made Owen all kinds of nervous.

A car backed up next to him, and the uninterested glance he threw at the driver suddenly became very interested when Owen recognized the wolf hunter he'd last seen in the bar.

Owen lifted a hand, shouted, "Hey!" but the guy pulled onto the highway and accelerated. Within seconds, his taillights were specks at the outskirts of town.

Where was Chief Deb when you needed her?

Owen had just pulled out his phone, thinking he would call Becca over and over until she either answered, or he heard her cell ringing and ringing from wherever she lay unconscious, when Reggie tugged on the leash and practically dragged him to one of the motel room doors, where he promptly sat and stared at the doorknob.

As if his stare was magic, the knob turned, the door opened, and there she was—along with a bunch of people Owen had never seen before.

For an instant Owen thought she might slam the door in his face. But Reggie barked and bounded inside. She patted his head, then murmured, "You too."

"I . . . uh . . ." The woman who'd said she was Becca's sister—maybe Owen did know one person in the room—glanced at Becca helplessly.

"I'll be in touch," Becca said, and began to leave.

"Nuh-uh." Owen crowded her into the room. Inside

he counted two men and another woman. Strangers all, but since the guys both carried concealed, Owen meant to discover who they were.

He held out his hand to the nearest, a slim, dark-haired, blue-eyed man who'd stepped in front of Raye the instant Owen entered the room. "Owen McAllister."

The guy didn't hesitate to shake, which calmed Owen a bit. "Bobby Doucet. I'm Raye's fiancé."

The second man, also blue eyed with dark hair, though his held flakes of gray, wore a suit that screamed fed. He confirmed it with, "Agent Nic Franklin, FBI." He even showed his badge.

"That explains your weapon." Owen glanced at Bobby. "How about yours?"

"I'm the police chief in New Bergin."

He might be lying, but why?

Owen's gaze flicked to the tiny woman with the white streak in her short dark hair.

"My associate, Cassandra," Agent Franklin said.

"Just Cassandra?"

"There aren't too many out there, but my last name's Murphy these days."

What did that mean? Owen decided to let the question go in favor of a better one. "What's going on here?"

They all exchanged glances; no one answered.

"I just saw the creepy wolf-hunter guy leaving." He glanced at each of them in turn. "Did he shoot Pru?"

Raye blinked at the name, cast a quick glance at Becca, whose tiny shake of the head made him both mad and sad. What was she hiding? Why was she hiding it from him?

Owen crossed his arms and leaned against the door.

Reggie, ever alert to his moods, left Becca—who'd been scratching his ears in just the right way—to stand at his side.

"Someone better start talking," he said.

No one did.

There were ways to make people talk. But he probably shouldn't especially with the FBI and a police chief in the room.

"So, your mom's the local witch?" the FBI agent asked.

Owen didn't answer. When he'd said someone should start talking he hadn't meant they should ask *him* questions.

"Smooth," Cassandra murmured.

Franklin shrugged. "We need a lead. Something. Anything."

"His mom isn't a witch," Becca said.

"But she did try to kill someone."

"Wasn't the first time," Owen said.

"That's right." The fed glanced at Becca then back at Owen. "You ever figure out why she tried to kill you?"

"No," Owen said shortly. He hadn't really tried. Talking to his mom back then had usually yielded gibberish. Not much had changed since.

"I'm sorry—" Becca began, and he shook his head.

"It isn't a secret." Though he wished it was. "He could have found that out pretty easily just by asking around town."

"I told you, Owen's mom isn't well," Becca said.

"She was well enough to escape from a psychiatric facility, then try and kill . . ." Franklin's lips pursed. "What was his name?"

"Dr. Jeremy Reitman," Becca said.

"Pet detective," Owen muttered, and Cassandra snorted. "Shouldn't you be more worried about the woman who *did* kill someone rather than the one who only tried?"

"If at first you don't succeed," the fed singsonged.

"You think she'll try again?"

"Why wouldn't she?"

"If my mom wanted to kill a witch, why didn't she kill Peggy when she had the chance?"

"You're saying she wanted to kill Dr. Reitman in particular?"

"Who wouldn't?" Franklin lifted an eyebrow and Owen shrugged. "He's a pretentious ass."

"Stop holding back," Cassandra said. "Tell us how you really feel."

Owen liked her more by the minute.

"Jeremy didn't have to drive all the way up here to help us out," Becca protested.

"He didn't drive here to help us. He drove here to see you."

She blinked. "Huh?"

"He's got the hots for you."

"Takes one to know one," Cassandra said.

Owen shrugged. He didn't care who knew it. Not any more.

"That's cra—" Becca snapped her mouth shut. "Sorry."

If Owen took offense every time someone used the word *crazy* he'd spend most of his life pissed off.

"Where would your mom hide?" Franklin asked. "A place where they both could."

"Both?" Owen repeated.

"Her and Mistress June."

Owen shook his head. "I don't think so."

"Mistress June killed your mother's keeper, and now they're both gone."

"Mistress June killed Peggy because she thought she was a witch, not to . . ." He made quotation marks in the air with his fingers. "Free Mary."

"She *thought* she was a witch?" Franklin repeated. "You know there *are* witches, right?"

"Are we talking broomsticks and warts witches? Or Wicca-practicing women?"

"And men." Bobby shrugged. "Reitman."

Owen bit back his opinion of Reitman and his witchery or lack of it. Now wasn't the time. "I don't know where my mom would hide, but I do know that she wouldn't take Mistress June with her."

"Because?"

"She called the woman 'bitch-whore' at first sight."

Cassandra's cough sounded like a laugh. "Sounds like they've met before."

"Doesn't it?" Franklin asked.

"Problem is, my mom also thinks she's a witch." Owen lifted his hands, lowered them. "Sometimes. Wouldn't Mistress June kill her too if she got the chance?"

"Probably."

"Therefore, I doubt they're hiding together." And if they had been, he was a lot more worried about his mom today than he'd been yesterday.

"I'd still feel better if we found either one of them," Franklin said.

"So would I."

"Does your mother have any friends she might go to?"

"She doesn't have any—" He paused. "Peggy said she made a friend in the facility recently who was as interested in witches as she was. Though I doubt my mother would run back to a place she just ran away from."

"Maybe she told this friend something that could help us." Franklin drew out his cell phone. "Who is she?"

"Peggy never gave me the woman's name."

And now Peggy was dead.

"I'll see what I can find out," Franklin said.

"Good luck with that," Owen murmured. Not only were there privacy issues he didn't think even the FBI could get around, but if this woman were in the same facility as his mom, he doubted she'd be coherent for questioning any more than his mom had ever been.

"So . . ." Owen rubbed his hands together. "You wanna go check on the wolf in your clinic?"

What he really wanted was to get Becca out of here. He was pretty sure he could find out more from her than from anyone in the room.

"Pru's gone."

"Gone how?" As she'd seemed well enough the night before, Owen didn't think "dead and gone."

"Ran off," Becca said.

He also hadn't thought she'd been well enough to be "long gone." Then again, what did he know?

"How much have you told him?" Franklin asked.

"Enough."

"Define *enough*," Owen said. "I know that Raye thinks they're sisters."

"Thinks?" Bobby asked. "Have you looked at them?"

"Fine," Owen admitted. "They're sisters. But what that has to do with the *Venatores Mali,* witches, and wolves is a mystery."

The room went silent.

"Maybe you two should go somewhere and talk," Bobby said.

Owen's gaze met Becca's, and he opened the door. "You read my mind."

As I started for the door, Raye caught my arm and whispered, "You need to tell him everything."

I *did* need to. I just didn't want to.

Owen, Reggie, and I climbed into the pickup. "Where to?" he asked.

"The clinic." Not only did I have work to do, but if this went badly—and how could it not?—I'd rather be in my own place, instead of having to walk back to it from the cottages. Have people pass me on the road, stop, and ask what the hell? That was just embarrassing.

Owen drove the short distance, waving at those who waved at us—quite a few. Townsfolk seemed genuinely happy to see him. I could tell it mystified him still.

The sight of the empty dog bed in the corner made my eyes burn and my throat thicken. Pru was fine. She was healed. But bizarre as it was to admit, she was my mother, and I wanted more time with her. Maybe once this was over, I'd get it.

Reggie trotted to the cushion and circled, then lay down. I started for the reception area. "I'll make coffee."

"I don't need coffee."

"I do." What I really needed was something to occupy

my hands, a way to stall while I figured out not only what to tell him but how.

Owen moved around the room, stopping in front of the pictures—photos Joaquin had taken of patients; the kid had a knack with a camera—shuffling magazines, straightening the furniture.

"Sit," I said. He was driving me bonkers.

"You first." I pressed the start button on the coffee-pot, turned, and ran right into him.

He caught my elbows. His hands were big and hard and warm—like him. I couldn't help myself. I leaned in, rested my cheek on his chest, felt his breath stir my hair. I never wanted to be without him again. But he needed to know the truth. All of it.

I straightened. He clung. I let him for just a minute, or maybe I let myself. Then I stepped back, and his hands fell away. I took the seat I'd wanted him to and spilled.

Sister triplets. Ghost-father Henry. Wolf-mom Pru. Scotland. Witchcraft. Time travel.

He took it pretty well. At least until I got to the part about me.

"Hold on." He'd been pouring himself coffee. He set the pot back where it had been with a sharp click, wrapped his hand around the mug, and turned. "You think you're one of these sisters who was sent through time?"

"You saw Raye, didn't you? We're identical. Or close enough."

"There's a better explanation for that than magic and time travel."

"If you have one, I'd be happy to listen."

He scowled. "You think you can hear the thoughts of animals?"

"I told you that when we were kids."

"When we were kids, I believed you."

"You don't now?"

"Becca." He let out a sharp breath. "Really?"

I was both annoyed—he didn't believe me?—and afraid. He didn't believe me!

"Reggie!" I called. A few seconds later Reggie appeared.

What?

Yeah, what?

"Ask me something that only Reggie would know."

"This is crazy."

"Ask me," I insisted.

"How would I know what he knows? *I* can't talk to him."

That had sounded more sarcastic than I cared for. If I couldn't prove that I could hear the animals, maybe I could prove my other talent.

"How do you think Pru was well enough to run out of here this morning?"

"She's a wild animal. They heal quicker than the wind blows."

They did. But not the way she had.

"Reggie's better," I said. "You're better."

"You think you did that?"

"I know I did."

"If you could heal me as good as new, why didn't you?"

I couldn't help it; I dropped my gaze.

"That's what I thought."

I lifted my eyes, thinking I'd see anger in his because he understood that I'd been selfish, that I'd stopped healing him last night because I didn't want him to go. Instead I saw pity, and it confused me. Until he spoke.

"Maybe we should talk to a professional about this."

"My mom and Raye are about as professional as it gets."

"I didn't mean that kind of professional." He sat in the chair next to mine, took my coffee mug, and set both it and his on the magazine table before he took my hand. "I know a lot of people who could help you, Becca."

The light dawned. "You think I'm crazy?"

Why did I sound so angry? Why wouldn't he?

"Listen to yourself." His fingers tightened around mine when I would have yanked away. "Your sister is an air witch. She can levitate. Move things. See ghosts."

"Ask her."

He didn't even respond to that. "And you think you can hear the thoughts of animals. That you can touch them, touch people, and make them whole."

"I can." I tugged on one hand, and he let it go. I set my palm over his injury. Energy snapped. Heat flared. "Let me heal you."

He stood, practically tripping over his feet to get away from me. I wanted to cry.

"If there's one thing I learned from my mother's insanity it's that I shouldn't buy into her delusion. I'm not going to buy into yours."

"Owen, I can heal you. You can g—" My voice broke.

After I healed him, he would leave. This time he might never return. But I couldn't be selfish. He and

Reggie had saved countless lives. Just as he'd let me go all those years ago so that I could have the life I'd dreamed of, I had to do the same now.

I got to my feet. Reggie stepped between us with a huff. His ruff lifted.

Splode.

I frowned. "What's going to explode?"

"Stop it!" Owen blurted, too loud, his voice broke.

Reggie woofed and crowded me back.

"I have to—" Owen yanked open the door. *"Hier."*

Reggie came, though he cast me an uneasy glance. He'd probably never seen Owen this upset. I hadn't.

My phone started ringing, so shrill I gasped and yanked it out of my pocket, hitting the mute without even a glimpse at the caller ID.

Owen closed the door. He never looked back.

Chapter 25

Owen had to get away. Not forever. Not even for long. But he needed to think. And when he could see Becca, hear her, smell her, touch her—or when she touched him—he couldn't.

He snapped Reggie's leash onto his collar, and the two of them began to walk. Without thought, Owen headed for the trees. He wanted to be alone. Or as alone as he got with Reggie, which was good enough. *He* couldn't hear the dog's thoughts.

The cool, calm, shadowed peace of the forest surrounded them. Owen liked it so much better than caves and sand.

"Who wouldn't?" he murmured, and suddenly . . .

He didn't want to go back.

Owen stopped dead on the path, and Reggie, nose down, sniffing at every swaying branch, kept going. He tugged the leash from Owen's hand—something that never happened when they were working unless Owen wanted it to—and he was gone. Owen didn't call him back. He was too caught up in this revelation, which wasn't much of a revelation at all.

He loved Becca. Always had, always would. No matter what.

Was she crazy? He didn't care. If she was, he'd help her. He was better equipped for that than anyone else.

"But what if she isn't?"

If she wasn't, he shouldn't have let her out of his sight.

Owen whistled. Reggie raced through the underbrush and leaped onto the path. It wasn't until they erupted into the parking lot that Owen realized something else.

He was running.

I stood in the waiting room, staring at the closed door. When my phone started vibrating in my hand, I was glad. It gave me something to do.

"Hello?"

"Becca! Thank God."

I hadn't looked at the caller ID this time either. Didn't matter. I knew that voice.

"I found something," Jeremy Reitman said.

The fog that had descended since Owen had left lifted a little. "What?"

"I have to show you. You aren't going to believe it."

Driving to Madison would take five hours, then I'd have to drive back. Wasn't happening.

"I have appointments today."

"This won't take long. I'm nearly there."

"Three Harbors?"

"I need you to meet me."

I was so glad I wasn't going to have to drive forever, then drive back—not to mention miss my appointments, reschedule them—that I said, "Sure."

"There's a place called 'Revelation Point.' You know it?"

Revelation Point was make-out central for all the surrounding areas. Located on the bluffs of Lake Superior, the area had a terrific view. Not that anyone spent time contemplating it.

I hadn't been there since high school. Hadn't had any reason to be. Not only had the idea of making out with anyone but Owen bored me, but I was no longer seventeen.

Thank God.

"I know it," I said.

"Hurry."

The line went dead.

As I had nothing better to do than brood about Owen, I got in my car and hurried.

Owen's palm curled around the knob on the clinic's back door. He twisted as he moved forward, smacking into the ancient wood with all of his exuberant momentum when he discovered it was locked.

The door made a nasty crunching sound and popped open. Owen stood there for a second, flummoxed. Breaking down doors was never that easy in Afghanistan.

Reggie bopped his nose against the wood and went in.

"Becca?" Owen followed. "I'm sorry about the—"

Reggie began to howl.

Terrified at what he'd find, Owen hurried toward the sound. Only to find the dog alone in the middle of the waiting room. A quick tour of the rest of the building, upstairs and down, revealed it empty.

Owen glanced out the back door. Her car was gone. If he hadn't been so determined to find her he would have noticed, and saved her a door.

"Dude." Joaquin stepped inside. "Was it like that when you got here?"

"It was an accident."

The kid snorted. Owen *had* sounded like a five-year-old after he'd broken Mom's favorite vase.

"Shouldn't you be in school?"

"Why does everyone keep asking me that?"

"Who else asked you?"

"Doc Becca."

"You saw her? When?"

"Early this morning." Joaquin frowned. "Isn't she here?" He walked through the exam room and into the office/waiting area. Owen followed. "We have office hours soon."

The unease Owen had been feeling since he'd returned intensified. Becca wouldn't miss her appointments.

He pulled out his phone, dialed her number, got voice mail. He almost disconnected without leaving a message. What could he say?

I'm an ass.

He figured she knew that already. In the end he made do with a short, "Call me," and hung up.

Joaquin appeared as concerned as Owen. "Should I cancel her appointments?"

Reggie blew air out his nose the way he always did when he was excited, revved, ready for a mission. Owen turned.

The wolf was back.

Reggie licked her face. She rolled her eyes, the amused disgust in the mannerism as human as her green gaze. Then she spun and ran out the still open door, pausing just outside to look back.

"You see it, right?" Joaquin stood at Owen's side.

"The wolf? Yeah."

"Look at her wound."

Her stance gave Owen a perfect view of her shaved flank. The wound that had nearly killed her was gone.

"How does that happen?" Joaquin asked. "Becca said wild animals heal fast, but that's ridiculous."

Owen didn't have the time to explain magic, even if he could. Then the wolf yipped—high, impatient—and Reggie rushed to join her. The two disappeared from view and Owen bolted after them. By the time he caught up, they were trotting down the sidewalk.

"Hell," Owen muttered, as locals and tourists did double takes, then scrambled out of the way.

"It's okay," he called. "She's tame. Not a threat."

He wasn't certain how true that was, but he didn't need anyone playing the hero, trying to grab either Pru or Reggie. Pru would probably be better behaved about it than Reggie would be.

"What's going on?" Joaquin had followed him outside.

"You need to stay here," Owen said.

"Not."

"The door's broken. Anyone could get in. Besides, I think you *are* going to have to cancel Becca's appointments."

The wolf had seemed agitated. That couldn't be good.

"I don't—"

"Becca would expect you to do your job," Owen said.

She would also expect Owen not to bring along a fifteen-year-old kid in his search for her. Considering all that had happened since Owen had gotten home, he doubted what was to come would be anything short of dangerous.

"I'll call you when I know something." Owen hurried after Reggie and Pru.

The townsfolk, who had parted like the Red Sea at the sight of the dog and the wolf, flowed back together like the ocean. Owen had to take to the street to keep up. At least everyone was keeping their distance and not following them.

A flash of metal to his right drew Owen's gaze as a man stepped out of the hardware store with a rifle. He sighted on Pru. Owen snatched it out of the guy's hands.

"Hey!" The fellow—someone Owen didn't know—tried to snatch it back. "There's something wrong with that wolf."

"I'll take care of it," Owen said.

"The wolf or my gun?"

"Yes."

Picking up speed, Pru left Carstairs Avenue. She wasn't a fool. Best to get where they needed to go before someone else appeared with a firearm.

Like Chief Deb. Where had she gotten to? Owen hadn't seen her since the incident on Route GG.

Ahead lay the coffee shop/motel. The wolf trotted right up to the same room Owen had been in that morning, bopped her head against it—once, twice. When it opened she went in.

Reggie glanced back, saw that Owen was close, and went in too.

For probably the fiftieth time since I'd bought my Bronco I was so glad that I had. What had once been a shitty, gravel road leading to Revelation Point was now a shitty, rock-strewn, overgrown dirt path leading to the same. Apparently kids no longer came here to smooch. Had to wonder why.

It wasn't until I shot out of the trees and put the vehicle into park that it occurred to me to call someone and tell them where I was. By then it was too late. My phone read *no service*. Maybe I could borrow Jeremy's. Different carriers covered different areas, and his might work.

As if the thought had conjured him, his Jaguar emerged from the forest and stopped behind mine. He had to have scratched the undercarriage badly on that trail. Weeds clogged the wheel wells and pine needles stuck in pine tar all over the hood. He must have something pretty damn important to show me.

I wondered for an instant why he didn't pull his car next to mine instead of behind it, but then he got out, all smiles, and I forgot.

Jeremy wore perfectly pressed charcoal-gray trousers and a red Polo shirt. I had an instant to think that he should have brought a coat—it was chilly enough up here on the ridge above the lake that I was thankful for my own—before he enveloped me in a hug. "Thanks for coming."

"No problem." My hands slid down his arms.

Electricity flared. Sparks flew, reminding me of the last time I'd touched his arm, in the parking lot after someone had tried to smother me.

My gaze fell to his forearms, both scratched badly— one worse than the other, but healing even as I watched. The really strange thing—and that was saying something—was that the scrapes matched my fingers. As if I had raked my hands down his arms and—

I had raked my hands down his arms. Then I'd touched one arm and it had healed just enough to make it seem like he hadn't tried to kill me. But he had.

Jeremy caught my wrists as I drew back, capturing me, holding on tight.

"It was you," I said. "In my apartment, with the pillow. The ring. The ski mask."

He didn't speak. He didn't have to. Owen had been right.

I yanked free. "Why?"

"Witches must die."

"But . . . you're a witch."

"I only pretended to be one to discover their identities."

"Being a witch is that big of a secret?" I asked.

I had to figure out what to do. Behind me lay a cliff, the drop straight to the rocky shores of Lake Superior. Jeremy stood between me and my car. The forest was an option, but I'd have to disable him first. He was fast. Much faster than me.

"The identities of the elemental witches, the ones with true power and real magic, like you, are a secret. It's those witches we need to kill. They're dangerous."

He was dangerous. But I didn't mention it.

"You mean to tell me no witches but elementals have been harmed?" I asked.

He shrugged. "I'm sure a few pretenders have died along the way."

His casual dismissal of lives chilled me.

"What makes you hate them"—hate *us*?—"so much?"

"I don't hate you, Becca." He shook his head, his

expression that of a professor admonishing a dumbass student. He'd no doubt used it a hundred and one times before. "But I do need to kill you."

I could tell he believed it, was, in fact, looking forward to it. How had I missed the crazy before? Or had he become crazy only recently?

"Roland speaks to me. In my dreams, my mind."

Recently then. He couldn't have hidden that for very long.

I needed to keep him talking, maybe talk him out of this. I had a pretty good idea how.

"If you've been chatting with McHugh, you know he wants to kill me and my sister."

"Sisters," he corrected.

He *had* been talking to McHugh, or reading *Venatores Mali* propaganda.

"He wants to wipe out our line. He won't be happy if you beat him to it."

"He doesn't care who kills you, he just wants you dead."

"Swell."

"I need a sacrifice to bring him forth. The one who raises him will stand at his side."

"Whoop-dee-doo," I muttered.

"A man who can return from the dead is a very powerful man indeed. There'll be no stopping him."

"If Roland could return, he would have. That he needs help—your help—means you have the power, not him."

He blinked. Maybe I shouldn't have told him that.

"I still have to raise him," Jeremy said. "He insists."

"You should probably talk to someone about that voice in your head."

Jeremy reached into his pocket, took out his keys, popped the trunk. Then he reached inside and withdrew a two-sided knife, the blade a distinctive S shape. I'd never seen it before, yet still I knew it.

The athame of Roland McHugh

"I wonder if I can brand you with this." He frowned at the head of a snarling wolf carved into the handle. "It'll have to do. You took my ring."

He backhanded me with no more emotion than swatting a fly. My cheek seemed to explode. I bit my tongue and tasted blood.

I wished for Raye's abilities. Levitation and telekinesis—either one would be handy right now. Toss the knife over the cliff—oh, what the hell, let's just toss the knife *and* its holder too—or lift myself high enough to kick him in the face.

In the distance thunder stirred; the wind picked up, bringing with it the scent of rain. Strange. On the drive here there hadn't been a cloud in the sky.

"Where'd you get that?" I had to keep stalling.

"She gave it to me." He pointed into the trunk.

A dead woman lay within. Her brown hair was wrapped around her neck a few times, but the ends brushed her breasts. Between them a stain the shade of mahogany bloomed on her once white shirt. She was a big girl. She barely fit inside.

I'd only seen her once before, and under vastly different circumstances—she'd been alive—yet still I knew her.

"Mistress June."

"Now *I* have the most witch kills," Jeremy said, and slammed the trunk.

Chapter 26

Raye appeared in the doorway of the motel. She frowned at the rifle in Owen's hand. "Where's Becca?"

Owen's gaze swept the cars in the lot, recognizing none of them. "I was hoping she was here."

Worry cast over Raye's face, and she beckoned him inside. Everyone who'd been there earlier remained.

"No one's heard from her?" Owen asked.

"Not since she left with you," Raye said.

"Her car's gone, and there wasn't any sign of a struggle."

"You left her?"

Owen had no excuse. He just nodded.

Fury sparked in Raye's eyes. Her fingers twitched. Owen took a step back, even though he hadn't meant to. Bobby took Raye's hand. "Won't help."

"I'll feel better." Her gaze remained on Owen.

"We need him. Conscious."

She gave a sharp nod. Owen had the feeling he'd just avoided grave bodily injury, and he'd have deserved it.

The fed took the rifle from Owen and set it in the corner of the room. Probably a good idea, though Owen missed the weight of it.

He needed to focus. Becca was gone. Pru was here.

Why? His gaze went to the wolf, which stared at Raye as if she were trying to communicate through osmosis.

"I'm not the dog whisperer," Raye muttered.

"Not a dog," Bobby pointed out.

"Henry!" Raye shouted.

Everyone waited.

"Anything?" Bobby asked, and she shook her head.

"I could do a spell to bring him here," she began, and Pru snarled. "Calm down. I won't."

"Why not?" Owen demanded. "Wouldn't he know where Becca was, if she were in trouble?"

"He might," Raye said. "Henry's attached to me because we share the ability to speak with ghosts. Pru's attached to Becca because of their shared affinity with animals."

"Then why is she here when Becca isn't?"

"Pru's not a supernatural wolf."

"She isn't a natural wolf either."

Case in point. She was sitting in a motel room with five people and a dog.

"True," Raye agreed. "But she can't morph in and out."

"Like Henry."

"Right."

"Get him to morph in," Owen ordered.

"Henry comes when I call if he can. If he doesn't that means he's involved elsewhere. For all I know he might be saving Becca's life. If I do a spell that drags him here then . . ." She spread her hands. "Bad things happen."

"So we do nothing?"

The unnatural sensation of helplessness nagged at Owen. In Afghanistan he always knew what to do. He was the guy who did it. He saved lives. He had a plan. He was the man. Or at least Reggie was. Unfortunately, as talented as the dog was at finding people and things, he wasn't going to be able to find a Bronco the way he found an insurgent.

Pru got to her feet, her gaze on an empty corner. Reggie growled in that direction.

"Henry," Raye said. "Thank God. We can't find Becca."

She listened. Pru glanced over her shoulder, a worried expression in her green, human eyes.

"What is it?" Owen asked.

"He can't find her either. He was looking, trying, which was why he didn't come."

"How can—"

Raye held up her hand, and Owen fell silent. "The only way to keep him from finding her would be to ward the place where she is."

"Why would she do that?"

"She wouldn't," Raye said. "She couldn't. Becca only discovered who she was yesterday."

"It's not that hard to ward against ghosts," Bobby said. "Rosemary does the trick just fine."

Owen cast him a glance. How did he know that?

The man lifted his chin toward the invisible Henry. "There are some things a father shouldn't see."

He had a point, and the idea that Becca's real father might have seen even more than her adopted—or whatever Dale was—father made Owen cringe.

"Rosemary," Owen repeated. "Thanks." He put buying some on his mental to-do list.

"Have you come to the dark side?" Cassandra asked. "You believe?"

Owen wasn't sure when, or how, or why that had happened—beyond Becca's needing him to—but . . .

"Yeah," he said. "I do."

"If it weren't for the warding, I'd think Becca had gone on a call, visited a friend or family, or gone shopping," Franklin said. "But for her location to be deliberately shielded, and not by her, indicates she's been taken."

Owen's heart seemed to stop, then start again with a painful jolt.

"All right," Raye said, but she wasn't talking to any of them, she was talking to Henry. She faced the room. "I need to scry for her location."

"You know how?" Bobby asked.

"No." Her gaze met Cassandra's. "But I bet you do."

"Why would an FBI consultant know how to scry?" Owen asked. He wasn't even sure he knew what scrying was.

"Voodoo priestess," Cassandra said.

"Excellent." The more magic, the better. Anything to find, save, protect Becca.

Anything.

The storm was heating up. Wind, thunder, lightning. The lake roiled like a cauldron. Becca could smell distant rain.

Jeremy produced a few zip ties from his fancy pants. "Hands."

"Fuck you."

He sliced my wrist with the athame. The way the blood sprayed, he'd hit a vein. I slapped my free hand onto the wound. Sparks flew. I steeled myself against the sickening lurch in my stomach as flesh knit together. Jeremy wrapped the zip tie around my wrists and pulled.

He was damn quick for an asshole.

He grabbed the front of my shirt with one hand, then lifted the other in front of my face and opened his fist. Green flecks that smelled pleasantly of an herb I couldn't place sprinkled against my skin, catching in my bra, sifting across my stomach, and gathering where I'd tucked in my shirt.

"What the hell?" I asked, but he just smiled.

When he bent to bind my ankles, I kneed him in the chin. His teeth clicked together. As he fell backward, he stabbed the athame into my thigh. From the spread of the blood on my jeans, he'd nicked my femoral artery. He was so good at this I knew he'd done it before—many times.

I reached for the athame with bloody fingers. If I wanted to heal the wound the blade had to come out. The instant I touched the handle, lightning fell from the sky, so close every hair on my body seemed to sizzle.

Had I done that? I didn't think so. If I'd brought the lightning, I'd have brought it down on him.

Blood dripped off Jeremy's chin. He lurched to his feet, and I jabbed at him with the knife. He kicked it, and my hands were so slick, the weapon flew.

While he chased the thing, I ran, staggered, then slid in the blood spreading out from my feet like a pool. I wasn't thinking clearly, probably from blood loss. Running wasn't an option until I healed myself. If I didn't do it soon I might bleed out.

I slapped my palm over the wound, gritting my teeth as it came together with a sickening slurp.

Jeremy's arm went around my neck; the knife pricked my skin. "Try anything else and I'll slit your throat. I only need to sacrifice a witch. It doesn't have to be you."

I stilled. He could keep cutting me; I could keep healing myself. But eventually I'd be too weak to move. I needed to quit while I still had enough blood left to fill my head so I could think. What else did Jeremy need to raise Roland?

Sacrifice of a witch by a *Venatores Mali* with the most kills. Chants of the worthy believers. Plural. Right now there was only him. Wasn't there something about the moon too? It was morning. Which meant I still had time.

He bound my arms to my sides with a bungee cord he'd pulled from somewhere then shoved me toward the cliff. I was half afraid he meant to throw me off. But a few feet from the drop he grabbed my collar. Was he afraid I'd jump?

I should have jumped! Except I wasn't ready to throw in the towel—or my life—quite yet.

"Lie on the stone." He poked me with the athame. Blood trickled between my shoulder blades.

"What st—"

Then I saw it. Right at the edge of the world, camouflaged by the roiling pewter sky and long summer grass, lay a long, flat, smooth gray rock. A perfect natural altar.

He poked me again, and I did as I was told. Rain spat in my face as he looped a zip tie around my ankles and pulled. Then he stepped back, took out his cell phone, scowled.

"No service?" I murmured. Welcome to my world. "Bummer. How will you summon worthy believers?"

Jeremy's head lifted; his gaze turned toward the trees. Tires crunched on stone. Seconds later a Three Harbors PD cruiser appeared. Chief Deb climbed out.

I had no idea how she'd come to be here, but I was so glad she was. Jeremy was armed, but so was Deb, and as in every action movie from now until the end of the world—gun beat knife. All the time.

Then my gaze lit on Jeremy, and my hope wavered. Why was he smiling?

Cassandra opened her bag and withdrew a chunk of black stone.

"What's that?" Owen asked.

"Black obsidian." She took out a white candle.

"You carry around scrying materials?" the fed asked.

Owen was impressed Franklin knew what they were. It made him wonder what else the guy knew.

"Never can tell."

"Tell what?" Owen wondered.

"Exactly."

Cassandra moved to the table, set the stone in the center. The overhead lights sparked against the obsidian like stars. She flicked them off.

"Can't have anything reflected in the stone but what we want to see." She motioned Raye into the chair on one side of the table then took the other. After setting the candle next to the stone, she lit it, then held out her hands. Raye took them.

"Close your eyes, and think of your sister. In a few minutes, we'll open our eyes, look into the stone's center."

"And then?" Raye asked.

"Then we'll see what we'll see."

"What about us?" Owen asked.

"Maybe you'll see too."

Cassandra and Raye closed their eyes. Bobby, Franklin, and Owen stood in a semicircle around the table, no doubt feeling as foolish as they appeared.

Owen closed his eyes and thought of Becca. Couldn't hurt. Unfortunately all he saw was the inside of his eyelids.

Raye gasped, and Owen's eyes snapped open. In the depths of the obsidian, smoke swirled. He leaned in. The mist cleared, leaving behind nothing but a blank, black stone.

"What did you see?" Cassandra asked.

"Nothing." Raye lifted her gaze. "But I did hear wolves."

"Really?"

"Didn't you?"

Cassandra shook her head, then chewed her lip.

Owen released his pent-up breath in a rush. "What are we going to do now? Henry can't find her. You couldn't see anything."

Cassandra held up a hand. "I didn't say that *I* didn't see anything."

"You did?"

She nodded.

"Where is she? How is she?"

"I didn't see Becca. But I did see a long, flat, raised stone."

"A natural altar." Raye had gone pale. "The perfect place for a sacrifice."

* * *

Deb started in our direction. "What's going on?"

"He—" I began.

Jeremy cut me. High up between my neck and collarbone—not an artery, not yet—but with my hands bound together and my arms tied down, I couldn't heal the gash. Blood dripped onto the stone.

Chief Deb had her gun out, but she wasn't pointing it at Jeremy, she was pointing it at the trees, which were shaking with the force of the storm.

"Who's there?" she shouted.

I could have sworn I heard the distant howl of a wolf, and for a minute I feared Pru would leap out. Bound like this, I wouldn't be able to heal her if she were shot. But when the sound died, I dismissed it as the wail of the wind.

Then Owen's mother emerged from the forest. She raced at Chief Deb, arm raised. The watery, gray light of the cloud-covered sun revealed a knife—plain old butcher—but it would . . . butcher.

"No!" I shouted.

Chief Deb was here to save me.

"Die, wi—!" Mary shrieked.

Boom!

Mary jerked. Blood blossomed on her shirt in almost the same pattern it had made on Mistress June's. The knife tumbled to the ground. Mary followed.

Chief Deb turned, gun still in her hands. I waited for her to shoot Jeremy. Instead, she put the gun back in her holster.

"About damn time you got here," Jeremy said.

Chapter 27

"Do you know where a stone like that might be located?" Franklin asked.

Owen shook his head. Panic threatened. Becca had been kidnapped. Cassandra had scried for her location and seen an altar. One and one equaled—

"Someone's going to sacrifice Becca to raise Roland McHugh."

When no one argued with him, Owen sat on the bed because his legs couldn't support him any more. Reggie laid his head on Owen's knee. Owen didn't have the energy to pet him and the dog whined, concerned.

"The wolves," Raye said.

"What about them?"

"I heard them when we scried for Becca's location, which makes me think they're near her. And they would be, because animals, especially wolves, are drawn to her."

"Go on," Franklin said.

"So far I share with Henry the ability to see, hear, communicate with ghosts, as well as his power of telekinesis. Becca, like Pru, has an affinity for animals. But Pru could also call the wolves." Her gaze went to the wolf, which already stood at the motel room door.

"Let her out," Owen said.

Cassandra, who was the closest, did. The instant Pru was outside, the long, lonely, chilling howl of a lone wolf lifted toward the sky. The faint outline of a moon occupied the horizon. Owen had always thought the days when both the moon and the sun were visible kind of creepy—as if they lived on a different planet altogether.

"I thought we had more time." Raye's gaze remained on the spooky daytime moon.

"What are you talking about?"

"Sacrifice of a witch by a *Venatores Mali* with the most kills, while the worthy believers chant, skyclad, beneath the moon. I thought that meant night." She pointed at the watery, silver orb. "But apparently not."

Owen's chest tightened. "We need to hurry."

Pru howled again. A moment later, what sounded like a dozen wolves, maybe more, maybe less, hard to tell, answered from a distance.

"How are we going to find them?" Owen asked.

Raye held up a hand as Pru howled a third time. When the wolves answered, they were a lot closer.

"We should probably head in their direction," Bobby said. "A pack of wolves running down the street is going to cause more trouble than we need right now and waste far too much time."

"Henry," Raye snapped. "Tell Pru to hold them at the edge of town."

The wolf loped in the direction of the woods at the opposite end of the street from Becca's clinic. Reggie took one step after her.

"Bly'b."

The dog glanced at Owen, then back at the figure of Pru in the distance. His expression was so melancholy

Owen would have been amused if it wasn't for . . . everything.

"She might be okay with you, pal, but her friends won't be." Reggie still belonged to the Marines. If Owen brought him back in several pieces there'd not only be hell to pay, but a lot of money. The dog was worth more than Owen was. *"Hier."*

Reggie came, but he wasn't happy about it.

Owen looked around for his pickup, then cursed when he remembered it was at the clinic, along with his Beretta. He glanced back at the motel room, missing the rifle he'd confiscated, and saw that Franklin had brought it along. Good man.

Owen flicked a finger at the cars in the lot. "Which one?"

Franklin headed for the dark sedan. Why had Owen even asked?

"I have a bigger car." Bobby pointed at a Suburban, which barely fit into a single parking space. Everyone piled in, including Reggie, and they trolled after Pru. The ghost would have to get there on his own.

"I wish Edward was still here." Franklin gave a half shrug at the incredulous glances thrown his way. "The guy's damn good in a fight."

"Problem is . . ." Cassandra jabbed a finger at the windshield. "It would be damn hard to keep him from fighting that."

Spread across the road that led from Three Harbors and into the woods were at least twenty wolves.

"Y-y-you," I managed. My teeth had begun to chatter, whether from shock over the blood loss, cold from the rain that now stung my face like icy needles, or the re-alization that Deb wasn't my savior, I had no idea. Didn't matter.

Chief Deb *was* one of them, and I was dead.

She ignored me. I hadn't really said anything worth answering.

"Let's get this over with," she ordered.

"Fine by me." Jeremy raised the knife again. "You know the chant?"

"I . . ." Deb's face creased. "You got a cheat sheet?"

"Amateur." Jeremy lowered the knife.

"It was you," I blurted. "The animals. You were prac-ticing."

Deb shrugged.

"Why did you come to me about the ones that were missing if you took them?"

"Figured someone would ask you sooner or later and it would seem suspicious if I hadn't done something about it before that."

I *had* wondered why it had taken her so long. Hadn't considered she was the one doing the grab and gut. Why would I?

"I didn't think you'd find them. Of all the people in this town to go anywhere near the McAllister place, you were the one I'd bet the farm wouldn't."

She had a point.

"Like I said," Jeremy repeated. "Amateur."

"If you hadn't tried to kill her right in the middle of town, we wouldn't be in this mess," Deb snapped. "I messed up the crime scene as much as I could, but sheesh. Wearing a ski mask? Why not just wear an 'I am a serial killer' sign?"

"Fuck you," Jeremy said. "I saved your ass. Why would you keep your practice kills around? You should have tossed them in the lake. I did."

"You disposed of evidence?" I asked.

Jeremy rolled his eyes. "You think she's gonna arrest me? She works for me."

Deb made a soft sound of derision, and Jeremy's eyes narrowed. "I've killed a dozen witches. What have you done?"

"I just killed one now, didn't I?" Deb pointed at Owen's mom.

"She isn't really a witch," I said.

"She thinks she's one." Deb glanced at Jeremy. "Doesn't that count?"

"No."

"She meant to say 'die, witch hunter,'" I murmured. "Not 'die, witch.'"

Both times she'd been interrupted—tackled by George, shot by Deb.

"There you go." Jeremy withdrew a small notebook from a back pocket, flipped it open, and handed it to Deb. "I figured you'd be worthless. Read that."

"What language is this?"

"Latin."

"I don't speak Latin."

"You don't need to. Just read along. Try to keep up."

He slashed my neck again. From the sharp pain and the incredible head rush, the wound was deeper than the last one.

Jeremy drew his shirt over his head, shucked his pants and everything else. He lifted an eyebrow at Chief Deb. "Skyclad."

She sighed, but she got naked too.

"Skyclad beneath the moon," I said. "You gonna stand around until it rises?"

He lifted his gaze to the stormy sky. "Just because we can't see it, doesn't mean it isn't there."

He began to chant. Chief Deb joined in, lamely but gamely. I struggled against the zip ties. Foolish, since even if I got them off, I doubted that Jeremy or Deb—or his knife and her gun, which she'd kept in her hand even after she'd lost the uniform—would let me go. But I couldn't just lie there.

I was a witch. If I weren't, I wouldn't be here. I should be able to *do* something. But what? Talking to animals wasn't going to help. Neither would the laying on of hands. Not for the first time I wished for a more active—i.e., destructive—power.

In the air above me a face appeared. As if made from the air, or perhaps *behind* it, trying to get out.

I blinked. It was still there. In fact, it was *more* there, and I recognized it.

Roland McHugh was trying to push his way out from wherever he had been the last four hundred years.

Help! I scream-thought. *I'm at Revelation Point. Please come.*

I had no idea who I was talking to, but oddly . . . it felt right.

The wind, or the wolves, picked up again. They sounded closer. They sounded here.

Though I didn't want to take my eyes off Jeremy and his knife, nor the creepy Roland-face that expanded and retreated from the air above me, I had to see if I was right.

I turned my head just as the first wolf emerged from the trees.

They weren't two miles out of town when a storm descended. Wind and rain slammed into the vehicle. Thunder shook the earth. Lightning split the navy sky, tossing silvery sparkles across the herd of now drenched wolves.

"That's weird," Cassandra said.

"Storms come up." Franklin shrugged. "They gotta start somewhere."

She glanced out the back window. "Huh."

Everyone but Bobby, who was driving, followed her gaze. Behind them, the sun shone from a cloudless sky. In front of them, the moon played hide-and-seek with the storm.

"Henry," Raye said. "Knock it off."

"Henry's doing that?" Owen asked.

"He says no."

"But he could?" Owen clarified. "If he wanted to?"

"He has the power to influence the weather."

"But you can't?" Cassandra asked, and Raye shook her head. "Becca?"

"Not that I know of." Raye faced front. "If she isn't, our other sister must be doing it."

Bobby glanced at her then back at the road. "What does that mean?"

"No clue."

"Can we focus on one sister at a time?" Owen pointed ahead as the wolves turned in a graceful sweep onto a dirt road.

Bobby slowed to follow, then slowed even more and

switched the car into four-wheel drive to make it up the now-muddy incline.

"This is Revelation Point," Owen said. "Used to be make-out central."

"Why would the *Venatores Mali* come here?" Cassandra wondered. "Is there a rock altar?"

"Not that I remember, but—" He shrugged. "I wasn't looking for that the last time I was here."

The last time he'd been here he'd been looking for the unlock mechanism on Becca's bra. As he recalled, she'd ended up unlocking it for him.

The car shimmied and ground to a halt. Bobbie shifted into four-wheel low. The tires spun and he slammed it into park. "We can try and get unstuck."

Owen opened the door and stepped into the mud. "Or we can run."

He didn't wait for them to climb out; he took off on his own. The road was washed out. The trail led uphill. He slid backward nearly as much as he moved forward. Finally he stepped into the woods, where the trees had blocked some of the rain, and the leaves on the ground and the roots and the pine needles gave him some traction.

It seemed like an hour—but was probably only a few minutes—before he reached the edge of the trees and saw two people upright, one on the ground.

His chest tightened when he recognized Becca prostrate, loosened a bit as he identified Chief Deb, then contracted when he saw the athame in Reitman's hand. He and Deb were not only naked but chanting in a foreign language. That couldn't be good.

The wolves formed a semicircle, quivering as if waiting for an order, a signal, a treat. Then the earth shook, the heavens spilled lightning, and the storm stopped as quickly as it had begun. All seemed frozen, shrouded. Each living thing held its breath.

The others burst from the trees behind him. The wolves surged forward. Owen shouted, "Becca!"

Her gaze met his; her lips formed: *Owen*.

And the athame plunged into her chest.

Chapter 28

In the midst of the darkness there was light, and I went toward it. I was a step away from going into it when someone called my name.

The man who emerged from the gloom to stand with me at the edge of that light was dressed in black, hat to boot. His hair was dark; his eyes were too. I'd seen him once before.

"Henry," I said.

He had Raye's eyes. Or she had his.

"Mo leanabh," he murmured, his voice bringing to mind the misty lochs of a Scotland I'd never seen. Or maybe I had. "Don't go."

"I—" I turned toward that light, and in the darkness just to the right of it, something slithered.

Henry stepped in front of me as the shadow became a man.

"Roland," we both said at the same time.

"One down." McHugh's whisper seemed to swirl in the air, stir my hair, slide across my skin like a slug. "Two to go."

"I won't let you hurt them," Henry said.

"You won't be able to stop me any more now than you were able to then."

"Watch me," Henry said, and lunged.

*   *   *

Raye screamed, "Becca!" and swung her arm in a wide arc.

Jeremy Reitman flew over the edge of the cliff and disappeared. Unfortunately he left his athame buried in Becca's chest.

She wasn't moving. From here, she didn't appear to be breathing. But that couldn't be right. Owen wouldn't let it be.

He ran across the open grass. He didn't even notice, or maybe he just didn't care, that Chief Deb had whirled in their direction. She might be naked but she still held a gun.

He never knew if she was shooting at him or one of the others. The shot fired harmlessly at the sky as Pru plowed into her. Deb's fury was cut off mid-shriek. From the gurgly sounds that followed, Pru had torn out her throat. From the snarling and slavering, the other wolves were tearing other parts. All Owen cared about was Becca.

He reached her side. There was so much blood. More outside than in, it seemed, which might be why she was so still, ice white. At first he thought she stared at him, then he realized she merely stared.

"No." He grasped the curved knife, yanked it free, and shook her. Her head lolled.

He had to do something; he didn't know what. He couldn't heal—

Heal.

He used the athame to cut the bonds on her arms, her hands, then he grasped her wrist and placed her palm over the wound.

Nothing happened.

"Owen?" Raye stood at his side. At first he thought the rain had started again. Then he understood the drops on her face, on his, were tears. "She's gone."

"She can heal." His voice was desperate, but so was he. "We just have to give her a chance."

"She can't heal dead, Owen."

"How do you know? She's never tried."

"Exactly." Raye sounded as sad and hopeless as he felt, which was why he listened. "Powers require energy, life force, heat. She has none."

"There has to be a way," he insisted. "What good is magic if she's—" His voice broke.

Raye set her hand on his shoulder then shouted, "Cassandra!"

Both the priestess and the fed turned away from the wolves and what was left of Chief Deb. Owen had the presence of mind to look for Reggie and discovered the dog pressed against his leg like a leech. At least he wasn't snacking on the police chief.

"Good dog," he said.

"You know how to raise the dead." Raye pointed at Cassandra, who blinked then glanced at Franklin.

"I—uh—"

"We need her. Get her back."

"I couldn't even if I wanted to."

"Why wouldn't you want to?" Owen asked.

"Because to do so I'd have to be a shape-shifter, and that's just asking for a bullet to the head."

Owen had no idea what to say to that.

"Things happen for a reason," Cassandra began, but Owen interrupted.

"There's no reason for this beyond evil and asshole."

"He has a point," Franklin observed.

"It's impossible," Cassandra said gently. "I'm sorry."

Becca's hand had fallen off her wound, and Owen picked it up and held it there again. "Come on, baby, come on."

He could feel the others exchanging pitying glances, and he hated it, hated them, this, himself. Why had he left her? Then or now?

"Nice toss." Bobby peered over the edge of the cliff. "He's toast."

He returned to Raye's side and put his arm around her, tugged her close, and she laid her head on his shoulder. Owen lowered his gaze as his throat went thick with longing.

"Though I'm surprised Henry didn't get to it first."

"Me too," Raye agreed.

Owen's head lifted. "Henry can toss things?"

"Of course. I inherited my power from him."

"He's a ghost, but he still has his power."

"That's right, but I don't—" Raye stopped speaking. Her gaze flicked to Owen's, and her mouth made an O.

"You can summon ghosts?"

She nodded.

"Do it."

"Henry?" she called. Her gaze swept the clearing.

They waited, listening, though no one but Raye would hear him or see him.

"Well?" Bobby asked.

Raye shook her head. "I'll have to do a spell to summon him."

"What do you need?" Bobby asked.

"My things from the car."

Frustration flared. They'd left the damn car half a mile back.

"Here." Franklin tossed a bag. Bobby had to catch it or eat it. "I figured someone might need that."

"Always prepared," Cassandra said. "Is that the FBI motto?"

"Boy Scouts."

"Same thing."

Raye pulled black candles out of the bag, a bottle with a few green sticks inside. She dropped to the ground and held out her hand. "Knife."

Owen still had it. He slapped it into her palm like a scalpel. She dug a five-pointed star into the earth, set a candle at each tip, took one of the green sticks and placed it in the center then lit the wicks. She leaned in so close her breath fluttered the flames when she spoke.

"I call the spirit of Henry Taggart. Come in peace or not at all. As I will so mote it be."

Owen listened, looked—which was stupid because he wouldn't see him or hear him even if he did come. And while he'd insisted on doing this, he still didn't think it would work. How could it?

"I call the spirit of Henry Taggart," Raye repeated. "Come in peace or not at all. As I will so mote it be."

She continued to say the words over and over in a singsong rhythm until she swayed trancelike to their tune. Owen felt entranced himself.

"Not working," Bobby murmured.

Owen wished he could help. He'd do anything but he wasn't the one with the power. The only thing he knew about witchcraft was that rosemary kept away ghosts.

Shit.

"Rosemary," he blurted.

Raye's eyes opened. They were unfocused, seemingly elsewhere for a moment before she blinked. "Right. We couldn't see her. But saw this place. She was warded. That might be keeping Henry away too."

Owen tore open Becca's shirt, studiously avoiding the sight of the horrible wound that had killed her. Green flecks sprinkled her stomach and stuck in the blood.

"Water," he said in the voice of someone lost in a desert.

He peered around frantically—they had a lake and a lot of puddles, but no way to get the water from there to her.

"Here." Franklin tossed a plastic bottle of water, which he must have scrounged from one of the cars.

Owen caught it, opened it, poured it over her, rubbing away the blood and picking off the flecks until she was clean. No more blood pulsed from the wound. Why would it? She had no pulse.

"Hurry," he said.

Raye began to chant again. Owen began to whisper the chant too. He could have sworn he heard Bobby, Cassandra, and Franklin do so as well.

Please, he thought. *Please*.

The air stilled. Everyone caught their breath. Pru howled and the wolves joined in. Reggie sat on Owen's foot. Raye's eyes snapped open.

And the candles went out.

Henry grabbed McHugh by the throat.

"He's already dead," I said. "Not breathing. Can't strangle him."

"But it feels so good," Henry muttered.

The wind that wasn't, couldn't be, stirred my hair, and I caught the scent of flames. I didn't like it.

"Henry," I began, and then I saw McHugh's face. He was smiling.

The breeze picked up, so strong it made me step back. I heard chanting in the distance, but I couldn't make out what was being said.

The wind pulled harder, and I had to lean into it to reach Henry. I wrapped my fingers around his arm just as lightning flashed, thunder rumbled, and Roland McHugh began to laugh.

The next thing I knew I stood in the clearing at Revelation Point. Jeremy was gone. Chief Deb too. Pru and the wolves were here, though they were eating . . . a woman's arm.

That explained the absence of Deb.

The others were gathered in a semicircle around Raye, who was on her knees, bent over unlit candles.

"What's going on?" I asked.

Raye's head went up. Bobby Doucet stiffened, shifting his shoulders.

"Becca's here," Raye said, though she didn't turn my way.

"Where?" Owen asked. He didn't look so good.

I hurried over. Reggie yipped.

"Hush," I said to him, then touched Owen's hair. "What's wrong?"

He didn't answer, didn't seem to see me, and I turned to Raye. I caught a clue an instant before I caught sight of my dead self still on the rock.

"Fuck me."

"Nice," Raye said.

"I'm not a kindergarten teacher." I hadn't had to watch my language even when I'd been alive. "Why am I here?"

"I don't know. I summoned Henry." She waved at the candles, which were set on a pentagram carved into the dirt. I wished, and not for the first time, that I knew half as much as she did about witchcraft. Maybe then I wouldn't be dead.

"If I'd been thinking clearly I would have just summoned you."

"Why?"

"Physician heal thyself." Raye pointed to my body.

"Huh?"

"Remember when you were attacked and Henry tossed your attacker into a wall?"

"A little random there, Raye, but . . . yeah."

"Henry's a ghost. With powers. Now, you're a ghost."

"I still have my powers?"

"Why don't you try them and see?"

I didn't need to be told twice. I moved to my own side, got a freaky shimmy of déjà vu when I stared into my own eyes. I laid my palm on my bloody chest.

Nothing happened.

No spark. No sickening slurch of skin coming together. Nada.

I pulled back my hand. Raye stepped up next to me.

"Try it again."

I did, and understood. I couldn't touch things as a ghost. "I'm not . . ." I didn't know the word.

"Corporeal," Raye said.

"You would know. Now what? I need a body to heal my body."

"Too bad I don't have your—" She stopped. "Wait. Possess me."

"Not," I said at the same time Bobby blurted, "No, Raye," and Cassandra choked.

"Without you the three is two," she said. "Make that one since I have no clue where our other sister is. You think this is bad?" She waved a hand at dead me. "It's going to get worse if I'm all that's left between the *Venatores Mali* and the witches."

"You aren't all that's left. You have them." I lifted my chin toward the others.

"They don't have powers."

"Do too," Cassandra muttered.

"And so do Henry and Pru."

"That's worked out great so far. You're dead."

She had a point. Still—

"Possession, Raye?"

"It got a bad rap because of *The Exorcist*."

"Ya think?"

She closed her eyes. "Do it."

"Do what?" I had no idea how to possess someone.

She opened one eye. "I don't know. Jump?"

So I did.

Owen had been reluctant to breathe for fear he'd miss a single exchange between Raye and the ghost of Becca. Not that he could hear anything but Raye's responses, but as long as she was making them he knew that Becca was here.

He'd certainly come a long way from thinking they were all nuts. If they were, he was too. While once that would have terrified him, now he almost embraced it.

Without Becca he'd gladly consent to being locked away and medicated forever.

"Jump," Raye said, and Bobby reached for her, but an instant before his fingers touched her arm, she changed.

Not physically. Not really. But something in the air shifted, and then so did she.

Bobby snatched back his hand, then rubbed his fingers along his jeans as if they'd been burned.

Raye stood differently, like Becca, though Owen wasn't sure exactly how Becca stood. Maybe he was just hoping for this to work so badly. Her hair stirred, and in the depths of the dark strands, streaks of red waved.

"Raye?" Bobby said, and his voice shook. He saw it too.

She glanced over her shoulder and everyone gasped. Her eyes were much lighter, hazel instead of brown.

"It's all right." The voice that came out of her mouth was an echo—two voices not one. She turned back. "I know what to do."

She placed her palm on Becca's wound and sparks flew, so many more than there'd ever been before. Thunder rumbled over the lake, and clouds billowed on the horizon.

Owen whispered the word that had become his personal chant. "Please."

Then Becca sat up with a gasp that was more like a shriek, and Raye collapsed like a marionette without strings.

One second I was in Raye—I *was* Raye, and she was me, I knew things about her, saw things that had happened, felt what she had felt, knew what she knew—the next I was myself.

It hurt. I hurt. The world spun. I saw Raye fall, and I wanted to go to her, but the instant I moved, I had to put my head between my knees or pass out. Coming back from the dead was a little harder than it looked.

"Becca?"

I kept my cheek on my knee so my head wouldn't fall off my neck. Owen hovered just out of reach. I held out my hand, and he took it.

"You okay?"

The dizziness faded. Raye sat up. Bobby held her hand too. The others stood between us, uncertain.

My shirt was open. Someone had tried to wash away all the blood. Some remained, but I could clearly see that where the athame had been only a thick pink scar was visible.

"Close enough." I allowed Owen to help me up. He hovered nearby, hands out to catch me if I fell. I knew he always would. But I was good. I was fine. I was better than fine. I was here.

I kissed him. I planned to keep on kissing him until someone made me stop. He kissed me back the same way.

Someone cleared their throat. I ignored it until they did it again. We parted. From the corner of my eye I could see Bobby and Raye parting too.

"Don't ever do that again," Owen said.

"No problem."

"I've called in help." Franklin shoved his cell phone into his pocket then gazed at the wolves still gathered around what had once been a police chief. "The rest of you should clear out. I'll wait for the cleanup crew."

"Cleanup crew?" I repeated.

"The Jäger-Suchers have a whole division to make stuff like this go away," Cassandra said.

"What about Owen's mom?" Franklin asked.

"What about my mom?"

Everyone exchanged glances.

"He doesn't know?" I asked.

"Know?" Owen echoed.

I tightened my fingers around his. "Come with me."

Mary lay where she'd fallen, at the edge of the trees, the long, mossy grass all around. Considering what had been going on near the cliff, I understood why Owen hadn't seen her.

"I'm sorry."

He picked up the butcher knife that lay a few feet away from her outstretched hand.

"I think she was trying to save me. She was definitely trying to kill Deb."

Owen went to his knees and took her hand. "She never meant to kill a witch. She was after the witch hunters."

"I think so."

"She was on our side."

Our side. His. Mine. Us.

"Yes."

"Maybe she's finally at peace."

I hadn't seen her in that gloomy room. I'd like to believe she'd already gone into the light. Why wouldn't she? If Henry hadn't been there waiting for me, I would have.

"Raye?"

My sister, who had been whispering sweet nothings to her fiancé, looked up.

I indicated Mary. "Is she . . . around?"

Raye's gaze swept the clearing, then she shook her head. Owen's shoulders sagged, and I set my hand on one of them.

"Owen?" Franklin was there. "What do you want me to do about your mom?"

"What are my choices?"

"I could have her taken elsewhere and found, then you could move on from there with a service and burial."

"Or?"

"She could disappear."

Owen remained silent another moment, then he patted his mother's arm and stood. "Make her disappear."

"You're sure?" I asked. "What if you want a place to visit?"

"She wouldn't be there any more than she was here my whole life." He lifted a hand. "I know she couldn't help it. She was sick. But it'll be easier all around if she's just . . . gone."

"Got it." Franklin returned to the others, who waited near Bobby's car.

There was one more person here than there should be—a man all in black, with his hand on the head of the sleek dark wolf.

I could see Henry.

I hurried over, Owen in my wake, just in time to hear Henry demand, "What did you do?"

"I summoned you," Raye said. "But Becca came too. She healed herself. All's well."

"Not exactly. Show me what you did."

Raye led him to the candles, spread her hands.

"What about the sage?" he asked.

Leaning down, Raye picked up the green stick that lay in the center of the star.

"You didn't light it."

Raye stilled. "Shit."

"What does that mean?" I asked.

"Burning the sage keeps evil spirits from getting out too," Henry answered.

I remembered Henry with his hands around Roland's neck, my hand around Henry's arm.

And Roland's smile.

"Where is Roland?" I asked.

"Wait a second." Raye glanced back and forth between Henry and me. "You can hear him?"

"See him too. Must have been when I was you and you were me and—" I flapped my hand. "More importantly, Roland. Where?"

Henry shook his head. "Haven't got a clue."

"How?" Raye asked. "He needed worthy believers."

"He had them," I said. "They chanted, skyclad, beneath the moon, which was freakishly up in the daylight."

"He didn't get out the last time."

"Last time there wasn't a sacrifice. You didn't die. I did."

"Are you sure he's out?" Raye asked.

From the direction of Three Harbors a siren wailed. Pru began to howl. We went to the edge of the cliff and peered west. There was one helluva fire in town.

Henry, Raye, and I exchanged glances.

"He's out," I said.

Epilogue

Edward's minions made it look like my clinic went up in flames because of a gas leak. The man has amazing minions. They came, they saw, they explained away every damn thing.

We arrived in time to see that the fire had been started from a pile of wood around a single wooden stake. A pyre built just the way the *Venatores Mali* liked them.

Joaquin stood across the street, herding cats—literally. After canceling my appointments, he'd hung around in case we had any walk-ins. Luckily he'd smelled the fire, called it in, then opened the cages in the kennel and let all the residents out.

Though the building was a loss—Roland McHugh made a damn good fire that burned hot and fast—the animals were saved. Joaquin was a hero. I gave him permission to dole out the poor homeless fur babies to several giggling girls who'd gathered around. From the admiring gazes cast his way, Joaquin wasn't going to go friendless, or dateless, much longer.

Owen, me, Reggie—as well as Grenade—slept that night at the cottages. So did Cassandra, Franklin, Raye, Bobby, and my parents. My birth parents.

Took some fancy talking by Franklin to get Kyle to agree to let Pru sleep inside. But he did. I'm sure the fed had to pay plenty. Kyle isn't the kind to care about a shiny FBI badge.

But we can't stay in Three Harbors. We have to go where no one knows us. Now that Roland's free, and he's discovered matches, no one and nothing is safe.

I spoke with my other parents. Told them I'd be leaving for a while. I hope that by the time I come back, I've figured out what to say to them. Maybe nothing beyond *thank you*. They might have lied, but they loved me; they protected me and accepted me. I always knew something was off, but only someone like me, with supernatural abilities, would have.

Though possessing Raye was weird for both of us, the exchange accomplished one important thing. I can see Henry and Raye can hear Pru. So far just them—no extra ghosts for me, no whispers from Fido for her. I kind of hope it stays that way. I have enough voices in my head already and so does she.

The morning after, I woke in Owen's arms. The sun slanting through the window told me we'd slept half the morning away. I wasn't surprised. After dying, rising, watching my livelihood burn, we'd come back here and proved we were alive the best way we knew how.

Reggie and Grenade lay on the couch all curled together. Neither one of them even lifted their heads as I sat up. The sun lit Owen's sleeping face, revealing every line that he'd earned. I drew back the sheet then placed my palm on the thin white line that still marred his thigh. One more dose ought to do it.

The spark woke him. He slapped his hand atop mine. "What are you doing?"

"You're good as new."

"Okay." He sat up, leaned over, kissed me quick. "Thanks."

"You can go back now."

"Back?" he echoed as if I were speaking in tongues.

"To the Marines."

He snorted. "Right."

"You said if you don't do your job, people die."

"If I leave, you might die. I can't risk that. The only people I care about, Becca, is you."

"But—"

"You think I don't know what you're doing? You're trying to get me out of harm's way."

"In Afghanistan?"

"Probably safer."

Definitely safer. "You should—" I began.

"Marry you. I know."

"Wait. What?"

"I'm not leaving you again. Ever. So we should probably get married. Okay?" he asked.

"What about Reggie?"

"He can get his own girl. I think he kind of likes your mom."

I thought he kind of liked her too, but—

"She's only got eyes for Henry."

"Poor guy." Owen sighed. "Reggie's going to have to go back."

"Why?"

"He belongs to the Marines. He was trained to sniff bombs. He's really, really good at it, and it's what he loves to do."

"He'll miss you."

And Pru. But right now it was probably best if Reggie was gone so that he stopped growling at corners after magazines smacked him on the nose of their own accord. People would start to talk. Which would cause any *Venatores Mali* that might be lurking about to become suspicious. We needed to keep a low profile.

"I'll miss him too," Owen said. "I'll put in a request; when he's retired, he can live with us."

"Maybe by then this will all be over."

Owen lay back and pulled me against his chest. "Once it is over, we can come back to Three Harbors."

"We don't have to."

"I don't mind, and I think there's a couple people here who would be great to work with."

"Doing what?"

"Breeding, raising, and training MWDs."

"That would be great!"

"Billy knows a lot about dog breeding."

"Billy the prophet? He does."

"And that kid who works for you . . . Joaquin—"

"He doesn't any more." Mainly because my clinic was rubble, not to mention we were going on the road. Joaquin had agreed to take Grenade—at least until we got back.

"Then he'll be glad for a job."

"How long do you think it's going to take us to end this?"

"No idea, but we'll do it. Together. You, me, the others." His arm tightened around me. "Roland isn't going to know what hit him."

I was glad Owen was confident. I was nervous. Two untutored witches, a ghost, and a wolf against an ancient evil witch hunter and countless serial-killing cronies.

Even with the FBI, a voodoo priestess, and whatever Edward was—

"The odds suck."

"Not once we find your third sister."

"How are we going to do that?"

A knock came at the door.

"Better put on some clothes," Owen said. "I called a meeting. First order of business, a plan to find that sister. Second order of business—figuring out what those mean."

He pointed at the athame with the wolf head carved into the handle, which lay on the kitchen table next to the necklace we'd found around Mistress June's neck. A pentacle similar to the one Raye wore, which according to Raye had been taken from one of the witches June had killed in New Bergin. We had no idea why.

However, when we'd put the athame, the pentacle, and Raye's wand on the same table, the legs had begun to vibrate so hard we'd been afraid the thing might self-combust. Raye had snatched up her wand; the table had stilled, and she had taken the wand with her when she went back to her own room.

The knock came again. I leaped out of bed and grabbed the nearest pair of pants. Owen did the same.

"And here I was afraid you'd miss the Marines, that you'd need more than . . . this."

I tugged a T-shirt over my head, and when my face popped out, Owen stood right in front of me. He drew me close and set his forehead against mine.

"All I need is you," he whispered, and when he kissed me I knew that he was right.

Read on for an excerpt from the next book in
Lori Handeland's Sisters of the Craft series

Smoke on the Water

Available August 2015 from St. Martin's Paperbacks

Chapter 1

"Do I know you?"

I glanced up from the book I wasn't reading to find one of the inmates—I mean patients—of the Northern Wisconsin Mental Health Facility hovering at the edge of my personal space. In a place like this, people learn quickly not to get too close to anyone without warning them first. Bad things happen, and they happen quickly.

"I'm Willow," I said. "Willow Black. But I don't think we've met."

I'd seen the woman around. The others called her "Crazy Mary," which was very pot/kettle in my opinion, but no one had asked me. She was heroin addict skinny. I gathered she'd done a lot of "self-medicating" on the outside. A lot of nutty people did. When you saw things, heard things that no one else did, you'd think you'd be more inclined *not* to take drugs that might make you see and hear more. The opposite was true. Trust me.

"Mary McAllister." She shuffled her feet, glanced at the empty chair next to me, and I nodded. She scurried over, sat, smiled.

She still had all of her teeth, which was an accomplishment around here. I had mine, sure, but I was only twenty-seven. Mary had to be . . . it was hard to say. I'd take a stab and guess between thirty and sixty. Give or take a few years.

Mary looked good today. Or as good as she got. Her long, wavy graying hair had been brushed free of tangles. She'd had a shower recently, but she still wore the tan jumpsuit issued to problem patients. The more you behaved like a human being, the more you were allowed to dress like one. I, myself, was wearing hot pink scrub pants and a white T-shirt that read NWMHF, which placed me somewhere between Mary's solitary confinement jumpsuit and the jeans and Green Bay Packer designer-wear of the majority of the visitors. Not that I ever had any visitors, but I'd observed others.

Mary had been incarcerated a while. The powers that be didn't like to call us "incarcerated," but a spade was a spade in my opinion, and if you couldn't waltz out the front door whenever you wanted to, I considered that "incarcerated." Mary spent a lot of time either doped into zombie-ville or locked away from everyone else. She was schizophrenic, but around here that was more the norm than not. Sadly, Mary was on the violent side of the spectrum—hence the doping and the locking away.

"Willow." She rubbed her head. "I don't think that's right."

"What isn't right?"

"Your name isn't Willow."

"It is."

"No!" The word was too loud. She hunched her shoulders, glanced around to make sure none of the orderlies were headed our way. None were.

Yet.

"It hasn't always been. It was something else. Before."

Very few people knew about my past, or lack of it. Mary McAllister certainly shouldn't. Unless she was part of it.

I'd been abandoned at birth. Found beneath a black willow tree on the banks of a babbling brook. Lucky for me it had been July, and there'd been a huge town picnic going on nearby. I'd been found almost immediately, or I'd have been dead.

I'd often wondered why the State of Wisconsin hadn't named me Brook instead of Willow, though I guess Brook Black is a bit of a tongue twister.

"Your hair was red." Mary leaned in close. "Your eyes were greenish-brown."

Mary might seem good today, but she was still talking crazy instead of truth. Even if I'd dyed my hair from red to blond, which I hadn't, I didn't think I could change greenish-brown eyes to blue, unless I wore super expensive contact lenses. As I didn't have enough money for new shoes, and putting anything near—never mind *in*— my eyes wigged me out, that hadn't happened either.

"You have me confused with someone else," I said. "That's okay. Happens to everyone."

Mary shook her head. But she didn't argue any more than that. The silence that descended went on so long, I nearly went back to my book.

"I know what you are."

I hadn't shared what I was with anyone, though I guess it wasn't a secret that I was here for the same reason Mary was.

"What am I?" I asked.

Might as well get the truth out in the open, although *murderer* was a bit harsh. The man hadn't actually died.

No thanks to me.

"A witch," Mary answered.

I laughed, but when her eyes narrowed I stopped. I'd been in here long enough, with people like her, to know better.

"Why would you say that?" Had I done something to her without realizing it? Or did she just think that I had?

"Because I'm one, too."

"When you say witch, you mean . . . ?" I'd been thinking "bitch" but—

Mary cackled like the Wicked Witch of the West.

Maybe not.

That interpretation made more sense. If Mary thought she was a witch, it followed that she'd think I was as well. Which meant everyone in here was a card-carrying broomstick rider—at least according to Mary.

"You see things," she continued, "then they happen."

Since becoming a resident of this facility, I'd told no one of what I saw when I looked into the water. I'd stopped insisting that those incidents would occur. I wanted to get out of here while I was still young. So how did Mary know about my visions?

"I don't understand what you mean," I lied.

There wasn't much that could be done about what was wrong with me. No amount of medication made the visions stop. Talking about them with my shrink certainly hadn't. Pretending I didn't have them was my only option, and I was getting better at it.

"You know any spells?" Mary lifted a bottle of water to her lips and sipped. The sun sparkled in it like a beacon. Images danced.

I closed my eyes, turned my head. "No."

"We'll have to find some."

"Find spells? How? Where?" I should have asked, *Why?* My first mistake.

The sound of water splashing onto the floor made my eyes snap open. Second mistake.

The puddle on the ground at my feet reflected the ceiling tiles and the fluorescent lights for just an instant before I saw something that should not, could not, be reflected there.

A room with books, books, more books. I recognized the library here at the facility even before I saw myself at the center—green scrubs, blue shirt, bare feet. I was alone. On the floor lay a volume. The title: *Book of Shadows.*

I seemed to be searching for something, or maybe someone. I appeared frantic—pale, scared, trembling. What had I done this time?

Then a face appeared in the water, blotting out both me and the library. A man slightly older than me. Longish dark hair, scruffy beard. I'd seen him many times before. He was important, but I didn't know why. He would keep me safe; he would save me. But I didn't know from what.

"Ladies." The mouth in the vision formed the word; those lips curved.

Strange. It was almost as if—

I lifted my gaze. He stood in front of us. Had I conjured him from my vision in the water?

I snorted. Conjured. Right. Mary's witch talk was invading my head.

"Something funny?" he asked.

I reached out, my fingers trembling as they had in the vision, and he took my hand with a gentle smile. A spark flared where we touched, and I tried to pull away, but he held on, though his smile faded to a frown. From the zap of electricity? Or my odd behavior?

This could not be him. He wasn't real. Even though he felt very much so.

I got to my feet, lifting my free hand toward his face. He was so tall I had to stretch. In my dreams of him I'd known he was big, strong. How else would he protect me from . . . whatever it was that he would?

He stilled, gaze on mine, but he didn't stop me from touching him. I pushed aside his tangled hair. The tiny golden hoop in his ear made my eyes sting.

"It really is you," I whispered.

Then I fainted.

Sebastian Frasier caught the girl before she hit the ground, swung her into his arms, then stood there uncertain what to do with her.

The other woman, older, wearing a tan jumpsuit, which seemed to have come from the In Custody Collection, beckoned. Sebastian followed her to a room halfway down the hall.

The Northern Wisconsin Mental Health Facility had been built to follow the Kirkbride Plan of asylums in the mid-19th century. Psychiatrist Thomas Kirkbride had the idea that the building itself could aid in a cure. With long, rambling wings that allowed for sunlight and air, the structures were massive enough to provide both privacy and treatment. Built of stone, they were set on equally large grounds, often former farmland where the inmates could work as a form of therapy. They were damn hard to escape from, which was why this one had been designated by the state as the go-to facility for the criminally insane.

Inside the room were two beds. Made. Two dressers— one with stuff on top, one empty of everything but dust. Two closets—one also with stuff, the second just dust.

"That one's hers." The woman jabbed a skinny finger at the bed next to the non-dusty dresser.

"Hers?"

The woman jabbed her finger again, and Sebastian laid his burden upon the mattress she'd indicated. He'd thought the girl an employee—nurse, orderly, maybe another doctor. She was dressed in scrub pants and a facility T-shirt. No ID tag, but he didn't have one either. At least not yet.

Nevertheless, her lack of one, and this being her room, meant she was patient, not staff. She hadn't looked crazy. But he should know by now that a lot of them didn't. Her companion wasn't one of them. Sebastian knew a lifer when he saw one.

"I should probably . . ." He glanced around for a button, a phone, some way to call a nurse, but he didn't find one.

He stepped to the door, glanced into the hall. No nurse. Although he apparently wasn't very good at spotting them.

There was only one name on the door. *Willow Black.*

"Is this Willow?" He returned to her bedside.

"Yes."

"Has she been ill?"

Though Willow was tall, she was also very thin, her

skin so pale he could see a fine trace of veins at her temple. Her hair was so light a blond it seemed silver, and her eyes before they'd fluttered closed had been such a vivid blue they'd seemed feverish.

He set his palm on her forehead, but he couldn't tell if she had a fever that way. The only way he'd ever been able to discern one with his sister had been to press his lips to her forehead.

In this case . . . bad idea.

"Would you get . . ." Sebastian paused. "What's your name?"

"Mary McAllister," the woman said, but her gaze remained on Willow and not on him.

"Would you get a nurse, Mary?"

"Nope."

"Why not?"

"First time she sees you and her eyes roll up, she goes down. You think I'm leaving you alone with her. I might be crazy, but I'm not crazy."

"I'm Dr. Frasier, the new administrator."

Mary eyed him up and down. "Sure you are."

At six-foot-five, two-fifty, Sebastian was huge, and his hands, feet, biceps reflected that. People often back-pedaled the first time they saw him. He didn't blame Mary for being leery, though she didn't appear scared, just protective. Considering the fey frailty of Willow, he could understand that. Even if he did work here, that didn't mean he wasn't a creep.

"You're right," he said. "You stay with her; I'll get someone."

"If you're a doctor, why do you need to get anyone?"

"I specialized in psychiatry."

Mary gave him another once-over. Sebastian didn't look like a psychiatrist. Although, really, what did one look like? He'd never met any who looked quite like him.

He could have tried to fit in better. Wear a suit and tie rather than a leather jacket and motorcycle boots. But as he'd driven his late father's Harley from Missouri, wearing a suit and shiny shoes would have been awkward. He could have changed. Should have changed. But there'd been an accident near Platteville, then construction north of Wausau. He'd been lucky to get here on time.

He'd figured he could transform himself—as much as he could considering his hair, his beard, and his dead sister's earring, which he would not take from his ear, ever—in his office. But he'd been distracted by Willow Black.

As a result, he was wearing a black leather coat and black dusty boots. His overly long hair was matted from the helmet, and he hadn't shaved in several days. The guard at the front door hadn't wanted to let him inside until Sebastian had shown him his license. Then the man had hesitated so long, frowning at the years-old photo of Sebastian sporting a nearly shaved head, a completely shaved face, and no earring, that Sebastian had become concerned he'd never get inside.

"Head doctor's still a doctor," Mary said.

Sebastian *did* have medical training. Not that he'd used it much.

He sat on the bed, then set his fingers to the girl's wrist. Her pulse fluttered too fast. Which could mean anything or nothing at all.

Now what? He had no stethoscope, no blood pressure cuff, no thermometer. He was out of options.

"You have any idea what happened?" he asked.

"She saw something that upset her."

In the hall there'd been the two women and himself. Sebastian might seem big and tough and scary, but he'd never had anyone faint at the sight of him before.

Mary shook the half-empty bottle in her hand. "I dumped it on the floor."

"Accidents happen."

"Not an accident. I wanted her to stare into the water, to see."

"Microbes?"

Mary wouldn't be the first psychiatric patient he'd met who was a germaphobe. She was probably nearer the hundredth.

Mary cast him a disgusted glance. "The future."

"You think Willow can see the future in the water?"

"I know she can."

"And does Willow believe this, too?"

"She's never said so."

"Can't imagine why." Sebastian returned his gaze to Willow's beautiful, still face. What was it about her that called to him? His ridiculous need to save everyone, which had gotten worse after he'd been unable to save his sister?

"Why do you think Willow can see the future?" Sebastian asked.

"Wouldn't you like to know?"

As the explanation probably involved headache-inducing kooky talk, not really. Sebastian was saved from answering when Willow began to come around.

Her eyes opened. He was struck again by how very blue they were. Sebastian had never seen eyes the shade of a tropical ocean. He'd never seen an ocean—tropical or otherwise—although he'd always wanted to. It was on his to-do list.

Willow smiled as if she knew him, as if she'd known him a long time, and just as she had before, she reached out to touch his face. He should have gotten to his feet. He should not have let her touch him, but he was captivated by the expression in her eyes. Her palm cupped his cheek, and his heart stuttered.

"You're here."

Her voice made him shiver. Or maybe it was just her words, which also indicated that she thought she knew him. And that couldn't be true no matter how much he might want it to be.

"Miss Black, I'm not—"

Her fingers flexed, her nails scratched against his three-day beard. "You are. I'm touching you. You're real."

"You have difficulty understanding what's real and what isn't?"

Her smile deepened. "Never."

Sebastian lifted his eyebrows, and she laughed. This time his stomach twisted, and lower, in a place that had no business doing so anywhere near a patient, he leaped.

He stood so fast he bumped into Mary and had to grab her before she landed on her ass. "Sorry."

She gave him a look like his mother always used to whenever he'd thought something he shouldn't. Mothers were like that. Then she took his place on the bed next to Willow.

"Run along, Doc. She'll be fine now."

"Doc?" Willow repeated.

"Sebastian Frasier," he said. "I'm replacing Dr. Eversleigh."

"Shiny new paper pusher," Mary muttered.

"Among other things." In a small place like this, the administrator also treated patients, just not as many as the rest of the doctors. It was one of the reasons he'd accepted this position over the others he'd been offered. Sebastian liked being a practicing psychiatrist. He also liked being the boss.

His superior, Dr. Janet Tronsted, was in charge of state health services. When she'd appointed him the administrator of this facility, she'd said, "You're in charge. Unless there's a problem, you won't be seeing me." Then she'd peered at him over the top of her vintage cat-eye reading glasses. "You do *not* want to see me."

As this Janet reminded him of another Janet—Janet Reno—same haircut, same biceps, same build—he'd had to agree. Her reputation preceded her. She was hands-off as long as you did your job. If you didn't, her hands would be around your throat—figuratively, he hoped—and they'd definitely be all over your record. You'd be lucky to get another job anywhere. Ever.

Someone called his name in the hall. "Should I send a nurse to check you out?"

"No." Willow sat up. She wasn't as pale. Her hands didn't shake. "I'm embarrassed more than anything. I—uh—didn't eat breakfast."

"Mary thought you might have had a vision."

"No," Willow repeated, scowling at Mary, who scowled right back.

Did that mean she hadn't had one now or that she never had?

Sebastian's name was called again—louder, closer. Not the time to press the issue. Really not his issue but her doctor's. He made a mental note to find out who that was and have a chat.

"It's nearly lunchtime," he said. "You should eat."

"I will."

As he had no more reason to stay beyond a strange desire to keep staring at her, Sebastian left. He headed back the way he'd come, just as the nurse who'd been calling for him barreled around a corner and bounced off his chest.